ESCAPE!

Common sense told him to turn back. Even if he scaled the barbed wire fence now, the clouds might break before he even got across the clearing. Then the guards would shoot him in a second.

But he kept pulling himself up. Something drove him and he knew he wouldn't turn back. They'd have to stop him. Even if he fell he'd just climb up again.

He didn't fall. He reached the top—resisted the temptation to leap down and hurt an ankle —and eased himself down, strand by strand, until he had only five feet to go. The urge to jump came again, but he resisted. He wouldn't get hurt but the fence would vibrate. They'd know someone had gone over. So he inched down until he felt the ground. He turned and fled into the jungle.

Missing in Action

BILL LINN

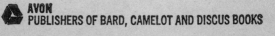
AVON
PUBLISHERS OF BARD, CAMELOT AND DISCUS BOOKS

MISSING IN ACTION is an original publication of Avon Books. This work has never before appeared in book form.

The author is grateful for permission to use the following:

Excerpt from "On Meeting Li Kuêi-Nien Down the River," by Tu Fu, from *The Jade Mountain: A Chinese Anthology*, by Witter Bynner, translated by Witter Bynner, Copyright © 1929, 1957 by Alfred A. Knopf, Inc. Used by permission of Alfred A. Knopf, Inc.

Excerpt from *Soliloquies in England and Later Soliloquies*, by George Santayana, Copyright © 1967 by The University of Michigan Press. Used by permission of The University of Michigan Press.

AVON BOOKS
A division of
The Hearst Corporation
959 Eighth Avenue
New York, New York 10019

First Avon Printing, March, 1981

AVON TRADEMARK REG. U.S. PAT. OFF. AND IN
OTHER COUNTRIES, MARCA REGISTRADA, HECHO EN
U.S.A.

Printed in the U.S.A.

The author acknowledges the assistance of Creative Artists Program Services, Inc., which provided a CAPS fellowship for the completion of this novel.

for Ruth—

"So long as the world goes round we shall see Tipperary only, as it were, out of the window of our troop-train. Your heart and mine may remain there, but it's a long, long way that the world has to go."

—George Santayana

I

The first thing he felt was the hot sun reaching into him with its sharp fingers. His eyes were closed but the redness shone through. He didn't feel any pain—only the heat and the dryness and the weakness. The weakness was the worst. He didn't have the strength to stand—he couldn't even crawl. It was all right now, though. He didn't mind. But in an hour or two he wouldn't be able to stand it, and then what would he do?

A little later, he felt the bugs for the first time. They started at his feet, crawling under the pants where they'd been pulled out of his GI boots and up the legs. They didn't bite, but he could feel them crawling. "In this country," Kurowski had said, "they got more bugs than raindrops." He felt them on his hands, then his face. *It's OK*, he thought, *just as long as they keep away from the wound.*

But he knew they wouldn't. Sooner or later they'd find it, and then the pain would start. He'd seen the corpses with legs and arms torn off, the raw stumps covered with insects. Millions of insects. All kinds—like people at a country market.

"Man, those damn bugs sure like that blood," said Kurowski. "New blood, old blood, dried blood. Like rats in a cheese factory."

He had laughed then.

"You're sick, K," he said.

"Yeah, maybe so," said Kurowski, and he blew out a big puff of smoke. "We all have our problems."

Early in the afternoon, they finally got to the wound. At first, it felt like only a tickle, like a feather moving over the edges of his open side. Then he felt them crawling toward the gash, following the blood. When they got to the center, it felt warm. Then the pain grew. By three he had passed out.

When he woke, the first thing he noticed was the darkness. He could see nothing, and he thought for a second that he must be dead. Then he reached down and felt his body. There was a bandage wrapped around him. *Well, if I am dead, they have good nurses in heaven,* he thought.

He lay in the darkness for a long time. Then a door opened and someone came toward him. The light blinded him and he couldn't see the face, but he felt someone changing the bandage.

"Who is it? Who are you?"

There was no answer. Or if there was, he was too delirious to understand. That was probably it—he was probably out of his head.

He slept again, for a long while this time, and when he awoke he felt much better. The room was still dark, but shafts of light penetrated around the edges of the door. He felt the bed. Then the sheets. They were rough but clean. The room was hot, stiflingly hot. *Not one of those R and R places in Tokyo,* he thought. *They're all air-conditioned. They must have taken me to the Philippines—maybe Olongapo City. Wouldn't mind that.* And he thought of all the stories he had heard about the whores in "the City." They said that they approached men in bars and did it right there, in plain view, standing up or on the bar. "Most God-damned wonderful town you ever saw," said Kurowski. "Yeah, yeah," he said, "if you want the siff."

The door was opening now. He saw a figure—an Oriental dressed in an orange medical gown. He came to the bed and stood over him, looked into his face for a minute, checked the bandage, then turned to go.

"Wait, wait!" he said. "Where am I? I want to know so I can write. Can you get me some paper and a pen?"

"That is not possible," said the man. He was surprised by the man's English. It was clear and American, not British like most Orientals' English.

"Look, man, they'll worry. I mean even if my parents were notified, they'll worry until they hear from me."

"I'm sorry, but there is nothing I can do." Then the man walked to the door, opened it, and left.

He had noticed the man's feet. No shoes, only sandals. Black rubber sandals. *Must be some little provincial hospital,* he thought. *Maybe somewhere up in the mountains north of Manila.*

The next day two men came to look at him. One was the doctor he had seen the day before. The other was older. His face was thin and long, and when he talked the younger man listened respectfully. Then they left. About an hour later, two men came and took him to another room.

There were several beds there. Three of them were occupied, but there were screens around them so he couldn't see the patients. There was one window, and through it he could see a mahogany tree; the leaves hung limply in the damp air. A few times he heard voices. They weren't speaking English, and they didn't sound like Filipinos. The voices were muffled. He thought that might be why they sounded so strange.

A female nurse brought him his meal that evening. She was slim with soft yellow-brown skin, and she moved with the quiet efficiency and grace that all Oriental women seem to have. When she collected the tray after he had eaten, she smiled at him. That night he slept soundly. Nobody had spoken to him about his parents yet, but he wasn't worried. *Orientals are slow,* he thought, *but in the end they're decent enough.*

The next morning the young doctor came, and there was another man with him. He wasn't a medical man—this he knew because the man was dressed differently and moved sharply with authority, the way professional soldiers do.

"My comrade is going to ask you some questions," said the doctor. "Please answer them carefully. It will be easier for you if you do."

That was the first time the truth dawned on him. The soldier spoke, and the doctor translated, stopping now and then to find the right word.

First, he was asked what his name was. He hesitated

for a minute, then remembered what he had been taught.

"William Tompkins. Specialist E 4 US852760521."
Then he was silent.

"What is your platoon number?"

He repeated his name, rank, and GI number.

"Where is your platoon stationed?"

"William Tompkins. Specialist E 4 US852760521."

The soldier frowned. The doctor looked at him and spoke softly.

"Really, it will be much better for you if you cooperate. Otherwise they will move you to a different hospital where it is not so good."

He shook his head, and the doctor smiled sadly, then turned and spoke to the soldier. They talked for a few minutes more and then left.

*

He was worried now and remembered what Kurowski had told him about POW camps.

"Man, they give you rat meat to eat and stale piss to drink. Or if it ain't, that's what it tastes like. Had a friend who was in one of them for eleven months. All his hair fell out, and he lost most of his teeth. Doctors said he had scurvy. He said that guys used to fight for half a mangy cat. Can you beat that? Fightin' to eat meow meat."

The next day at about noon, two soldiers came for him. They were dressed like the first only their boots were not polished, and he noticed that the doctor did not seem to be afraid of them. *Just enlisted men like me,* he thought. *It isn't any different over here.* As the doctor left, he wished him good luck. The last thing he saw was the mahogany tree. One side of it was eaten away by some kind of rot. He hadn't been able to see that from his bed.

The place where they took him couldn't have been far. The truck ride took about two hours. For the first hour, the going was smooth; later he felt the ruts and ditches as the truck tossed from side to side. There were two other prisoners with him. One had a scar over one eye and his arm in a sling; the other was a black who slept for most of the trip.

14

Finally the truck stopped. The back gate was opened, and a thin soldier in a brown uniform motioned for them to get out. His cap was pulled down over his eyes so that all one could see of them was a glimmer.

The bright sun blinded the prisoners for a few minutes. Rifles prodded them and they stumbled ahead, their hands shading their eyes. Then there was a shout, and they stood still.

Someone was speaking to them. The voice was shrill, and they couldn't understand it. Then it stopped and another voice started, this one softer with a funny singsong rhythm. This time, though, it spoke English.

"The prisoners are to stand at attention, arms at sides."

He kept his hands over his eyes. Then he heard the first voice again. This time it was shriller. Hands grabbed his arms and forced them to his side. He squinted in the bright sunlight. Shapes loomed up in the glare. Two men were standing in front of him. One was short and strong-looking, dressed in a black uniform with red stripes at the shoulders. The other was taller and leaner, wearing spectacles and olive fatigues. The man in black moved his mouth, and the shrill sounds started again. He was excited, and beads of sweat covered his forehead. Then he stopped, and the other voice started.

"The prisoners have been assigned to Muong Lam Prisoner of War Camp. They are responsible for following the rules of the camp. All breaking of rules will be severely punished according to the Geneva Convention."

K had said, "Those suckin' gooks think Geneva is a place where rich people go for a vacation. A place polluted with millionaires. They make their own rules, and some of 'em would make Dracula sick. Real sneaky little devils with broken glass for hearts."

The shrill voice started again. When the man spoke spit sprayed from his mouth. Then he stopped, and the translator started again.

Now accustomed to the light, the prisoner looked around. Behind the two officers was a row of soldiers standing at rest with their rifles at their sides. He looked at their faces. Most were unsmiling, staring ahead, bathed in sweat. On one or two, he could detect a half smile.

The lecture went on for about fifteen minutes. Then

15

the commander turned and walked away briskly and the prisoners were marched to the barracks. They had to pass through two chicken wire gates, topped with strands of barbed wire. *Easy to climb over that,* he thought. Later he would remember that thought and how wrong he'd been.

II

The room he was in was about fifty feet by twenty. The floor was wooden, but the walls and roof were sheet metal and the heat was intense. There weren't any beds, and men were stretched out on the floor, lying on straw mats. It was so hot that nobody was moving. He wondered why no one went outside; then he remembered the sun and knew that it was even worse out there.

He looked for an empty space to claim. At the farthest end from the doorway there was about ten square feet of empty space, so he walked over and sat down. He leaned against the wall, closed his eyes, and tried to rest and collect his thoughts. When he had first realized that they would send him to a POW camp, he had been scared, but it hadn't really gotten to him. *Whatever it is,* he thought, *I'll handle it OK.* He had confidence in himself. It wasn't that he was that tough, but he knew what he could take. *Things don't get to me,* he thought. *I roll with the punches.* Now that it was real and he was in the camp, it was a little different. The walls and the barbed wire and the guards were real, and it all made him feel different. He wasn't afraid, but he wasn't so confident either.

The drive had tired him more than he had thought, and his side was hurting. The wound had healed pretty well, but when he moved it felt tender. The bouncing on the truck hadn't helped any. After a while, he dozed off. When he woke, it was dark and he felt hungry. He wondered when they ate and leaned toward the body he could see lying closest to him on his left.

"Say, buddy, when's chow time around here?"

The sleeping man rolled over and turned his back to him. He got up and walked down the empty space that formed an aisle in the center of the room. His eyes became accustomed to the darkness, and he could make out figures on both sides of him. Most of them were sleeping, their snores making a soft lullaby.

Finally he came to the end of the room where he knew the doorway was. It was open, and he walked outside. The moon was overhead—an orange tropical moon—and he could hear the hum of insects and the sound of guards talking by the first fence that surrounded his section of the compound. He thought of asking them about food but then realized how stupid that would be, so he just stood, taking in the night and feeling the soft breeze that rose every now and then. After a while, he went back inside and went to sleep again.

*

He awoke when he sensed men were stirring and moving around him. He could hear their voices. They didn't whisper, but there was a softness in the way they talked that bothered him. He opened his eyes and looked around. Most of the men were sitting against the wall. A few were smoking; most were just staring ahead. He sat up, then turned toward the man he had tried to speak to the night before.

"When do they give us something to eat?"

The man looked at him. He had dark hair and the beginning of a beard. There was something contemptuous in his expression.

"Not for another half hour."

He frowned and the man smirked.

"When you see the stuff they give you, you won't be so hungry."

17

The man on his other side turned to look at the newcomer. His face was thin, and his eyes seemed enormous. The man started to speak, then stopped. He had a twitch on one side of his face that made his eyebrow dance.

The prisoner said his name and offered his hand to the man. The man looked at it for a second, then stuck his own out. The prisoner noticed how weak the man's grip was.

"How long have you been here?" he asked.

"Six months," said the man. "I came on June 24—six months ago."

He thought for a second. It was only August, but he decided not to tell the man.

"Which outfit were you with?" It was the man with the smirk and the beard.

"The hundred and fifteenth," said the prisoner.

"Heard they all bit the dust, heard they were all wiped out at Canh Trap. How'd you make it?"

"Don't know. When I woke up, they had me in a field hospital. First thing I saw was one of their doctors putting a bandage on me."

The man looked at him for a minute, then smirked again. "Lot of people here from platoons that don't exist no more. Most of 'em sorta left at an opportune moment —just a little before it was too late to do any leavin'."

The prisoner looked at the man but didn't say anything.

An Oriental was standing in the doorway. "Prisoners assemble for morning meal!"

They stood and formed a line. The guard watched them, took a quick count, then signaled that they should follow him, leading them out the doorway and through the first gate. Soldiers stood on each side of the gate. They had rifles and held them loosely, watching the men file past. It was hard to tell what they were thinking. He had been in the Nam for a half year, and he still hadn't learned how to read Oriental faces.

They passed through the second gate. There were more soldiers here and two machine guns behind sandbag bunkers about ten yards behind the gate in the open space in the middle of the compound. The soldiers manning them sat in the shade of small awnings.

18

The prisoners were marched into the middle of the compound; then the guard stopped and they all stood. He could feel the sun already. He looked at the sky. From the position of the sun, he guessed that it was only about nine. They waited. The men started to sweat; a few of them sat. Then the door of the small building in the center of the compound opened, and the short fellow in the black uniform came out. He said something to the guard, and the guard turned toward the men.

"Prisoners will all stand at attention. Prisoners are not permitted to sit in presence of commander. Rules of Geneva Convention."

The sitting men struggled to their feet. The little man looked at them, slowly running his eyes up and down the line. Then he spoke. He didn't look as angry today, but still the spray came from his mouth. When he stopped speaking, his face froze, his mouth a line, his eyes staring at them.

"Today, after morning meal, the prisoners will report to work area. They will assemble machinery to repair villages destroyed by their bombers. They will try to help stop suffering which they have caused among the people."

The translator stopped speaking and stood at attention. The short man in black turned and walked back into his office. Then the translator turned toward the guard and said something, and the prisoners were led to a place on the far side of the compound shaded by a big awning.

Two men ladled the food out of a big pot. Both were skinny and had the dried-out, emaciated look that people in the Orient have when they are consumed by parasites and never see a square meal. *Christ,* he thought, *what graveyard did they dig up these two gooks from?* The stew was a thick brown paste. He could see a few bamboo shoots but nothing else solid. It had a strange taste, salty and sweet at the same time.

The prisoners ate in silence. Tea was poured into the cups that each had carried with him. The man pouring noticed that the new prisoner had no cup, so he took one off a table and handed it to him, motioning that he should hold it up to get some tea. While the man was pouring the tea, he said something that the prisoner couldn't understand, then laughed and moved on to the next man.

19

The tea tasted good; he could feel it seep into his body, and for the first time since his journey in the truck, he felt a little stronger. When the men had finished their tea, the guard came back, ordered them to stand again, then marched them to the work area.

It lay behind the building that the little man in black had come out of. There were a few trees here, but they were scrawny with long, snakelike, yellowish leaves that didn't make much shade. There was another awning in the middle of the trees, and a half dozen soldiers were sitting on chairs underneath it, laughing and playing a game that looked like dominoes. The prisoners were ordered to stand in a line, and two of the soldiers came out. One was tall—taller than any Oriental the prisoner had ever seen. The man had a thin mustache, and his skin was red-brown instead of yellow like the other soldiers'. The second man was older than the first. There were lines on his face, and the little bit of hair that showed beneath his cap was streaked with gray.

The two men spoke to the soldier who had brought the prisoners, then went down the line dividing the men into groups. They made certain that each group had at least one strong man. Then the other soldiers came out from under the awning, and each led a group to the trucks that were parked nearby and ordered the men to climb in.

*

The truck moved slowly at first, went over some bumps, then picked up speed. The prisoner looked at the other men. They all had that worried, worn look that he had noticed before. It wasn't really that that bothered him, nor was he bothered by the fear—they all had reason to be afraid. It was the resignation and dull hopelessness that unnerved him. There was no rebellion left in their souls. They looked as if they would eat dog shit without a whimper if they were told to. *I'll never become like that,* he promised himself. *No matter what happens to me, they won't be able to make me like that.*

After about a half hour, the truck came to a stop. The back was opened up, and the men were ordered out. He looked around. They were beside a river that ran

20

through a wide valley. Trees covered the hills, but the valley was open and grassy, and covered with rice paddies on one side. The water in the paddies shimmered in the sunlight. He looked down the valley, his gaze following the river. About a quarter of a mile away were the remains of a village. The buildings were reduced to rubble, and there were people moving through the debris, searching. The soldier ordered the prisoners to march, and they approached the village. The people who were searching through the rubble all stopped and looked at them.

It would be a long time before he forgot the expression in their eyes. It was not hatred, nor was it indifference. There was a coldness that he had never seen before. It was unnerving, but it wasn't the coldness that he would remember. It was the sadness and weariness. When he looked into their eyes, he could see bombs and fire and people dying and women weeping. He looked at the ground.

The soldier broke them up into groups, and they started to clear the rubble. Everywhere they went, people followed them, watching silently. This confused him; they looked too worn to be curious. And he knew they weren't scavengers. The VC shot scavengers. The prisoners started to remove the fallen beams and the rusted pieces of tin that had been roofs. Sometimes rats scurried out and ran about madly looking for new cover. Then they found the first body—an old woman, shriveled and twisted. A silk dress was wrapped around her legs, and she wore a purple shirt. But it wasn't really an old woman anymore, only a piece of flesh. It smelled.

The people moved closer. Suddenly there was a wail, and a woman pushed through the crowd and tried to embrace the corpse. A soldier stopped her and held her arm as she bent over the rotting body. Then two women came out of the crowd and led her away.

They dug some more. The next body was that of a small boy. Nobody claimed it. The next a woman with a baby in her arms. One side of the baby's head was squashed like a rotten orange. A man came out of the crowd and stood over the two corpses. Tears flowed down his face, but he made no sound.

21

The prisoner stepped back for a minute and looked around the village. He could see the other work crews with similar groups of people around them. He looked up at the sky. A few big black birds were circling. They looked like crows.

III

After four hours of clearing debris, tearing down broken walls, and scraping together rotting corpses, they were tired. The sun was burning into them, and they had stopped sweating, for there was no water left in their bodies. A man passed out. Then another.

Finally the guards stopped them and pointed toward a clump of scraggly trees about fifty yards away. They went over and sat under them, their backs against the trunks. The prisoner looked toward the man who was closest to him. His face was pale, and he was blinking in a funny way. He took some water from the bucket that the guards had placed in the center of the clearing and gave it to the man. He sipped it slowly, then leaned back and closed his eyes.

"Thanks, pal, I needed that."

"No problem," he said and went to get a drink for himself. There wasn't much water left, and another man was already there. It was the fellow with the sneer. The man started to pour all the water into his cup.

"Hold it, I want some of that," the prisoner said.

The man looked at him, smirked, and went on pouring. The prisoner grabbed his arm.

"Don't you hear me?"

The man rammed his elbow into the prisoner's gut and jumped on him. They were rolling in the dust. There were shouts, and the guards were on them. He felt a thump behind one ear, and then everything went blank.

When he came to, he was on the truck, bouncing over the ruts again. The men sitting opposite him looked just as they had looked in the morning with the same expressionless faces and the same staring eyes. Only now their faces were covered with dust and reddened by the sun. When he tried to sit up, the throbbing in his head started. It ached, and there was a sharp pain like a knife thrust on the right side.

"Those guards know how to do it, buddy. Don't worry, nothing permanent. It'll go away in three or four days."

He looked toward the voice. It was a fellow with a short haircut—almost a crew cut. His hair was blond, and there was a scar over one eyebrow. The fellow smiled—it was the first real smile he'd seen since he came to the prison camp. He reached over and helped the prisoner sit straight.

"Happened to me the second day here. I tried to get an extra bowl of rice but didn't know the Viet word for 'no.' I was laid up for two days 'cause the guy worked me over with his foot after I was down. The other guards didn't like that. They're professionals and they work neat. I think they sent the guy back to the field."

The man reached into his pocket, took out a cigarette, and handed it to him. Then he took a second for himself, lit it, and handed it to the prisoner to use as a light. They smoked in silence. The prisoner watched the smoke drift toward the ceiling of the truck. The tobacco tasted good—better than any cigarette he could remember. He felt someone watching him and looked toward the other side of the truck. The man with the sneer was staring at him. The prisoner looked him in the eye, and the man held his gaze. Hate flared, but the prisoner didn't look away.

The other man broke and looked down. The prisoner kept staring at him. The man tried to stare him down again, but the prisoner kept looking dead into his eyes, and the man couldn't match him. The man kept looking

23

up and then down, angry that he couldn't hold his stare. Finally the prisoner looked away toward the end of the truck. He could see the road rolling away behind them— red-yellow dust bordered by lush green grass and a few small trees. The land looked peaceful and calm—brighter and lusher than the corn fields of eastern Ohio that he remembered. Then there was a high pitched whine. The ground about twenty yards behind the truck suddenly exploded. The truck moved faster, then there was another explosion about fifteen yards to the right.

The truck veered off the road, and everyone jumped out and ran. The whining grew louder, and the ground blew up ten feet to his right. A man flew into the air and landed beside him. He looked like a broken rag doll. The prisoner ran on. In front of him was a Viet guard, breathing in gasps. He drew even with the guard just as there was another explosion, and they both dived forward and rolled. He started to get to his feet, but the man held him down. A flow of bullets passed over them and pounded into the ground about fifteen feet in front of them, making the dust rise.

After the whining finally stopped, they stood. Men were walking about aimlessly or standing in a daze. He could see four or five bodies—all of them prisoners—small humps in the grass. Then the guards yelled and held up their rifles, and they collected the bodies and moved back to the truck.

IV

"But they were our planes—don't they know who they're shelling? Don't they make sure first?"

The man with the blond crew cut was listening. A rueful expression came over the man's face, and he shook his head.

"They never check when they're on search and destroy. Their orders are to get everything that moves—men, women, livestock. It doesn't make any difference."

He looked at the men lying on their pallets. Some of them were sleeping, others staring blankly at the ceiling. He knew it was hard—that you never knew who was your friend and who your enemy. But they could check first. It wouldn't hurt to check. He said so to Crewcut.

"There's no way to check. They can't do it from up there, and if they come down lower they're liable to get winged by a sniper or one of those antiaircraft guns."

"So they just blow everything away," he said.

"Yeah," said Crewcut, "they blow everything away. Everything they can hit."

"That's precision warfare," he said, "the kind they talk about in training school?"

"War's not very precise business," said Crewcut. "At least not over here."

His head still hurt and his nerves were shot, but nevertheless he drifted off in a minute. At first he slept soundly, but then he started to dream. The dreams were filled with whines and explosions and bodies flying through the air. The attacking planes were striped red and white; the bombs they dropped were blue and speckled with white stars. He ran and ran, but the explosions were always there, always getting closer.

He woke in a sweat and sat up. He could hear snoring in the darkness. It was hot but a breeze was blowing, and it felt cool and good. If he had a cigarette, he would have lit up, but he didn't have any and he didn't feel right about asking Crewcut for some of his. Later, when he knew him better.

He looked to the right halfway down the room. That's where the Sneer was sleeping. He'd noted that before he dozed off. He could see the outline of a body. He'd have to watch that man. He had made an enemy, and he'd have to be careful. Crewcut said he was a tough nut and that no one should turn his back on him. The prisoner had known that kind before, and he could handle them, but this was different. There were no doors here and no rules—at least none that he could imagine would help him. He'd be careful all right, but if he got the first chance, he'd do what he had to. Sneer would only understand fear, and he would have to give him something to worry about.

V

The next morning they were paraded out into the center of the compound again. It wasn't as bright as the day before, and a thin haze almost like smoke filled the air. The men were silent as the guards herded them along. The food was the same, but the tea tasted strong and good. He laughed to himself. He was beginning to like the stuff; he would try to drink it afterwards when he'd left the place and gone home.

After breakfast they were loaded onto the trucks again. This time the ride was longer, up into the mountains, and the air became cooler as they climbed.

Finally the truck stopped, and they got out. They were standing on the top of a rounded hill. Below them was the jungle, and beyond that he could see the plain and the river winding through it like a snake. The guards pointed toward a clump of trees about fifty yards to their right, and the prisoners marched off.

When they entered the trees, the guards told them to stop. One man opened a large wooden chest, took out shovels, and passed them around. They were old, but the blades were polished from use. Then another guard marched the men deeper into the trees.

When they reached a clearing in the center of the trees, they stopped, and the man drew lines marking off rectangles about twelve feet by six feet and ordered them to start digging. They began to work. The ground was soft on top, but once they got down a foot or so it became hard and stony, and the work was slow. He talked to the man next to him as they dug.

"Whad'ya think this is for?" he asked, worried as he remembered stories of soldiers made to dig their own graves.

The man shrugged and threw a shovelful of dirt over his shoulder.

"Been here long?" he asked the man.

He shrugged again, and they worked silently for three or four minutes. Then the man spoke.

"About a year, maybe a little less." He became silent again and continued digging.

"They always make you work like this? I mean is this the usual routine?"

"Only been doing this for three months," said the man. "Before that we just sat in the compound all day."

The prisoner stopped for a minute to rest. He felt someone's eyes on him and looked around. A guard was watching him. The man's eyes were expressionless.

"They don't mind if you rest," said the man. "Most of them are farmers and they know what it means to dig."

The prisoner drove his shovel into the ground again.

27

The hole was taking shape. It was about five feet deep now. A guard came over and looked. He called to another man who came over and looked, too. Then one man took out a stick to measure the hole and indicated that they should dig some more.

It had grown hotter, and the prisoner wiped the sweat from his brow. A guard brought a big bucket, and they each took a ladle of water. It wasn't cool, but it tasted sweet.

When the hole was about six feet deep, the guard came over and measured again. This time he was satisfied and indicated that they should make the walls sheer and square the hole. This took about twenty more minutes. When they had finished, they moved to another place and started again. Finally they took a break and ate some cold rice. He found Crewcut and sat beside him.

"How you making out?" asked Crewcut.

The prisoner held up his hands and showed him a row of blisters.

"They'll break tonight and turn into calluses. Then you'll be all right."

"What do you think these holes are for?" he asked.

"Worried, huh?" said Crewcut with a chuckle. "Probably antiaircraft mortar. They usually plant them on the top of hills."

"That's against the Geneva Convention—the rules of what you're allowed to use prisoners for, you know?"

"Yeah, the Geneva Convention," said Crewcut, "the good old Geneva Convention."

After the break, they dug again. He was becoming better at working with the shovel and didn't waste so much motion now, but his hands were sore. Each time he plunged the shovel into the ground, it felt like the handle was burning into his hands.

When they finally stopped, it must have been after six or seven. He knew that it was later than they had worked the day before because the sun was lower. The truck lurched from side to side as it rolled down the mountain road. He looked at the other men. They were resting with their eyes closed. He could see Sneer. He was sleeping in the corner farthest from him. They had been eyeing each other from a distance almost all day. He could see his big shoulders and thick forearms. Sneer looked rough, and he wondered if he could take him. *It's been a while,* he thought, remembering the little bit of boxing he'd done. He recalled the feel of the heavy bag and the calisthenics and the ring—springy but taut. He had been able to take care of himself.

The truck rolled to a stop, and they got out. They were back at the camp. The guard pointed, and they headed for the mess tent. The food tasted better than the day before—there was more meat in it now. The sun was almost gone behind the hills—a bright red in a clear sky. Crewcut was watching his eyes.

"Beautiful country, huh?"

"Yeah," he said. "A nice place to visit, but I wouldn't want to take up permanent residence here."

"Me neither," said Crewcut. "It might get a little dull."

VI

The next day they went to another hill and dug another set of holes for more antiaircraft guns. The day was about the same, maybe a little hazier. His hands were so sore that he had to stop often, so after a while the guards gave him the job of carrying the water bucket to the other men.

Sometime in the afternoon, he brought the bucket to the group with Sneer. The ground was hard where Sneer's group was digging, and they had worked up a good sweat. Sneer eyed him while the men drank from the tin ladle. When it was his turn, he took the ladle, dipped it, and drank about half. Then Sneer stopped and looked at him, smiled, and threw the rest of the water in his face. The prisoner just looked at him. Sneer kept on smiling. Before the prisoner could do anything, a guard was beside him. He took the ladle from Sneer, said something sharp, then indicated that the prisoner should move on.

Crewcut was in the group nearby. The guard came up to him and spoke slowly. Crewcut listened. He knew a little Vietnamese. Then he went over to the prisoner.

"The guard says you aren't supposed to give him any more water. He says to let him dry up like a dead rat."

"Like to do more than that," he said.

"Wait till you have a better chance," said Crewcut.

He nodded and continued his rounds.

That night he read some newspapers. He guessed they were about a month old—he'd lost track of the days—but it was still good to read them. There were blocks of print cut out, but there was still war news. Mostly it told of Cong victories and South Vietnamese losses. This didn't interest him. He just glanced at the headlines of the columns dealing with the war, then went on. He was tired of war.

The papers were filled with news of the U.S. political scene. There were investigations afoot, and the word "Watergate" appeared over and over. He read but he didn't understand. It made no sense without the beginning of the story which he didn't have. Maybe Crewcut knew. He'd ask him later.

When he came to the sports page, he felt better. The Dodgers were three up on the rest of the league. The Orioles looked like they already had it sewed up in the American League. There was a picture of somebody sliding into third and Brooks Robinson tagging him out. Robinson never missed. They said he couldn't hit, but he hit when it mattered—when there were men on. And nobody got one past him at third. He was like a vacuum cleaner. *Best damned third baseman ever,* he thought.

After he finished with the paper, he gave it to the man next to him and lay back and stared at the ceiling. Then he turned and looked out the window. The sky was black —blacker than black—and filled with bright stars. He thought of his friends back home, going to ball games, spending evenings with girls, sitting in bars and shooting the breeze. He sighed, then looked around him, afraid that someone would hear. It was the first time he'd felt the isolation, the first time he realized how much he wanted to be home.

VII

They were up early the next day. The sun was bright again. It was already hot by nine, and they sweated as they marched across the compound to the mess tent. The tea made him sweat even more, but he didn't mind. He was getting used to it, and as he felt it seep into his blood he woke up. Across the valley he could see the hills shimmering in the heat. The sky was pale blue and the river glittered like gold.

After they finished eating, they were marched to the trucks again. This time the ride wasn't as long. It ended by a temple where they got out and waited. Two men dressed in orange robes with shaved heads appeared. They spoke to the guards for a minute, then walked toward the rear of the temple. The prisoners followed.

There were endless rice paddies here, about half of them unplanted. The guards divided the prisoners into small groups, and more monks came out of the temple so that there was one monk for each group. Then they waded into the paddies.

The young rice sprouts were collected in barrels at the sides of the paddies. The monk in the prisoner's group took some sprouts and showed the men how to plant them. He pushed into the soft mud under the water, pressed the sprout in, then smoothed mud over it. After doing this once more, he handed out rice sprouts and watched as the men worked.

They were clumsy at first, and half the sprouts floated to the surface. The monk gathered these, put them back in the barrels, and continued watching the men. They got better at the planting, but their backs became stiff and after a short while they had to stop and stand. The monk watched them, his face expressionless. After about fifteen minutes he motioned that the prisoners should continue, and they went back to work.

The prisoner didn't mind so much. This was easier than digging holes, and the water was cool and felt good. The sun bounced off it, though, and the glare bothered him, so he took some mud and daubed it on his cheeks the way he had when he played baseball on bright days. That helped some.

When the sun was straight overhead, the monks signaled that the prisoners should stop, and they led them back toward the temple. Across the paddies he could see the other groups of prisoners moving in the same direction. They went around to the flat space in front of the temple, and the monks indicated that they should sit. After a few minutes, two men came out of the temple carrying a big bronze pot suspended from a pole which they were balancing on their shoulders. One monk ladled something out of the big pot into small bowls, and the men filed up and got one, together with chopsticks, and went back to their places and ate.

The food was good. It was rice mixed with vegetables and some sort of fish. It had a pinkish color and was hot, and as he ate, he could feel strength growing in his body. When they finished, another monk moved among them, filling their bowls with green tea from a big brass pot. The tea had a minty flavor that complemented the rice and fish perfectly.

The monks let the men sit for about fifteen minutes after they had finished their tea, then signaled that they should stand and marched them back to the paddies.

During the afternoon, the heat increased. They took a break at three, and the monks brought them some more tea. When evening came, the monks marched them back to the temple, the guards reappeared, and the prisoners boarded the trucks and were driven back to the compound.

He had his first dream of home that night. He remembered the old church he had attended on 8th Street off Detroit Avenue. The church was red brick, and there were small pine trees surrounding it. Those were the only pine trees he'd ever seen in Cleveland, and they looked strange growing there, almost in the heart of the city, only two blocks from Detroit Avenue where heavy traffic rolled by day and night.

In the dream he attended services. The priest stood in the pulpit and gave a sermon. But the man in the dream was not Father Winder whom he remembered. Father Winder had been a slight, gray-haired man with rimless spectacles. The priest in the dream was bald—like the monks—and he spoke slowly, his face expressionless. The prisoner sat in a pew near the front of the church. At first he couldn't understand the words of the sermon, but then they became clear. The man was speaking about mercy. That was the first virtue, the one his parishioners must cultivate. Without it, they would be empty vessels.

The prisoner felt uncomfortable and looked around at the other people in the church. Their faces were empty of expression. He looked at the walls of the church. There were flickering candles there. Then suddenly they exploded and the walls started to burn, but the people just sat, doing nothing, and the priest continued speaking. The fire spread, and soon the people themselves started to burn. Still no one moved. Their skin charred, and their eyes popped then melted and ran down their faces. Still they sat.

He woke in a sweat and looked into the darkness of the barracks. He could see the familiar faces and hear the snores. Then the dream came back to him. It left him with a strange feeling—not the panic that he had felt while dreaming, but a sadness and dull anger and confusion that he didn't understand. He slept fitfully for the rest of the night, and when the guard summoned them to mess in the morning he was still tired.

VIII

They spent two more days working in the rice paddies behind the temple. The prisoner's back ached from the work, but he had begun to feel a strange satisfaction in it. He liked the monks, and he looked forward to the rice and tea. The men were still guarded, and they were worked hard, but there was a feeling about the place and the work that calmed him. He wanted it to go on.

*

Near the end of the second day, he found a chance to get Sneer. Sneer was in a different group, but it was only about fifteen yards from the prisoner's. Several times he felt someone's eyes on him. When he stood and looked about, he saw Sneer standing nearby with his hands at his side, staring at him hard. The stance made his shoulders and arms look even bigger than they were, while his legs appeared shortened because they were in the water. Suddenly it occurred to the prisoner that Sneer looked just like a gorilla.

He waited until he felt Sneer staring again, then he jumped up and made a loud noise. Everyone in the vicinity stopped working and looked at the prisoner. He pointed to Sneer and began leaping up and down, making loud grunting noises and scratching under his arms. A few men began to laugh. Then the monks understood, and they started laughing too. One monk was toothless. The men looked at him and laughed even harder. Soon everyone was roaring, and men in the other groups stopped working to look at them. Through it all Sneer stood transfixed, and as anger rose in him his neck swelled, the veins bulged, and he looked more like an ape than ever.

After a few minutes the laughter subsided, and the men went back to work. The prisoner felt satisfied but vaguely uneasy. Then he shrugged. *What the hell*, he thought, *he deserved it*. He shot a swift, half-guilty glance in the man's direction. Sneer was staring at him again.

Another night passed. The prisoners had worked hard during the day, digging a trench at the north end of the camp. They had worked through the afternoon in the heat of the sun, and the prisoner was dead tired. As soon as he lay down, he fell into a deep sleep. After an hour he suddenly woke, filled with a vague anxiety. He looked toward Sneer's usual place. There was no one there. He listened for movement and strained his eyes. On Sneer's side of the room, he saw a shape pressed against the wall where no one ever slept. He watched it. The shape was moving slowly in his direction. He waited. It moved, then stopped. Then it moved again. The prisoner tensed himself. The shape was about ten feet away now, and he could make out the broad shoulders and thick neck of Sneer.

Seeing the body gather itself to spring, the prisoner cocked his fist. Then Sneer lunged and the prisoner quickly rolled over and heard him grunt as he hit the floor. In a second he was on top of Sneer, punching him in the face. Sneer tried to push him off, but he kept punching. Finally Sneer freed himself, and they were both on their feet, swinging wildly. He heard yells from the men around him, then the lights went on. Guards grabbed his arms and led Sneer and him away.

The prisoner spent the rest of the night alone in a small room. The next morning at about ten a guard came for him and took him to the small cabin in the center of the compound. Outside the door they halted. He could hear voices inside. Then someone gave a command, and they stepped in. The short, strong-looking man in the black uniform was sitting at a desk. On the wall behind him was a picture of Ho Chi Minh. Otherwise the room was completely bare. The man was studying some papers.

35

The prisoner and the guard stood in silence. Minutes passed. Finally someone else stepped into the room and saluted the man in black. He couldn't see the man because he was still standing at attention slightly behind him, but the prisoner thought it best not to move.

Then the man at the desk looked up and spoke. There was a pause before the new man spoke. It was in English.

"You have fought with one of your fellow prisoners. You have caused a disturbance which required the guards to intervene. Have you anything to say for yourself?"

If he denied the accusation, they probably wouldn't believe him. Still, it was worth a try.

"I was only defending myself," he said. "The other man attacked me in the darkness." Then he was silent.

The translator spoke, and he could see that the commander was listening. Then the commander looked at him. He stared into the prisoner's eyes, but the prisoner didn't look away. Finally the man wrote something on the paper before him, then spoke. The interpreter translated.

"You will be given extra work detail. Further disturbance will be punished with severe measures."

A command was given in Vietnamese. The guard turned, and the prisoner followed him out the door.

*

He spent the rest of the day in the barracks because he had missed that day's work detail. At midday the place was like an oven. The prisoner tried to sleep, but it was impossible, so he went outside. It was worse there, and he quickly returned to the barracks. The guard, sitting in the shade by the doorway, laughed when he saw the prisoner rush into the shade and sink to the ground, sweat pouring off him.

"Hot!" said the guard.

The prisoner was surprised for a minute, then looked toward the man and said, "Very hot."

The guard pointed to the water bucket in the shade, and the prisoner went over and took a drink. It tasted good, but he noticed something strange about it. He took another ladleful and smelled it. He felt the man

36

looking at him and turned toward him. The man smiled.

"Gin—good, huh?"

The guard had spiked the water. He took two more ladlesful, then walked into the barracks. He was high, and it felt good. He lay down and looked at the ceiling. After a few minutes, he dozed off.

The noise of the returning men woke him. He sat up. Crewcut was standing over him.

"You missed it today. We worked down by the river," he pointed off across the plain. "Cool as a cucumber."

"I'll bet," said the prisoner. "How were the leeches?"

"No leeches. Just water, cool water. All the water you ever wanted to drink."

"And dancing girls," said the prisoner.

"Yeah, but only two," said Crewcut.

"Too bad," he said. "Me—I passed my time sipping Tom Collinses in the shade."

"Yeah," said Crewcut. "And my uncle is Ho."

"No shit?" he said.

"No shit," said Crewcut.

IX

The next day they traveled to another temple. This was a much longer trip than the last. The truck bounced over rough roads for about an hour, then hit a smoother stretch. It was cooler, too, but they weren't climbing so he figured they must be in the jungle somewhere, underneath trees. After about an hour and a half, the truck started to climb. This went on for fifteen or twenty min-

37

utes, then the truck stopped. The back gate wasn't opened, though, and he could hear men speaking outside. Then the truck started again, climbing up a steep grade. They seemed to be turning and twisting. The road was rough, bouncing the men about. He gave up trying to sit on the bench and leaned against the metal wall, bracing himself by planting his feet and pushing.

"Some trip, huh?" said Crewcut. "We musta covered fifty miles."

"Where you figure they're taking us?" he asked.

"No way of tellin'. Probably to some fort up in the hills."

"I heard there was some action up there—that the guys on our side were still holding out."

"Which guys you talkin' about?" asked Crewcut.

"You know," the prisoner said, "the guys who're trying to hold back the VC."

"Oh, them," said Crewcut. "All five of them."

Finally the truck stopped again. The back gate was opened, and they stepped out. They were high on a hill. Behind them were a number of buildings with domes and spires. They were gilded with some sort of metal that glittered in the sunlight. Monks in orange robes were walking around. He had not seen so many monks in one place before. In front of him, the mountain dropped away sharply. There was gray rock for about a quarter of a mile, then some small shrubs, and then about a mile down the jungle began. It went on and on. They were on top of the highest hill, and all the others were completely covered with jungle. Far off in the haze to the east, he could see a thin twisting thread of silver. He guessed that was the river that ran through the valley near the compound.

The men stood, looking about them. The guards were looking over the jungle, too. There were only two of them on this trip. Before there had always been four. *They're getting lax,* he thought. *They don't think we have enough spirit to try anything.* Then his gaze went back to the jungle, and he laughed softly to himself. In this jungle, where would anyone go? One would die out there in a matter of days without help. And if he turned to a native for help, he would certainly be rounded up again—or maybe worse. The Cong knew what they were doing, and they weren't going to waste men on a useless guard detail.

Two monks were in front of them now, talking to the guards. One was very old. His skin was wrinkled and dry, his eyes reddened slits. The other was young; the young one did the talking. When he was finished, the monks left, and the guards talked among themselves for a minute. He watched the two monks walk away across a flat, dusty field and up some stone steps that led to a gate. Then they disappeared in the complex of buildings.

When the guards were finished, they signaled that the men should follow them and walked briskly toward a path to the left of the steps that the monks had taken. The path curved around the buildings, passing between rocks and pools of stagnant water. It led to the top of a small hill about 200 yards behind the cluster of buildings. Here they stopped.

At the highest point of the hill, there was a pile of stones cut in rough blocks near the foundation of a small building. Only the first two layers of blocks for the foundation had been set. The guards motioned that the prisoners should sit. The prisoner found a clear spot close to the pile of stones, and Crewcut joined him. They lay back and shut their eyes. The sun was hot, but the mountain air blowing over them felt cool. They could hear the faint tinkle of bells coming from the temple.

They dozed—he couldn't tell for how long—and were awakened by the guards. The two monks had returned and had brought a dozen men with them. Some of them were monks dressed in orange, others apparently were native laborers. The prisoners were divided into groups of three, and each group went with either a monk or a laborer. Stones were placed in small piles, and the men were shown how to stack them on the foundation wall so that they interlocked. Then a material like cement was taken from a big jug and pressed into the chinks between the stones. The prisoner noticed that it dried almost immediately. After showing them how to stack the stones, the monks stepped back, and the prisoners went to work.

They were sloppy and set the stones imprecisely. The cement they pressed into the chinks oozed out and ran down the sides of the wall. He looked at the monks' faces. The monks had always been impassive and expressionless—he had rarely seen one smile or show anger. Now, for the first time, he saw displeasure. Finally one of the monks spoke. The men stopped and looked at him. He was a skinny monk and the veins stood out on his arms. The prisoners stared at him as he babbled and made motions with his arms, showing them how to lay the imaginary brick.

But no one understood, and when he stopped and they went back to work, the results were the same. The monk watched for a while, then spoke again. This time he was really angry. He walked over to the wall and ran his hands over it. It was uneven and swayed outward about fifteen degrees. He pointed to it, looked at the men, then shook his head. Then he ran his hands over the wall again. They became covered with the cement which was oozing out of the chinks.

The prisoner looked at the two guards. He could see faint smiles on their faces. The skinny monk's voice rose, and the other monks standing around the foundation of the building turned toward him. Evidently everyone was having the same trouble. He waved his arms, and the other monks indicated that all work should stop. Then the guards gestured for the prisoners to form a circle around the angry monk. He pointed to the wall, then spoke. His words came out in bursts; the prisoner could see the spittle flying from his mouth. The monk had no front teeth, and this—together with his thinness—gave him a weird, ghoulish appearance. He railed on and on, walking to the wall, touching it, pointing to the cement on his hands, then pointing at the prisoners. Finally he spit on the ground.

Crewcut turned toward the prisoner and whispered into his ear. "This is it. Man, we're gonna be put on the shit list."

Then the monk stopped. There was nothing he could do. The prisoners didn't understand him—he knew this—and he was at a loss. He shook his head again and looked toward the guards. They said a few words to each other, then pointed toward Crewcut. The monk took him by the arm and led him to the wall. He took a new stone, set it on a part of the wall that hadn't been ruined yet, and lined it up. He had to work slowly to find the right space because each stone was shaped slightly differently.

When he found the right space, he turned to Crewcut and spoke slowly. Crewcut turned toward the men.

"You must not put the stone just anywhere. You must find the right place . . ." he stopped and looked at the monk and the monk said something else. Crewcut looked confused for a minute, then he laughed.

"His Reverence says that placing a stone is like making love to a woman. One must make sure that he finds the correct opening—otherwise the work will not bear fruit."

The men laughed. It was the first time the prisoner had seen them laugh, except in malice, since he had come to the compound, and it made him feel strange. The monk took some of the cement from the jug and pressed it into the chink beneath the stone. He ran his hands over it smoothly, almost lovingly, then turned to Crewcut and spoke again. Crewcut spoke to the men.

"When you place the cement under the stones use only as much as will fill the space. Too much will cause a mess"—he pointed at the sloppy walls the men had done so far—"too little will not fill the holes."

The monk watched Crewcut as he spoke to the men. When he stopped, the monk smiled and said something else. Crewcut translated.

"His Reverence says that cement is like semen. One should conserve it and use only as much as is needed for each job. That way one will have a long life and many children."

The men laughed again. Standing there, on the hill in the sun, the prisoner felt the breeze and heard their laughter and in the background there was the faint tinkle of bells from the temple. It was noon of the sixtieth day since he had been taken prisoner.

X

They continued working on the foundation of the building through the afternoon. By about six the monks signaled that they should stop and walked off quickly toward the cluster of buildings. The guards let the men sit for a minute, then marched them off along the path that the monks had taken. When they came out onto the field in front of the buildings again, the prisoner could see monks crossing it, all walking quickly toward the temple. Their number seemed to be countless.

The trucks weren't there yet, so the men sat. He walked over to a boulder in the middle of the field and climbed up on it. He could see down the mountain through the green undergrowth and shrubs to the jungle below. Men were climbing up the hill toward the temple. They were all dressed in bright orange robes which stood out against the green and gray of the mountain. There must have been ten thousand. Then the bells started again. Not deep and throbbing like the church bells he knew, but tinkling and soft. They filled the quiet, but they didn't awe him. They were sweet, like the buzzing of bees or the singing of birds.

He looked at the other prisoners. Some were listening, standing and watching the scene as he was. Others were stretched out on the ground, sleeping with their hands over their eyes. The guards were sitting at the edge of the circle of men, talking softly. Every now and then one of them would look over at the prisoners. They had noticed him going to the boulder but didn't seem to mind, so he stayed. After about fifteen minutes the trucks came, and the prisoners climbed in and began the trip back to the compound.

As soon as the road entered the jungle, the heat increased. The air was thicker and heavier than he had ever felt it. As the truck jounced along the road, he looked out at the jungle. The leaves hung limp, and there was no breeze. Here and there, he saw a splash of color where wild orchids hung over the road. He never saw animals though—they were afraid of the roads and the men who traveled them.

That night after they ate, he sat with Crewcut and played cards. The deck was handmade from pieces of old cardboard. The men knew most of the cards by their backs because of the irregular edges, but they played anyway. Crewcut won ten cigarettes, the other players broke even, and Sneer lost ten. Sneer squinted up at Crewcut and muttered something as he reached for his cigarette case. Crewcut watched him closely, but Sneer didn't try anything. He was afraid of Crewcut; besides, he was still worried from the last fight. The commander had given him two days in solitary confinement, then made him dig latrines for a week. The guards said that he had started the fight.

Sneer eyed Crewcut, then went to his pallet and pretended to sleep. Crewcut looked at Sneer, then at the prisoner. A big smile covered his face.

"If there's anything I can't stand," Crewcut said, "it's a sore loser. You can always tell them by their faces. They're generally pretty ugly and they smell bad."

Crewcut looked toward Sneer, who still appeared to be sleeping. Then he looked at the prisoner and winked.

"Want a cigarette? I got extras."

The prisoner took one of the cigs and lit it, then blew smoke rings. Crewcut watched him.

"You makin' signals?" he asked. "You must be part Indian. We don't want any Indians around here. We got enough trouble with the gooks."

"Things are tough all over," he said.

"You ain't kidding," said Crewcut. "Life may be a bowl of cherries, but these cherries got plenty of pits."

When the lights were turned out and the prisoner lay down to sleep, he checked to see if Sneer was still in the same place. He looked like he was sleeping, but the prisoner couldn't be sure. Then he looked toward Crewcut's pallet. It was on the other side of the room diagonally across from Sneer. It would be very difficult for Sneer to get to him because he'd have to go halfway around the room along the wall—if he tried to go directly across the center of the room, he would be out in the open. Moonlight from all the windows focused there, lighting it like a stage. The prisoner felt better, and he started to doze off. Sneer wouldn't try anything tonight.

The next morning when he woke and stretched, he felt good. He had slept soundly—it had cooled off sometime after midnight—and he felt rested. He looked around the room. Men were sitting up, a few standing and talking to their friends. He looked toward Sneer's place. He was awake, but he hadn't gotten up yet and was lying with his hands behind his head, gazing out the window. Then the prisoner looked toward Crewcut's place. Crewcut was lying on his side with his back toward him; it looked like he was still sleeping. The prisoner got up, walked over, and nudged him. Crewcut flopped over and just lay there, staring up at him with lifeless eyes.

He looked toward Sneer. Sneer was staring at him intently; then he pointed his finger straight at the prisoner. "I'll get you, you son of a bitch!" the prisoner yelled and started across the room toward Sneer, but some men grabbed him and held his arms. Sneer stood calmly, waiting, his lips set. Hate flickered in his eyes.

The guards came then, and the men showed them Crewcut. Then they saw the others holding the prisoner, so they took him away and put him in a small room near the cabin in the center of the compound, locked the door, and left.

There were no windows and the sun beat down harshly. He thought. Maybe they'd blame him, maybe they wouldn't. The commander seemed pretty shrewd, and the translator would question the men. They were all afraid of Sneer, but someone would speak out—and if they didn't, the guards would tell the story. They'd seen Sneer in action. But no matter what happened, he would get the bastard. Even if they blamed him and put him in solitary he'd find a way.

44

Sometime in the afternoon they came for him. He was almost delirious from the heat, and he stumbled as they led him to the commander's building. The translator was there, standing by the doorway. The commander eyed the prisoner closely as he came in, then nodded to the guards. One left for a minute, then returned with some water for the prisoner. He guzzled it.

"Slowly," said the translator. "Slowly or else you will become even sicker."

The prisoner put the tin mug down and looked at the man.

"Can I sit?" he asked. "I am dizzy, and if I don't sit I'll fall."

The translator said a few words to the guards, then a chair was placed behind the prisoner and he sat.

"You have killed another prisoner," said the translator.

"I did not do it," he said.

"The guards found the others holding you," said the translator.

"I didn't do it. The man was my friend."

The commander said something to the translator.

"You have been accused. Another has seen you commit the crime."

"That man is a liar," he said.

The commander said something and again one of the guards left. They waited in silence. He could feel the men's eyes on him. Then the door opened and the guard walked in with Sneer, leading him to a place about ten feet from the prisoner.

"Tell us again what you said this morning!" commanded the translator.

"I saw this man strangle the dead prisoner," said Sneer. He looked straight ahead as he spoke, avoiding the prisoner's eyes.

The commander said something to the translator. Then he spoke to Sneer again. "If you saw this prisoner attacking the other, why did you do nothing?"

Sneer was silent for a minute. The prisoner noticed that the commander was watching Sneer closely.

"Neither of the men is my friend. What they do to one another is not my concern."

The translator translated for the commander who first

listened, then wrote. After a minute he stopped, looked hard at Sneer, then spoke to the translator again.

"You are to face the man you accuse," said the translator. Sneer turned and looked at the prisoner.

"Repeat the accusation!" ordered the translator.

Sneer looked at him. "This man strangled the dead prisoner," he said, and as he spoke, a smile curled his lips.

The translator translated and the commander looked at the two men again, then wrote. Then they were led away.

XI

They kept him alone for two days in a different building. This one had two windows, and although it was hot, it was bearable. From the rear of the building, he had a view of the plain and the jungle beyond. He guessed it was about a mile and a half to the jungle.

At night a man could make it, he thought. *He'd have to pick a dark night when there was no moon, and he'd have to be quick, but he could do it.* Then he thought about the jungle, thick with vegetation and filled with rushing streams. The only paths were beside the main roads, and the Cong traveled up and down those roads all the time. It was over 350 miles to South Vietnamese territory—or so he had heard; nobody knew for sure because the border was shifting all the time. It would be impossible. Whoever tried it would be caught before they got fifty miles.

That first night in solitary, he couldn't sleep. He stood by the window and looked across the plain in the darkness. The moon was bright—not silver as it was at home, but a deep yellow. It gilded the grass on the plain, and when a wind blew the grass rippled. *Christ*, he thought, *it looks like a wheat field.* Then he thought of home again. He wasn't sure, but it was probably mid-June. The wheat would be standing tall, growing fast and strong for the fall harvest. The farmers would be worried about the rain— too much and the wheat would rot, too little and it would dry up and wither. He had heard about the weather since he was old enough to understand from his Uncle John, who was a farmer.

He remembered the weekend trips to the farm. They would leave Lakewood early on Saturday mornings. By eight they would be on the highway, and by ten they would turn off onto the dusty county road that led to the farm. His Aunt Maude would be waiting for them and would hug everyone. Then he would run out into the farmyard, screaming like a wild Indian. If hay was in the loft of the barn, he would climb up and dive into it, burying himself and pretending he was playing hide and seek. When he came in later for lunch, Uncle John would be in from the fields. Hay would be sticking out of his clothes, and he would still be wild from the freedom and excitement of playing in the barn.

"Looks like someone has been in a hayloft," Uncle John would say with a wink. "Better keep outa' that place —found two boa constrictors there last week."

He would give Uncle John the raspberry, and his mother would frown and shake her head.

*

On the third day they came for him again and took him to the commander's hut. This time Sneer was not there. The prisoner was told to stand while the commander studied the papers in front of him. Then the commander spoke, looking directly at him. The translator spoke slowly to make certain he was understood.

"We have studied your case thoroughly. Unfortunately we have little information. No one saw the crime except

47

your accuser." The translator paused; the prisoner looked steadily at the commander. "Soldiers Minh and Ky have informed us of your fight with the accuser prior to the incident." The translator paused again, and the prisoner could feel both men watching him. "Still, we have only your word against his. What do you have to say for yourself?"

The prisoner looked at them. They seemed like decent men. The translator was young and thin; his spectacles made him look like a scholar. The commander was a bulldog but he did not seem unkind.

"I can say only what I said before. The man who accused me is the murderer. The night before the murder he lost at cards to the dead man who had insulted him. He took his revenge, and now he has tried to put the blame on me."

"You did not tell us about the cards and the insults," said the translator. "We will ask the others about these things." Then he spoke to the commander, and they dismissed the prisoner.

He was not sure, but he felt they would discover the truth. They would be slow, but they would be objective. He slept easier that night.

Two more days passed, then the prisoner was taken to the commander's hut again. Sneer was there this time. He looked more worried than before. The translator spoke first.

"We have learned about the card game and the argument between the victim and the accuser. What does the accuser have to say of this?"

Sneer remained silent, his face expressionless. Several minutes passed. *Maybe,* the prisoner thought, *he won't say anything. And if he does that, they will know.*

But then Sneer spoke. "Show me the man who said that I argued with the dead man. No one said such a thing except this man"—he pointed at the prisoner—"because it did not happen. He made the story up."

The commander spoke, then the translator turned toward Sneer. "We will bring the men. It will take a few minutes. You may sit." The translator called a guard, said something, then the guard marched off. "I have sent for the men."

The prisoner watched Sneer. He was pale, and there were beads of sweat on his forehead.

"It will be easier for you if you confess. We know the truth already." The translator had spoken slowly and clearly, looking directly at Sneer. "But if you do not, we have a way. You have perhaps seen war movies"—he smiled—"depicting the Japanese treatment of western prisoners in the last imperialist war. We know of such methods, and although we do not favor them, we use them when we must."

Sneer's face was twitching. Suddenly he jumped to his feet and dived at the prisoner, but before he could reach him the guard cracked him over the head with the butt of his rifle and he fell in a heap on the floor.

The commander was still sitting at his desk. He had not moved at all. He nodded to the guard, who went to the door and summoned two men to carry Sneer out.

"You will be returned to the barracks," said the translator. "He is the guilty man."

A guard turned and marched out, the prisoner following. Only after the men had returned from work that night, when he noticed how shamefaced they were and how they avoided him, did he realize that none of them had corroborated his story of the card game and the argument. Then suddenly it dawned upon him that the guard could not have been sent to get witnesses, for all the men had been away on the work detail during the day. It was strange where one met justice and what uniform it was apt to wear.

XII

The days moved slowly now. Sometimes he saw them strung out before him forever; at other times he forgot that he was a prisoner so far from home and that his family and friends probably thought him dead.

What does it matter anyway? he wondered. *That way at least they won't worry. If she knew I was here, Mom would worry herself sick.*

But it was strange what knowing that others believed you dead did to you. Some days it seemed he was moving in a vacuum. The trees and the plain and the road that the truck rolled over didn't seem thoroughly real. They were there—if he stubbed his toe on a rock it hurt—but he always had the feeling that they weren't quite real and he could wish them away. The other prisoners didn't seem like men. As he watched them sitting across from him, their noses and eyes seemed to break loose from their faces and float free. And when they talked, it was as if he were watching a pack of animals barking. He had no connection with them.

He dug the holes he was told to dig, built the walls, cleared the rubble—and it was all in a dream. Sometimes he floated away, and he would swear that he was over there—ten yards away sitting in the shade of a tree watching another man work.

The sun came up and the sun went down. Day ran into day. Some days the sun was red—like fire—some days pale gold. And the sky was always cloudless, and there was never any breeze at midday to soften the heat. But by five the leaves started to dance, first one or two, then all of them fluttering. And there was a soft whisper, and the sweat dried on his brow, and he could breathe again, knowing that the day would end and that it would be cool enough to sleep that night.

Then the rainy season came. They stayed in the barracks and stared out the windows or played cards while the drops pounded on the tin roof like bullets. It rained all day and then through the night. Sometimes it only drizzled, but then it would speed up and the drops would come faster and harder, and finally they would be pounding on the roof so hard that everyone stopped speaking because it was impossible to hear.

It rained hardest at noon and midnight. Then the drops were big and made great splashes in the pools of water in the compound. No one walked outside, and the men tried to sleep but couldn't. After fifteen minutes the rain would let up, and the drops would turn small, and he would watch them moving across the compound in waves. Then he could think again, and his mind would start back over the places he had been and the way they looked and the silence and the prisoners working slowly and steadily, never stopping, and the guards watching. Then his thoughts would roll back farther into the past, and he'd remember the battle and the flash and the pain and the sun and the bugs crawling into him. That part always passed quickly. Pain was funny. Once it was gone, you forgot it and couldn't even imagine what it had been like. But then he did not know real pain yet; he only thought he did. That would come later.

At first his mind stopped there. It was incomplete, but it was good because the thoughts filled the emptiness and there was nothing that he had much real feeling about, so it was like watching a movie. Thinking was good then, and it helped him pass the day.

Later that changed. It was like a door opening—nothing violent—but when he went through that door it was different. Then he remembered boot camp and his friends and the ones he had seen killed and the ones he knew must have died and the others who were probably dead, too. He could see Kurowski lying on his bunk with his boots on, his arms behind his head, smoking a stogie.

"All sergeants suck," K said. "And all colonels and all

51

majors and all one-star generals and two-star generals and three-star generals."

"How about the four-star generals?" he asked.

"They take it in the ear," said Kurowski, "in the left ear."

He remembered the card games and Kurowski winning and splitting his take with him.

"Because you ain't a sore loser," K said. "And besides, we're partners. When you play, I always win."

They had left Fort Benning together. They both thought they'd go to Germany.

"We'll drink wine and yodel and chase blondes," said Kurowski. "Ah, German women! They're strong—like oxen—something worth chasing after."

But he'd been wrong, and they were shipped out to Nam in the same outfit. They stayed together through it all—almost all. A week before the sun and the wound and the bugs, it had happened. It was routine. K was out with some men. They didn't come back. Not one. Later they found them. They'd run into a nest of snipers and were all mowed down, filled with holes oozing blood. *Nobody ever looks deader,* he thought, *than someone bleeding from six or seven places at once.*

"Like Swiss cheese," K had said once, "like fuckin' yodel cheese."

His thoughts stayed on K for a week. He saw his face and remembered his laugh and his stupid jokes and his bohunk sadism and his god-awful cigars. Then K was gone, and the prisoner felt better, and the catch in his throat relaxed.

Then for a while it was a picture show again. He remembered school and girls and football games and exams. It was strange the things that stuck, never the exciting things—the corner where he and the guys went out nights for hamburgers; the way the girl who sat in front of him in his American History class pushed her hair out of her eyes; streetcars and an afternoon when it rained and he went to the movies, then came home and drank beer and read *The Sporting News.* Pictures floated past him and he lived in them, but they seemed far away. He couldn't imagine being back there, and he wanted to so much. And he remembered strawberry ice cream and his brother

and the way they used to fight, and he wanted to be back
there only he couldn't. And the rain came down again.
They played cards some and he slept, and the pictures
floated back, and then he went and lay on his pallet, and
then he wanted to get up and do something only they
kept coming back, and he didn't want to do anything.

XIII

The rain lasted for three weeks. The first change he noticed was in its intensity. He wasn't wakened by the
pounding of drops on the roof at midnight, and the men
kept talking at noon because now they could hear each
other. Then there were stretches when the rain was soft,
almost like a mist, and he watched the guards walk back
and forth across the compound, making ripples in the
water that covered everything. When they came into the
barracks, they would be wet but not soaked through like
before, and the tea they carried in the big open kettle
would not be cooled and weak because of the rain water.
Then there were stretches when it didn't rain at all, and
birds waded in the compound's puddles, and the guards
would take potshots at them so they would have meat in
their gloop that night. The guards got excited when they
shot one. They were the worst shots he had ever seen—
that they were winning the war was amazing. And everyone would cheer when they got a bird, then they would
rush through the water and come back holding it by the
legs so that the prisoners could see.

Now he noticed the fence around the compound more
because it stood out, almost black against the gray sky.

He could see the lookouts on the towers and the guns mounted up there and the searchlights they never used, but which were there if they needed them.

After a month the sun still hadn't shown, but the grayness was fading from the sky and it was becoming silver. Finally there was a whole day when it didn't rain, and that night there was a strangeness in the air that he had never felt before—an electricity that got stronger and stronger until it seemed to crack. When he woke the next morning, he could see the edge of a cloud and the sun shining behind it.

*

In three days the sun dried up the water. In a week the roads were hard enough for the trucks to go out on work details, and they were digging holes and building walls again. There was no rubble to clear just then, and there were no rice paddies to plant because they were still flooded. The people beside the road looked the same, although he didn't see any wounded children with arms and legs covered with dirty bandages. That was because the bombing had moved north. But the people still looked thin, and the monks still walked erect and smooth with their faces calm, and the jungle was as green and lush as ever. Someone had told him that there had been fighting in Vietnam for a hundred years, and that the people were so used to it that the children slept through gunfire and bombings. They did not know peace and did not look past the next day, but they prayed and hoped. He thought these would be good things to learn how to do, so he looked closely at the people as the truck passed, but he could tell nothing. And when they looked at him he could see hate in their eyes, so after a while he stopped trying to discover their secret and looked, instead, at the sky or a tree or a bird. He could understand these things, and they hated no one. For a while they would have to be his counselors.

The men talked more now than they had before, but mostly it was only to complain. Some of them held up and others crumpled, and at night sometimes he heard sobbing, but they all went out on the work details each day. At the beginning, months back, this had amazed him. *Why do they keep working?* he asked himself. It would have been different if the guards threatened them, but he had never seen this. They watched and only showed the men what to do. The prisoners worked without coercion.

Now he understood. If you didn't work, there was nothing. The empty space in your life was worse, and the memories and the loneliness became stronger; and if you were not tired at night you couldn't sleep, and then the thoughts grew stronger. That was the worst time—when you were alone in the darkness.

And so now he worked as hard as the rest, steadily and smoothly. When he dug a hole, it was a good hole even if he thought it would be used for antiaircraft guns. The walls he built were straight and smooth and strong, and when it came time to plant rice, he pressed the shoots deep into the oozing mud. Doing these things made him feel better. He slept at night and didn't dream too much, and the days passed and he did not rot away. He kept thinking about freedom. He looked at the jungle and thought about how a man could live off it and travel to the south, avoiding villages, moving slowly at night. According to the newspapers they were given every two weeks, the Cong seemed to be winning all the battles and the Vietnamese were moving farther and farther south. At home the protests to end the war were growing. *If they end it,* he thought, *then we'll go free.* And he would breathe a little faster and thrust his shovel deeper into the ground.

But the end did not come. Month after month there were pictures of protests, but nothing happened and he stopped believing it would end that way. *They'll never do that,* he thought. *They can't. They've lost too many men already and too much is at stake. They can't do it.*

Then he would look at the jungle again, and his mind would race as he saw himself crouching in the shadows of the trees, waiting for the night so he could move south. *I've got to try it,* he thought, *otherwise I'll go crazy. I've got to!*

XIV

For a week the moon had been covered with clouds, and the plain was dark. He couldn't see the jungle. It was so black he couldn't even make out the guard tower.

I should plan it, he thought. *I should have a map and food and a plan.* But he didn't, and he couldn't wait. *If I start putting things aside someone will notice,* he said to himself. Then he laughed. No one would tell—none of the other prisoners cared, and the guards would never notice. He should have been ready, but he had no time. It had to be now while the nights were dark and he could cross the plain without being seen.

The air was thicker now, and sounds lingered in it. At night he could hear the guards talking in the tower. He had never been able to hear them before, and it worried him. They would be able to hear him when he crossed the plain. They might get him—maybe wing him—and they'd be sure to catch him then even if he made the jungle, because he wouldn't be able to move fast enough. Speed—that was the thing he would need. He wouldn't have any food, and he wouldn't be able to stop anywhere because if he did they'd catch him, so he'd just have to keep going. He could drink from the streams, but there would be no way to get anything to eat once he left the compound. And it would take him at least a week to work his way south—that was if he was lucky and found a good trail and didn't have to hole up. No man could go for a week without food and cover twenty miles a day.

When he thought of all that, he wanted to give it up.

He looked at the other men in the barracks. Most of them were lying on their pallets, staring at nothing with that empty, hopeless gaze he had come to know so well that it no longer startled him. A few men were in a corner, playing cards. He looked out the windows at the black of the night, then back to the men. He was just like them, no different. In a few more months he would be doing the same—staring into nothing, passing the evenings at cards, living for another smoke and dreaming of home. His soul would then be dead—completely dead—and all he could do would wait like a child for someone to liberate him. Already he could feel the tug, the desire to give up and relax into the nothingness of not caring.

He looked out the window again. The blackness had turned into a smoky gray. He could hear a wind rising, moving across the plain and then over the jungle. He imagined the dancing leaves. Then the rain started to fall, not steadily but in bursts like machine gun fire. Mixed with the sound of the drops was the rustle of the grass on the plain as it swayed in the wind.

The evening moved on. The lights went out. The rain continued, and the wind grew stronger. He listened in the darkness. There were snores and some groans. In the corner, someone was crying. The sobs were quick, not loud but choked and fast the way a baby cries. He quietly got to his feet, walked to the door, then silently moved out into the compound.

The rain cut into his face. The wind was whipping in from the southwest, slanting the drops toward the jungle. He moved across the open space, then came to the commander's cabin. He stopped, hunched over, and walked cautiously around the building. Then he straightened up and ran toward the back of the compound, the area farthest from the tower with the guards and the guns and the searchlights.

The first of the two barbed wire fences that surrounded the compound was before him. The strands of wire were horizontal, about six inches apart. He lay down, pushed the bottom strand up, then slid under. He was surprised that it had been so easy. Then he came to the outer fence. This was mesh with barbs running both horizontally and vertically. He tried to push it up to make a space at the bottom, but it wouldn't move. He dropped to his knees to inspect it. The vertical strands were driven into the earth. He grabbed a wire and pulled. It didn't move. He tried again. His hands tore on the wire, and he let go. For a minute he stood there, collecting himself. The only other way was to climb over the top. That wouldn't be easy. He'd tear his hands going up, and he would be a sitting target. If the clouds broke, even for a second, he would be completely visible, and they would have him in a flash like an insect trapped in a spider's web. But it was the only way.

He started up. As he pulled himself upward, he felt the barbs push into his flesh. He gritted his teeth, then climbed on. When he got up about ten feet, he looked up. He had made it about halfway, and already his hands were in shreds. He reached and tried to pull himself up but lost his grip and fell. As he felt himself falling, he pushed out with his foot so he wouldn't slide down the wire. If he hadn't done that, the whole fence would have vibrated, and they would have heard him.

He lay on the ground. He couldn't tell how long, but he thought he had passed out for a few minutes—not from pain but from fear. No, he was mistaken—he only imagined it. He hadn't passed out. He knew what he was doing. He was just resting, getting his strength back, getting ready to try it again. The rain came harder then, and it made his hands sting. He tried to look at them but couldn't because of the darkness. He put them to his mouth and tasted blood. *Maybe,* he thought, *I should wrap them. That way I'll be able to stand it.* He tore two strips from the bottom of his shirt, then tied it in front. He couldn't leave it, for in the jungle the insects would eat him alive without it. The natives could stand it—the bugs didn't even bother them—but a white man would almost be driven crazy with pain in an hour. He had seen it happen.

He wound the strips around his hands, covering the palms but leaving the fingers free. Then he started up again. Five feet . . . ten feet. He looked up, and he could see the top of the fence against the sky. That meant it was getting lighter. Morning was coming already. He had no way of knowing how long he'd been in the compound. Common sense told him to turn back. Even if he got over now, he'd probably never make it across the plain before light. And even if he did, they would discover that he was missing at the morning check, and he would only be able to get a mile or two into the jungle before they caught him. It was wiser to turn back and sneak into the barracks before anyone saw him. That was his best plan. He could try it again another night, maybe even tomorrow. The black nights might continue for a month. There would be plenty of time to try it again.

But he kept pulling himself up. Something drove him, and he knew he wouldn't turn back. They'd have to stop him. He'd keep trying, and if he fell this time he'd climb up again.

He didn't fall. When he reached the top he hovered for a second, tempted to push off and leap down. That would be easy but stupid. If he jumped there was a good chance he would hurt an ankle; then he'd be done before he even started.

So he eased himself down, strand by strand, until he had only five feet to go. The urge to jump came again, but he resisted. He inched downward until he felt the ground, then the prisoner turned and fled over the plain.

It was still dark. The grayness in the sky had only been temporary, and the blackness had returned. The wind became stronger. It was at his back, driving him on. He flew forward in bounding strides. After a half mile, he looked over his shoulder. The compound was still in darkness. They didn't know or else they would have switched on the searchlights. He ran faster. Now he could discern the edge of the jungle ahead. His heart pounded. He would make it.

At the edge of the trees, he stopped for a second and looked back. The sky was lighter now, and he could see the silhouette of the fence and the watchtower against the brightening clouds. That meant he had about an hour and a half before the first check—not much time. He pushed back the leaves and moved into the forest.

XV

At first the going was easy because the jungle closest to the plain was not dense, and he could weave his way between the trees easily. Farther in, it was different. Here the trees were closer together, and even though there were places where the light came through, the going was slower. Sometimes he had to circle to keep moving ahead, and he wasn't even sure that he was always moving in the direction he wanted to go. If he could have seen the sun, he could have oriented himself, but all he saw of it were arrows of light shooting down from the gaps in the trees high overhead.

At least it was dry—not wet as he had imagined—so he didn't have to worry about leeches. He still felt strong, and he was making good time.

After about three miles the ground started to slope upward. He had entered the hills. He remembered how they looked high up from the temple—endless rolling hummocks, all covered with green. They had gone on and on, and everywhere there were trees. There was only one road—the one that ended at the temple. If he could keep moving and if he stayed away from the road, he'd be OK. It would take a thousand men to find him in that jungle.

He imagined the scene back at the compound, the commander questioning the guards, the men in the tower searching the plain with binoculars. Then guards would be loaded on trucks and sent out. They would probably guess that he'd gone south into the jungle—that wouldn't be hard. But there were only about fifty soldiers at the compound—he had counted them—and the most they could spare was twenty, and twenty men could only cover so much ground. He just had to keep going, that was all. His adversary wasn't human now; it was vegetable and animal. It crawled, and it swayed in the wind, and it had thorns and claws.

He kept going all day, stopping only twice to rest for about a half hour each time. His legs were tired and his side hurt, but he knew he could keep going like that for at least another day. He was hungry, but it didn't matter. He expected that, and he could stand it. When it became completely dark, he stopped. If he kept going, there was a good chance that he would lose his direction, and he might circle or veer west into the real mountains; then he'd never make it. He could die there, and no one would ever find the bones.

So he groped in the darkness for a place to sleep. He wanted a flat rock—there would be fewer insects, and he imagined that he would be safe from snakes. But after a half hour, he still hadn't found one. Then he remembered that he had seen no rocks like that during the day. He knew he was wasting his time, so he chose a spot in front of a big tree and lay down.

He slept long and deep, but when the first light filtered through the trees he woke immediately. He felt his arms and legs. They were lined with small lumps where something had bitten him. He ran his hands through his hair, felt two insects, and pulled them out. They were small and black with bright red spots on their backs, and they had big pincers like tiny lobsters. He threw them to the ground and crushed them; then he stretched. His legs were sore, but they weren't weak. He could go far today. He took his bearing from the tree, remembering that he had come straight at it the night before. If he wanted to continue south, he would have to pass at a diagonal to the lowest branch. Then he walked on. His feet hurt, so he stopped and took off his shoes. Blisters covered the soles of both feet. His hands hurt, too, only the pain was different there. He looked at them closely. The left was all right, but one place on the right was badly torn and looked infected, as if a piece of a rusty barb from the fence had lodged in it. He pressed to work it out, and the pain made him gasp.

By noon he had covered about five miles, but he was thirsty and hadn't found any streams. He couldn't understand that because he had seen hundreds of them when the truck carried him up and down the jungle roads on the work details. Some days after a rain, there were so many flooding the road so badly that they had to turn back and return to the compound. Now, when he needed one, there was none.

In the afternoon he pressed on. He had already climbed up and down ten large hills—he kept track of this—and he was pretty certain he was moving south. The ground seemed a little rockier, and the trees were fewer here. He had the feeling that he was gradually moving into higher land. The air was cool, and occasionally a breeze stirred the leaves. He could see ahead —his eyes were accustomed to the half-light, and it was a little brighter. He could see the black trunks of mahogany trees, thick and squat, and here and there the thinner, graceful stands of bamboo. Toward the middle of the afternoon, he was startled by a strange cry. It sounded like a man calling for help, repeated over and over, echoing through the trees. He stopped instantly, crouched behind a tree, and peered in the direction of the cry. It came again—a screech, half-human, half-animal. Then he saw the crier—a blue bird with a long green tail. It walked a few steps, weaving in an "S" pattern, then arched its neck and the cry came again, three times. He watched it strut elegantly between the trunks, then he walked on.

*

The ground was climbing again, and for the first time he could see the sun, orange and burning. It was sinking, and he lined it up with his right shoulder. He had been going in the right direction, perhaps a little more toward the east than he had planned, but he could not have been off by more than five degrees. He had no way of telling how far he had come, but he guessed that he had covered nearly fifty miles. That meant he had about 300 more to go—a long way, but he still felt strong.

Now he slackened his pace a little. He would move steadily and not overdo it. Persistence was the key. Ten more days and he could make it if he kept up a good pace. Uphill, downhill, resting twice a day, sleeping when he needed to. He remembered seeing maps of the country. There were towns stretched along the coast but only a few inland, and most of these were along the road that went south from Hanoi all the way to Saigon, paralleling the coast for 800 miles. He was east of that toward the Laotian border, and there were only mountains and jungles there. He would go south as far as he could, then east. If the Americans hadn't left yet, he would eventually find them near the coast, in tent cities with guns and tanks and Viet whores. They'd be there; they wouldn't leave. They had too much at stake, and besides, the gooks didn't really want to drive them all the way out, not yet. He didn't know why, but he was pretty sure of that.

XVI

The third day he started to feel weaker. He had found water just before nightfall on the previous day, and so at least he wasn't dehydrated. But he could tell that his strength was going, and he knew he was slowing down. Sometimes he felt lightheaded and now he had to stop more often. He had been foolish in thinking that he could go for a week without eating. He had imagined that something would turn up—some berries or perhaps fruit—that would enable him to keep going. But there was nothing. Except for the blue bird, the only living things he'd seen were insects. He was not that hungry yet. If it came to it he'd eat them, but now they'd only make him

sick, and that would make things worse. It had been stupid not to have tried to get the bird the day before. That
would have filled him for at least three or four days. He
would have had to eat it raw, but he could have done it.
He listened for more cries, but there was no sound except
the buzzing of insects.

When he stopped toward evening his legs were cramp-
ing, and he was so weak he couldn't walk anymore. This
time he found a flat rock—the ground was stonier here—
and he lay down. *At least the bugs won't eat me,* he
thought. *God, there's not enough left for them and me
both.*

Then he slept—not a deep sleep but a half stupor. He
could still see the light coming through the trees and here
and there even a patch of blue. He imagined he would
think of food, but he didn't. Instead he remembered the
time he'd gone camping in the Rockies with two friends.
They had hiked all morning and at noon had crossed the
timberline, coming into snow fields. He was eighteen that
summer, and his high school graduation present was a
sleeping bag and a backpack. He remembered the mountain air and the wonder of seeing snow in the summer and
the bright glare and the way his friends looked in sun-
glasses, marching across the whitened slopes without their
shirts. The first night his friends were burned so badly
they couldn't sleep; they hadn't felt the sun because of the
cool air and the wind. He'd been smarter and had kept
his shirt on. He slept soundly that night and wakened the
next day to watch the sun come over the mountains. It
was the most beautiful thing he'd ever seen—the sky
turquoise, the sun pink, then gradually growing red, then
turning to orange.

Eventually he fell into an uneasy sleep, awoke shiver-
ing about midnight, then slept again. When the morning
light came through the trees, he opened his eyes and tried
to rise, but he couldn't. He fell asleep again and finally
awoke around noon.

It was hot, and he was sweating. The rock was in the
middle of a small clearing, and the sun was shining directly on it. He sat up, then stood. The weakness was
worse than the day before. He had hoped sleep would
help, but it hadn't. He had to find something to eat or

else he would never make it. He climbed off the rock and moved toward the trees again. Just as he left the clearing, something prompted him to look back. There were dark spots, holes, near the base of the flat gray rock on which he had been sleeping. Then he recalled that snakes liked rocks. The holes might be snake holes.

He went back to the rock, but he didn't know how to begin. It would do no good to plug up the holes. It was midday, and the snakes would be inside, keeping out of the heat. All he could do was wait. He sat down about fifteen feet from the three likeliest-looking holes and waited. Time passed. The sun moved to the right; then it was gone behind the trees, and the shadows started to cross the clearing. When they reached the rock, he tensed. If there were snakes in that rock, they would come out soon.

He didn't have long to wait. Two came out of the first hole and slithered toward the jungle. They moved in a continuous "S" and were so fast that they were gone before he could do anything. Quickly he moved closer. Another came out of the middle hole. He smashed it with a small rock, catching it just behind the head. The snake started again, moving slowly, and he picked up the rock and pounded its head. This time it lay still. Then he went back to the holes. Another came out, and he hit it with the rock. This time he got the head on the first try, and it stopped moving. More snakes were coming out, and he rushed back and forth, pounding them with his rock. The rock in his hand was now slimy from the blood, and when he swung his arm down, it slipped out. He grabbed for it and felt a hot sting at his wrist. When he raised his arm, a snake came with it, its tail wiggling and its fangs buried in the flesh of his forearm. He shook his arm frantically, but the snake would not let go. Then he grabbed it and started to pull, but the pain was worse and he had to let go.

He bent over and found another rock. Laying his arm on the ground, he started to pound the snake just behind the head. After three blows, it let go and slowly slithered away.

He looked at his arm. There were two small holes oozing blood about halfway between his hand and elbow. He put the wound to his mouth and sucked, then spit. He did

65

it again. He didn't know if the snake was poisonous or not. He didn't think so because usually only the smaller ones were, but only time would tell. He should have put on a tourniquet to keep the poison in the arm, but it was too late. He'd just have to wait and see what happened.

He turned to the dead snakes. There were four of them, and they were pretty big. They were gray-brown with bluish, bullet heads. Two were almost five feet long, the others were between two and three feet. *Well,* he thought, *I'd better start. They'll taste the same in an hour.*

He skinned the smallest snake, then held it up. The flesh was pink and smooth, almost like chicken. He would have given a hundred dollars for matches then, even if the smoke did give away his position. Roasted, the snake wouldn't be so bad, but when he looked at it now, it seemed to be still trembling. He knew the longer he waited the worse it would get, so he bit into the flesh, tore out a big chunk, chewed it, and swallowed.

He felt his stomach turn over and waited a minute until he calmed down. Then he took another bite and chewed. The flesh was soft and juicy. He swallowed.

After he had swallowed six or seven mouthfuls, he stopped. That would be enough for now. More would probably make him sick. He took the rest of the snake, wrapped it in a leaf, and stuffed it into his shirt. He strung the other snakes on his belt, cinching it tighter to hold them. Then he walked on. There were about two hours of light left, and he wanted to cover as much ground as possible. Every step brought him that much closer to freedom.

XVII

By the seventh day he reckoned he had covered 125 miles. He had been going at a good clip from the beginning, excepting the third day, and he had made up for that. He still had one snake left. The flesh was dried and hardened, but it would still be edible. At first he had been afraid that it would rot, but the air dried it, and the sun seemed to cure it. A few days earlier, there wouldn't have been enough sunlight. But now he was in higher country, and the air was cooler, and the trees much more sparse so that he walked in flickering sunlight almost all day.

Sometimes he stopped and sat under a tree to rest and study the country. All around him were hills, each one like the next with small trees covering them, their yellowish-green leaves fluttering in the soft breeze. The breeze always came from the southwest, blowing toward the China Sea, and it was almost as good a compass as the sun or the North Star. If he kept up this pace for seven more days, he would be in territory held by the U.S. There was no way he could miss.

Fortunately, he had a good memory and could call a rough map of the country to mind when he needed to. If he kept going as he was, he would cross back and forth over the border into Laos a couple of times. The Cong would not be watching these borders, for they all lay in the mountains where the only people were hill tribesmen. There would be rivers along the way, but there wouldn't

67

be big ones until he got to the south. He'd worry about them then.

That night he ate half of the last snake. Tomorrow he'd have to start looking for food again.

He woke at dawn to the sound of birds, but when he searched the tress he could see nothing. Already he was thinking of food. If he had trouble finding some, he would be slowed down again, and the need to move haunted him. The country was green, but he saw nothing edible. If he was a native, he would know where to look. The gooks could make a meal out of anything. But he didn't know which roots to try, and he was afraid that if he ate the wrong ones, he'd get sick.

Toward noon he saw a bird. It was a small, dull brown one with a black tail, sitting on a branch about fifteen feet above the ground. He picked up a rock and moved cautiously toward it. It continued to preen itself, pecking under one wing with its bill. He threw the rock but missed. Still the bird sat. He searched frantically for another rock, found two, and fired them both at the bird. The second one hit the branch and the bird flew off.

That night he took only four bites of the snake. He had enough for another day, maybe two if he ate sparingly and didn't try to cover too much distance.

The next day was hot—the hottest weather he'd encountered so far—but he was in high country now, so there wasn't much humidity, and he walked easily. About noon he sensed that he was getting burned and looked for a place to rest until the sun had moved to the west, but couldn't find any cover. Everywhere it was the same —sunlight filtering through flickering leaves, dappling the ground and dazzling him. He kept walking.

That night he was very thirsty. He hadn't found water in two days, and his mouth tasted of salt. He decided to eat only two bites of snake—that way it would last a while longer. He lifted the snake to his mouth and started to bite into it, then noticed a strange smell. The meat had changed color—it was purplish, and flies were buzzing around it. He looked closely to see if any of it was still unspoiled, saw that it wasn't, and threw it away, cursing himself for not having eaten it the day before while it was still good.

He began to get depressed. He had left the compound ten days ago and by his reckoning had not even covered half the distance to freedom. He still felt strong, but the solitude was starting to bother him. The chirps of crickets kept him awake, the wind seemed loud, and the sound of the grass swaying in the night breeze irritated him. He imagined the blades of grass sawing at each other, tearing their fibers apart. *You're going around the bend,* he thought. *You'd better think about sex.* So he manufactured some fantasies. That made him feel better and eventually he fell asleep.

The next day he woke with a dryness in his throat. When he rubbed his face, it felt hot and parched like old leather. The skin at the corners of his eyes and mouth was split. He stood up and looked over the hills. They were spread out all around him as far as he could see, brownish yellow, covered with small trees. He squinted and stared into the distance, looking for the glimmer of water. He saw only more hills. He sat down again. He didn't feel weak as he had on the third day, but he just couldn't make himself walk any farther. He leaned against a tree trunk and peered up at the sky. It was blue, becoming paler and paler until it was almost white at the horizon. Far off in the direction he thought was west, he could see some clouds. *They must be at least fifty miles away,* he thought. In his depressed state, he couldn't imagine water anywhere between him and the clouds. He put his head on his knees and closed his eyes.

Toward noon the heat got worse. He had been dozing, but now there were flies—millions—small flies that bit. Soon they were swarming about him. He couldn't stand it anymore, so he got up and started walking again. He hardly cared where, but instinct pointed him south.

He walked through the afternoon, putting one foot in front of the other, moving like a zombie. The hills flattened out into a undulating plain, but still there was no water, and he knew there was probably even less chance of finding a stream here than there had been in the hills.

When twilight came, he lay down and slept, woke after an hour, then slept again. After midnight the air cooled, but he didn't waken. Just before dawn, he started to shiver. He felt feverish, so the coolness was refreshing, but his hands were shaking and his skin felt strange. He knew that if he didn't find water soon, it would be the end. He remembered the movies he'd seen about men crossing the desert. They hallucinated and fought among themselves and called out to God. It wasn't like that. He just felt weak and didn't care anymore. He tried to walk on but gave up. *There's no point,* he thought. *I'll never make it.* And he thought of the clouds so far away, and again he imagined that there was no water anywhere between him and those clouds. He started to sob, then stopped; the sound was strange—half wail, half rasp. It shocked him. *If I sound like that,* he thought, *I must be just about gone.* Then he shut his eyes and tried to sleep again.

*

At the first light of dawn, he saw them—a line of figures black against the brightening sky. They were marching about a half mile to the east of where he lay. He tried to stand but couldn't. Then he tried to yell. The sound was weak and not human. He tried to stand again. This time he almost made it before his knees buckled.

They were closer to him now, marching along a path that would lead them about 200 yards from him. He summoned all his strength and tried to scream. It came out as a strange, eerie wail, and the men stopped. The last man in the line pointed toward him. He raised his hand, then collapsed.

XVIII

When he came to, they were giving him water. It tasted sweet, but he choked. The cup was pulled away. He couldn't see their faces because the sun behind them was blinding him. Their hands were brown and lined, but that meant nothing. They could be Viet Cong or Vietnamese. Then the group around him separated, and he made out one man who was standing and looking down at him. The man gave a command, and he felt himself being picked up and carried. He was placed on a stretcher, a hat was put on his head, and the men resumed marching.

The men marched at a good pace, and the stretcher rocked from side to side. Still he fell asleep. In his dreams he could feel the rhythmic sway, but he didn't waken. He dreamed of water. He was on a small rowboat, which rocked gently as it moved through the waves. Two men were rowing, but he couldn't see their faces. The boat moved on and on. When he looked over the side, the water was clear, and he could see deep down into it. A million fish were swimming there, all of different colors. He reached his cupped hand into the water, then raised it to his lips. The water was cool and tasted like mint.

*

When he woke he was in shade, and he could see men moving around, setting up camp. They were talking as they worked. He looked for a guard but could see none. *They must be on our side*, he thought, *otherwise they*

71

would have someone watching me. He called to two men who were working near him, and one came over. He spoke to him, but the man smiled and shook his head. He looked at his uniform. It was olive green, but there were no markings so he couldn't tell. The man said something and gestured. He didn't understand. The man spoke and pointed. Now he understood. The man was pointing at a helmet on the ground nearby. There was a small yellow star on it. Some expression must have crossed his face because the man looked at him for a minute, then shook his head again slowly and patted him on the shoulder.

For three days they marched. On the third day, he walked with them. His face was sore from the sun, but otherwise he felt much better. The pace was fast, and they ate only twice a day—in the morning before they started and in the evening after they had set up camp. The sky was cloudless and blue, but ahead of them, where the plain met the jungle, he could see dark clouds hanging low over the trees. That place seemed to be about twenty miles away, but he couldn't really tell because the plain was flat, and each time he looked toward the jungle it seemed just as far away as before.

When he lay down to sleep on the third night, he thought about trying to escape. All he would have to do would be to slip off in the darkness. But then he remembered the thirst and the hunger. There would be other chances. *I'll do it when I'm stronger, and the odds are better,* he said to himself. While he thought this, there was another voice in the back of his mind, eating at him. It told him that if he gave in once, that would be the beginning of the end. He became angry. He hated that voice. It had no compassion. It was insane.

*

On the fifth day they entered the jungle. There was a trail marked and the ground was trampled, so he knew that they probably came this way often. He thought it was probably a supply line—a link between their northern and southern forces. He wished he had a map so he could mark it; that way when he escaped he could tell his side, and they could block the trail. *That would mess them up good,* he thought. *They would have to hack a new trail, and it could take months.* Then he laughed at himself. *When you escape. Yeah, when?* It was the voice from the back again. *That'll be a long time coming . . . a long wait.*

He tried to blot that out. If he listened to it, he would go crazy.

For three days they marched through the jungle. On all sides he saw nothing but green, and the jungle was so thick he could see only a foot or so into it from the trail. This was different from the jungle he had seen when riding in the truck on the work details. Then he had been able to make out individual tree trunks and catch a glimpse of a stream now and then, bubbling and twisting as it plunged in the darkness. Here there was nothing but leaves and vines. No birds, no water buffalo. Only insects, buzzing and whining. Sometimes the sky was blotted out for long stretches—perhaps a mile or so—and then he felt as if the jungle were closing in on him, swallowing him up in greenness. It made him dizzy. He focused on the back of the man ahead of him and kept marching, his anxiety giving him energy. He understood then why they had told him in boot camp that it was nothing for a man to march forty miles through the jungle in a day, but he was lucky if he could manage twenty-five in the open.

About noon on the fourth day, they came to a base. One minute there was jungle, the air thick, the insects humming, the next minute they were in the open, marching across a clearing, the ground covered with red dust in which he could see hundreds of footprints. In the center of the open area were three large buildings. A pole extended from the top of the biggest building, and a red Viet Cong flag hung from it. The men marched to the center of the compound, then stopped and formed a line. He stood at the end, feeling foolish and not knowing what to do. A man in a black uniform came out of the central building, interrogated the leader of the men for a minute, then barked some commands. The men marched off toward a ramshackle building with steel walls and a thatch roof at the very end of the compound. For a moment he thought of following them, but one of the men indicated that he should stay behind. So he stood alone, feeling the sunlight, looking at the red dust, and

73

watching the men he had been with for a week marching off. The man in black was talking to another officer who was dressed in black but without as many red stripes. After a minute the officer had finished, and both men looked toward him.

"Captain Van Thinh says that they discovered you in the plain at latitude 20° 40'." The man stopped as if he expected an answer.

The prisoner said nothing.

"We assume that you are an infiltrator, a member of the imperialist force that we have defeated and driven south. We punish infiltrators with death."

The words had the sound of finality, but they did not move him. He stood in the sunlight and stared at the two men—at their yellow-brown faces and slanted eyes and black uniforms—and suddenly it all seemed absurd, and he started to laugh. The men looked surprised. They spoke rapidly for a minute. He kept laughing. The trees and the flag and the red dust and the soldiers and the blue sky punctured by the bright orange sun—they all seemed unreal, like the pieces of a fantastic game, and he could not stop laughing.

Finally the man with fewer stripes walked off, while the other remained, staring at him.

"You cannot fool us by pretending to be mad. Many have tried that, and it has done no good. It will not save you."

He stared back at the man, then sat down, put his head on his knees, and continued laughing. Now and then he looked up at the man, but mostly he just shut his eyes and tried to relax. He was laughing so hard his stomach hurt. He wanted to stop, but he couldn't. Then he felt hands on his shoulders, and two men lifted him to his feet. Then two more men joined them, and they took him to a small building on the edge of the compound, opened the door, and pushed him in.

The door was locked behind him. He banged on it, but they didn't come back, so he went to the lone window. It faced a wooden shed, and in front of it were latrines. The smell was sickening. He went back to the door and banged on it again, but still no one came. Then he sat on the floor, leaned back against the wall, and stared ahead.

74

He knew he had appeared mad, but he also knew that it had been a lucky break. Otherwise he might already be dead. He didn't know how long he could keep it up, though. It had been a natural reaction, but the feeling was wearing off. In a while he would look like any other prisoner; then they would change their minds, and he would be facing a firing squad.

A breeze blew, wafting the odor of the latrines to him. It was thick and pungent. Almost without thinking, he went to the door, grabbed the bars of the small window, and started to moan.

"Jesus," he said. "Oh Jesus, let me outa here!"

Two soldiers were sitting about ten yards from the building. They looked at him, then laughed. One pointed to his head and made a circle with his finger. He roared again, this time louder, like a wounded animal. The men got up and moved away. He moved back from the door and sat against the wall again. It was hot—the sun was shining straight down on the roof and only the window in the door and the window in the back, by the latrines, let in any air. He was sweating, and he cursed. He cursed himself and the Viet Cong and the Vietnamese and the President and Ho Chi Minh and God. Then he shut his eyes and tried to sleep. The sweat soaked his shirt. He took it off, made a soggy pillow out of it, and lay down. Two flies came through the window, buzzed in a circle, then landed on his shoulder and promenaded there. He left them alone; it was too hot to move. *If I was a cow*, he thought, *I'd swat them with my tail*. Grazing cows passed through his mind, munching grass slowly. *But you are*, said the voice in the back of his mind. *A cow is a thing without horns, and that's you, baby*. He cursed the voice and continued to ignore the flies. Then they began to bite, and he tried to swat them—he missed. They buzzed away, circled, and came back. This time one landed on his neck. He could almost see it out of the corner of his eye. *You're a smart-ass little bugger*, he thought. *You've got balls*. He swatted at it, and it buzzed off, circled, and landed on the wall, waiting for another chance.

For a half hour the flies tormented him. They were battling flies, war insects, and they circled and dived, strafed him, then moved off. He got to his feet and swung his shirt at them and they buzzed away to the other side of the room. He ran after them, but they zoomed over his head and crossed the room again. He stood. *There's no sense in this,* he thought. He became afraid that he really was going mad. *Chasing flies,* he said to himself, *my God!* So he lay down again, and the flies started buzzing again. They were flying short distances now—advancing on him by moving three or four feet, then landing, scratching their legs together, then flying another short hop. Finally they were both on the ceiling directly over him. They dived, and with a roar he sprang at them, swinging his shirt wildly. He got one, and it fell to the ground. The other zoomed out the window toward the latrines. He went over to the dead fly, looked at it for a second, then started to laugh again.

XIX

The next morning a man came to see him. The prisoner had had nothing to eat or drink since they put him in the shed, so he remained on the floor when the door opened, too weak to stand even though he knew that it angered the Viet Cong officers when an American sat in their presence. The man was tall and thin, but he had very wide shoulders—wider than he'd ever seen on an Oriental—and almost no neck. His head seemed to sit on his shoulders, and the prisoner couldn't imagine how the man could look to the side.

"Prisoner will rise," said the man in the Oriental singsong of pidgin English. He tried to struggle to his feet, but couldn't make it and gave up. The man looked at him with contempt, then went out the door and returned with a soldier who gave the prisoner some water and rice in a bowl. Then the two men left, and he ate. About a half hour later, the officer came back. This time the prisoner stood. *Coward!* said the voice in the back of his mind.

"Prisoner is spy. This we know. Prisoner must tell us what installations he has seen, and where he is to report to his superior."

He looked at the man. He could continue to feign madness, or he could answer honestly. Instinct told him madness was the better bet.

He made a funny noise, laughed, and sat down. The man's eyes narrowed as he looked at him hard. The prisoner continued to sit, staring ahead. Then the man walked over to him and kicked him. He fell over. The man tried to kick him again, but he grabbed the man's leg and pulled him to the ground. Then he heard shouts, and men were around him. He felt a blow on the back of his neck, then everything went black.

*

When he awoke, he found himself in the same place, lying on his side. He rolled over on his back and stared at the ceiling for a minute. Then he tried to get to his feet. His neck was sore, and he had a headache, but otherwise he was OK. He looked at the place where the man had kicked him—it was turning black and blue. *Well,* he congratulated himself, *at least you didn't just lie there and take it.* The voice in the back of his head was quiet, satisfied for a while. He had played the game that he had chosen. Only a madman would attack an interrogator. If they weren't convinced before, they should be by now. He sat down and stared at the wall again, then looked out the window. When he sat, it changed his angle of vision, and he didn't see the latrines, only the tops of the trees at the edge of the clearing and the sky above. Some clouds were passing over, and he watched them. Then he saw five or six black dots swoop overhead, high

77

up at about 20,000 feet. He wondered which side they belonged to.

They did not give him any more food that day, and he could feel his stomach working. A little before dark he went to the door again, grabbed the bars, and roared. Men were passing back and forth outside, but no one turned. He lay down and slept.

The next day at about noon, they gave him another bowl of rice and some water. A little later the door opened, and the man with no neck walked in. This time there were two other men with him. They were both stocky and looked strong.

"The prisoner refuses to speak, and the prisoner has attacked an officer in the army of the people. He will be punished."

The two men pulled him to his feet and held his arms, and the four of them walked out into the sunlight. They crossed to the far side of the camp and stopped at a place where two poles were stuck into the ground about six feet apart. The men tied each arm to a pole, then moved back. He felt a crack across his back. It knocked his breath out and burned. Then there was another crack, and another. He wanted to roar again—*C'mon, show them!* he thought. *Put on a real show!* But something wouldn't let him, and he remained silent. The blows continued until he had been given twelve; then they stopped. The officer stood before him.

"The prisoner has been punished. Now we will ask questions again. What installations has prisoner seen, and where is he to contact his superior?"

He said nothing and the man nodded, and the blows commenced again. After ten they stopped, and the man asked the same questions. The prisoner's head was hanging. He felt someone grab him by the hair and lift his face.

"Prisoner will look at interrogator!"

Lights flickered in the background and he felt dizzy. He tried to focus his eyes but couldn't. All he could make out was No-Neck's black uniform, his wide shoulders and bullet head.

"Prisoner will speak!"

He moaned for a second, then tried to fake a laugh.

There was a sharp command from No-Neck, and the blows to his back started again. After five lashes he passed out.

*

He woke in the shed again, lying on his stomach. It was night, and the air was thick. He was bathed in sweat. When he tried to move, the pain came. It felt like his back held endless knives, each stabbing into him. He lay still, breathing heavily. Then he made another attempt to move, but it was the same, and he sank back and lay still, wishing for sleep. He closed his eyes, and his breathing slowed. The sweat was turning the lacerations on his back to fire. The burning warmed his whole body, filling him with fever, and he fell into a delirious state halfway between sleeping and waking. Shapes floated in front of him. He saw No-Neck and the green of the jungle and himself, alone on a hill, crying out for water and food. Then the burning became stronger, and he woke. He stared into the darkness, cursing the pain that ate at him. He could see the outline of the window and the blue-black of the sky. There were a few stars—silver, twinkling dots. He watched them. It seemed to him that they were beckoning him, and in his delirium he imagined himself floating up, rising in softness toward them. First he was above the camp, watching the soldiers walking back and forth to the gunsights and the sentries pacing at the edge of the clearing. Then he was higher, and the camp was a dark space in the midst of the great jungle, visible only by the faint flickering light of the fire where the sentries kept their tea hot. Then he was higher still, floating in the blue-black air over mountains and rivers. He was racing to the west, and a faint pinkish-orange glow lit the horizon. Then he had caught up to the sun and was passing it, crossing over the western coast of Africa. It was night there, the only sign of day a faint red on the horizon behind him. He was speeding on, swooping high over the clouds, turning northward, homing in like a pigeon. And there were the lights of the coast, and he could make out the Empire State Building and the flashing neon signs of Broadway. Then he went west again, over Pennsylvania

79

sleeping beneath him, past Pittsburgh and the stacks of the mills belching orange fire. And then he saw the lake and the lights that ringed the lakefront and Detroit Avenue and the trees and the broad streets and the big frame houses with people inside, all sleeping safely and dreaming of the day and their jobs and their lovers and the Indians and the Yankees and tomorrow and what it would bring.

*

Early in the morning two men came to see him. One of them had a canvas bag with him. They spoke for a minute, then one took something from the bag and spread it over the prisoner's back. It stung at first, but then a coolness started to spread over him, and he relaxed and breathed deeply and fell asleep again.

Toward midday he awoke. The men had returned and were putting something on his back again. One of them took him under the arms and lifted him gently until he was standing. When the man released him, his knees buckled, but the man caught him before he fell. The other man gave him some rice from a bowl and a drink of tea. He felt better. Then they lay him down, and once more he slept.

For three days they came to put salve on his back and feed him rice and tea. His strength returned, and he could stand now and walk. But his back still ached, and if he moved suddenly and stretched the flesh, his back would burn and he would break into a sweat. Now he knew the pain of what the man with no neck could do to him, and he was afraid.

On the night of the third day after the beating, he was wakened by a light shining into his eyes. There was a sharp command in a voice that he knew, and then hands roughly pulled him to his feet. He was blinded by the light, but he could make out a figure before him—a figure with wide shoulders and a bullet head.

"Prisoner will stand at attention while he is questioned!"

The hands holding him disappeared, and he stood unsteadily, raising a hand to screen his eyes from the light.

"Prisoner will keep hands at his side!"

His arm was grabbed and pushed down.

"Prisoner will answer questions!"

He waited. He knew what was coming, and he knew what he would do. He had thought about it for two days, knowing that it was only a matter of time before they returned. He had started on one path, and he would continue. If he broke and told the truth, it would do him no good because they would not believe him, so he really had no choice.

No-Neck began the questioning. The prisoner's eyes were accustomed to the light now, and he could see his interrogator's face. The eyes were narrow, and the cheek bones high—a strange-looking face, not unattractive. No-Neck had finished talking and was now looking at him intently. He gathered his courage—remembering the pain—and spat straight into the man's face. No-Neck swung out and hit him across the face, but the prisoner laughed. No-Neck hit him again, and again he laughed. No-Neck barked out commands, and the prisoner was pushed to the floor. They started to whip him again, and he felt the stinging, biting pain. He crumpled into a ball and covered his face as the blows rained down on him. He pretended to have passed out, and they continued for a minute, then stopped. Then the men left, and the door was closed. He lay in the darkness too filled with pain to think.

XX

All during the next day they let him lie without food or water. He burned with fever, then toward night, began to shiver uncontrollably. He felt his arms and legs vibrating and chills moving over him. He moaned and tried to curl into a ball to warm himself. That night he became delirious and screamed out. A guard came to the door, looked at him, then left. The wind carried the odor from the latrines. The leaves shook in the breeze. Toward midnight clouds rolled over the orange moon, and it rained. The roof leaked, so the water came in and soaked him. It was cooling, and he smiled and laughed. He remembered his first swim in Lake Erie—the cool waves lapping over his toes as he stood on the beach, and the thrill he felt when he dived into the water. Memories of home flooded him, and he tried to hold onto them but cried when they faded. Each time one memory faded, it was as if something had been taken away from him that he would never get back. He felt certain that he was dying.

The next morning the two men with the canvas bag came to see him again. This time they turned him gently and gave him some medicine and a cup of warm tea with quinine. Then he slept. Later he was awakened and given some more tea and a little rice. He slept for two days. Each day the men came several times to feed him, and once they sponged off his face and covered him with a thin piece of linen to stop the chills. On the second day he was already awake when they came. He studied them. Their faces were like a thousand others he had seen—yellow-brown and expressionless, with high cheekbones and sunken cheeks. They showed no emotion as he looked into their eyes, the light through the one window flickering on them. For the first time he was aware of how different they were. They were men, but he didn't understand them. What did they want? What did they fear? What did they dream of or long for? He would never know.

The next day he felt better. The cramped room and the smell from the latrines were getting to him, but he could feel his strength returning. *It's about time for No-Neck to come back,* he thought, reaching to his back and putting his hand under his shirt to feel the cuts. Some had started to heal and were covered with hard scabs like thin belts. These were from the first beating. Others were still soft and oozing fluid. He thought of No-Neck and shivered. *He'll come today, or he'll come tomorrow,* he said to himself, *but he'll come.*

He was right. The next day just after dawn, he was wakened by two men who took him out of the cabin and across the camp. The red dust was still damp from the morning dew, and the leaves in the trees hung limply. There was a faint glow in the sky to the east, and the top of the sun showed over the jungle. He heard the sounds of birds chirping and was surprised. When he was alone, wandering on the plain, he had listened for birds, expecting them to wake him in the morning as they had back home in Cleveland. But he rarely heard any and had assumed that for some strange reason birds didn't sing in the morning in the Orient. *Nothing works like it ought to in this damn place,* he had thought. But now there was chirping—thin and high, ending in a whistle—and he told himself that he would begin waking at dawn to listen for it. That would at least give him something to look forward to.

At the edge of the camp, No-Neck was waiting for him with an older officer who wore more red stripes. No-Neck looked at him, then repeated his questions. He said nothing. The older officer spoke to No-Neck.

"Commander Xuong says that you are fooling no one.

We know that you are an infiltrator, and we know that you are not mad."

The other officer spoke again, and No-Neck listened. The prisoner watched No-Neck and noticed that he looked at the officer with respect but was not afraid as most Orientals were around their superiors. *A model officer*, he thought. *He'll go far*.

"Commander Xuong says that you are foolishly hurting yourself with your stubborn refusal to speak."

He looked at the other man. His face was hard and lined, and the black peaked cap almost came over his eyes.

The two officers watched him for a minute, then the older man looked at No-Neck and nodded. The soldiers tied his hands to the posts again. The prisoner waited for the lash, but it didn't come. No-Neck gave a command, then he and the older officer left with the soldiers following them. One man stayed behind. He walked over to a nearby building, went inside for a minute, then came back out with a chair and sat down.

By about eight the sun was over the edge of the jungle. He could feel its rays like warm fingers playing over his face and body. It felt good. By ten the sun was at 45°, and he was sweating. A half hour later the heat was unbearable. His clothes were soaked through, and he had to squint because the salt was burning his eyes. His legs were aching, and he moved his feet. The dust was wet beneath him, almost red, but a minute after he shifted his position, it had dried to a yellow powder. His head began to ache, and he closed his eyes.

Toward noon he fainted. When he came to, the sun was still high, and his hands were numb because the ropes around his wrists were pulled tight, cutting off the circulation. He tried to stand again to relieve the pressure. His knees gave way. He waited a few minutes, then tried again. This time he made it. That gave him some courage, and he tried to pull himself together. *I can stand it*, he thought. *If they don't make me panic and give up, I can stand anything these stupid gooks try*.

After two it was better. He had learned that it was easier if he kept his eyes shut and stood for a half hour, then relaxed and hung, letting the ropes do the work. But the real secret was in his mind. If he thought about the heat and the sun, it became worse, and soon he felt he would go mad. But if he thought about other things, it was OK. So he tried women, but that didn't last. Then he tried water. That was better. There was a lake—a cool, blue-green lake—and he was swimming. He rolled over on his back and floated, thrashing the water into foam with his feet. Then he was walking in snow—deep snow—and it was so cold that his toes were numb and his fingers stung.

Early in the evening, his thirst became intolerable. He had sweated all day, and now he felt dehydrated. Cramps were wracking his body. First he felt that he would vomit, then the urge to defecate came over him. He tried to hold back, then, in panic, realized he couldn't. He saw the guard look toward him, then look away. Flies came. They buzzed and landed on him. They crawled over his pants, then up his shirt to his face. He shut his eyes and mouth, but he could feel them crawling into his ears and up his nose.

Darkness came. The air was still. He could hear men talking and laughing. Once a group of them came to look at him. Someone must have made a joke because they all laughed. At about nine a new man came and took the place of the guard in the chair. The night wore on. His legs were weak, and he found himself standing for shorter and shorter periods. Then his knees buckled, and he hung by his wrists again. After a while he started to get short of breath. He tried to stand because he knew if he could do that, it would be easier to breathe. But he couldn't. He cried out to the guard for help, but the man just looked at him then went back to sleep. It felt like he was choking, and he kept blacking out. Now when he tried to call for help, all that came out was a feeble gurgle.

Dawn came over the trees. The first pink rays woke him. He was still tied to the posts. He couldn't remember how he had passed the night. His hands were numb, but he could move his fingers, so there was still some circulation. That was strange because the night before his fingers hadn't moved. But more strange was the thirst—it was still there, but it wasn't as strong. It was as if he had had water, but he couldn't remember drinking. He looked toward the guard. The man was sleeping with his feet propped up on a crate.

At nine they changed guards. The two men spoke for a

minute, and the new guard came over to look at him. The guard seemed to be studying him. After a minute the guard shrugged, walked to the chair, and sat. For a second he thought he had detected a flicker of compassion in the man's face, but then he changed his mind. *He's only a gook*, he reminded himself, *just a gook, and no one ever knows what they're thinking*.

At ten he started to sweat again, and by noon the sun seemed to be stabbing him. When he looked toward the guard, he saw a dark figure, almost black, in the yellow-white glare. He shut his eyes, and everything turned red. He could feel the sweat pouring from him, and he felt nauseated again. He became afraid. If he vomited he would choke, and no one would come. He fought to control his stomach. Suddenly he retched and choked, but it was only stomach acid. It filled his mouth with sourness, and he retched again. The guard came over to him, then went to the building and returned with some water. As soon as he felt the edge of the cup in his mouth, he drank greedily and the guard pulled it away. Then the guard returned to his chair.

In the afternoon the flies came again, buzzing and swarming around him. They seemed to cover every inch of him. He screamed, but nothing happened. Through the slits that were his eyes, he could see the guard watching him.

In the evening No-Neck came back. The older officer was with him, and once again he asked the questions.

The prisoner said nothing. His neck felt like rubber, and his head drooped. No-Neck gave a command, and someone grabbed his head and forced it up.

"When interrogator speaks, prisoner must listen!"

The guard released his head, and it fell down again. No-Neck gave another command and someone hit him with the whip, but still he didn't lift his head. Then there was another blow. He tried to lift his head but couldn't. Again he heard No-Neck's voice, but this time before it had finished the older officer said something and no more blows came.

Then the men left, and he was alone. A soft wind began to blow, and he could hear the crickets in the jungle. He tried to lift his head because he wanted to look at

86

the sky, but he couldn't. Then he became nauseated and started to vomit again.

The guard came more quickly this time. He gave the prisoner water which he drank greedily. Then the man went back to his chair. The crickets chirped louder. He made one last effort to raise his head, then gave up.

XXI

The next day was a haze—afterwards he remembered none of it clearly. He had a vague sensation that someone was carrying him, then he felt the softness of a bed. It had been so long since he had lain in a bed that he didn't recognize where he was at first. Gradually things came into focus. First there were random details. There was the hand of someone who held the cup from which he was drinking. Then the face of someone who peered down at him and put a hand to his head to see if the fever had broken. Then the light that filtered through the window, golden and warm at the end of the day. Then the chirp of the crickets at night.

As he began to feel stronger, dread grew in him, and each day he expected to see No-Neck again. This time he would say what the interrogator wanted—he would make it up—but he knew it wouldn't do any good. They wouldn't believe him, and then they would start all over. When he thought that, he began to sweat and feel faint.

After almost a week No-Neck hadn't come, and his anxiety began to subside. *He wouldn't have waited so long,* he thought, *if he intended to break me. No, he would have started again on the third or fourth day if that was his plan.*

Then a visitor came—the older officer. The man looked down at him, then beckoned for one of the orderlies to bring him a chair.

"So," he said, "you are feeling better."

The prisoner was surprised to hear the words in English—American English. The man smiled at his bewilderment.

"University of Pennsylvania, Class of '40."

He nodded to the man who nodded back.

"My friend, Commander Duc Thang, is convinced that you are an infiltrator and that you have been sent to discover our supply lines for your Generalissimo Westmoreland." The man smiled again and took out a cigarette. "But Commander Duc Thang is young and zealous, and he judges all men by his own soul. He is a stubborn man and a fanatical patriot, and so he assumes you must be also."

The commander took an ashtray, set it on his knee, and flicked the ash off his cigarette. "I dislike this filthy habit," he waved the cigarette, "but I cannot get decent tobacco for my pipe. And so I must smoke these."

The prisoner said that was a pity.

"Before your President broadened this accursed war, I could smoke what I wanted—good burley with a touch of perique and latakia. Now there is nothing but weeds. My countrymen do not believe in luxuries."

An orderly passed, and the commander spoke to him. The man went away, then returned in a minute with a bottle. He poured the contents into two glasses. The commander offered the prisoner one. It was cool and mint-flavored, but he could taste the alcohol.

"Good, eh?" said the commander, taking a long drink. The prisoner watched him swallow. He was an old man, about sixty, but he was hard and muscular.

"Have you ever been in Philadelphia?" the commander asked. "That's my old stamping ground."

The prisoner said he'd been there once or twice.

"It's a pleasant place," said the commander, "not exciting but pleasant. I guess you would say it is a conservative town."

"Yes," he said, "that's what most people say."

He felt a warm glow in his stomach and realized that it was the alcohol. It was stronger than he had imagined. "What is this stuff?" he asked.

"Mintwater with *mao tai*—its like saki, nothing fancy. It's good when it's cold, isn't it?"

The prisoner agreed and asked if he could have another. The commander called to the orderly who soon returned with another glass.

"I'd go easy on that," said the old man. "You're still weak, and it will go right to your head."

"I might say things I shouldn't," the prisoner said and winked. The commander smiled but said nothing.

They talked for a while longer, then the old man left. The prisoner watched him walk away. His stride was springy and strong, but he limped on his right foot.

The next day the commander returned. It was the afternoon, and although the sun was bright, there was a breeze and the air was pleasant. The old man suggested they walk outside and helped the prisoner to his feet. Although still weak, he was glad for the chance to move.

They walked to the center of the camp, and the old man pointed to the jungle directly ahead of them.

"That is the South. Your forces are there now, but they have been driven all the way to the coast."

The prisoner shook his head.

"You don't believe me? Ah, the patriotic optimism of the young!"

The commander was then silent for a few moments, as if he was thinking. "I will try to get some newspapers for you. They should show you how the war is moving. They will be in English and slanted toward your side, but the truth is so overwhelming that nothing can hide it. You will see."

The commander sounded firm as he spoke, and the prisoner watched his eyes and the muscles of his jaw. He was a man who people believed—a man who had given hard commands and done hard things.

They sauntered on. When they reached the edge of the jungle at the north end of the camp, the commander stopped. "If we go in here, there must be soldiers with us, and we want no soldiers, so we will turn back."

They had gone a third of the way back toward the

medical building when he heard a high-pitched whine. The commander pushed him to the ground. There were three quick explosions and a building twenty-five yards to their right disintegrated. Fragments of wood and straw flew through the air. They both lay still. There was a low hum and then the whine again, this time louder, then the ground a few yards in front of them flew skyward and showered them with dust.

"Stay down," the commander warned. "I do not think they are through yet."

They waited. There was no noise except for the chirp of crickets and the distant thunder of a midday storm. Then the hum began again, and suddenly there was a sharp *rat-tat-tat,* and the ground at the south end of the camp began to give off small clouds of dust. The sound continued, and the prisoner watched, fascinated, as the dust cloud advanced across the camp toward them.

The commander sprang to his feet, pulled him up, and began to run. He followed. The old man dashed madly, covering the ground like a crab as he pulled his game leg after him. The prisoner was weak, but he kept pace. Then he felt his knees buckle, and he crumpled. The old man stopped, ran back a few steps, and pulled him to his feet. The *rat-tat-tat* was louder. He looked over his shoulder and saw that the dust cloud had reached the middle of the camp and was moving rapidly toward them.

"The trees!" said the old man. "That's the only safe place. Run—run even if it kills you!"

The prisoner took two steps and collapsed. The old man pulled the prisoner's arms over his shoulders and began running again, carrying him piggyback. When they reached the trees, the old man pulled him in and then collapsed, breathing heavily. There was a sound like hail falling, and the leaves overhead danced as the *rat-tat-tat* passed over them.

The prisoner looked at the old man. He was sitting now, propped against a tree, still panting.

"Your countrymen out for a day of sport," said the old man.

He looked back toward the camp. Several buildings were destroyed, and soldiers were searching through the ruins for wounded. He could see figures lying on the ground. They looked dead.

"Not a very successful raid," said the commander, "only a handful killed and three buildings destroyed. Hardly worth the taxpayers' hard-earned money. The bombs alone must have cost fifty-thousand dollars."

They got to their feet and walked back into the camp. The commander nodded to a soldier who came and took the prisoner back to the hospital building. Then the old man went to inspect the damage.

XXII

He didn't see the old man for three days after that. Each day an orderly took him for a walk in the camp, and he watched the men put up new buildings and bury the dead. There were several rows of mounds at the south end of the camp which he had never noticed before; now he realized that they were graves. He counted seventy-five. *They weren't all killed in air raids*, he thought. *Some of them probably died in ground fighting.* Then he remembered that the Cong never buried their dead after jungle skirmishes. For them a dead person was just so much meat, and they had more important things to worry about.

He remembered the old man and the expression on his face as he sat propped against the tree. It was a mixture of sadness and rage. *He's all right*, he thought, and he knew that if the man hadn't carried him into the jungle, he'd probably be under one of those mounds.

*

Two days later the old man returned.

"You are almost healthy again my friend," he said, tapping him on the shoulder with a cane. His limp had become worse, and he was now using a stick to walk.

"An old injury," he said, "aggravated by our run to the jungle. You'll never believe where I first got it."

The prisoner asked.

"Baker Field. The Penn Relays in '39. I was a pole vaulter and got tangled in the crossbar. I took third that day, but if I hadn't gotten hurt I would have won. I was really flying then—it was one of those days when everything goes right. A once in a lifetime day." The old man's eyes narrowed as he stared into the past. "Those were the days. No worries. Only studying and athletics."

They talked about Cleveland for a while. The old man had visited it once. He remembered the bleakness of the avenues and the cold wind that howled off Lake Erie in the winter. "A most inhospitable place," he said, then looked embarrassed.

"I hope I have not offended you."

The prisoner laughed and said that that was the usual reaction to Cleveland, especially in the winter, and that he concurred. Then they drank a glass of cold mintwater and *mao tai,* then the old man left.

He was well now, but they seemed in no hurry to move him. He passed the time re-reading the old newspapers that the commander brought him and sitting in the sun with the convalescing soldiers. He knew that he was lucky and tried not to think about what might happen if things changed and No-Neck got him again. From the sports page he learned that the Celtics had done well in the East and that Los Angeles was winning in the West. He wondered how the playoffs had gone. The papers were two months old, and they would be over by now. He thought about the guys in the fraternity he had belonged to. They bet heavily on the playoffs and watched them on TV in the guest room, swilling beer and eating stale potato chips and pretzels left over from the last frat party. Someone always had a story to tell about his latest conquest. He couldn't imagine himself ever doing that again —it was too much like kids' play. *They don't know yet what it's really like,* he thought, *and most of them never will.*

He remembered the green campus and the science building and the chem labs where he'd worked into the night, trying to discover some damned unknown. He knew he wasn't a bad chemist, but he also knew he didn't give a damn about chemistry and wondered why he'd ever decided to study it. Then he became bitter. *It's like everything—it doesn't make any sense. It just happens, that's all. And you're just there, and it happens to you.* He remembered his mother and his old man. They both wanted him to study a science, especially his old man. "That's real work," he had said, "something you can get your teeth into, something solid, not like business." He knew now that his father had been thinking of his own business and his own failures, and that he had probably ended up studying chemistry because of them. But it didn't matter anyway. He would change all that if he ever got out; he'd do what he wanted then. He was through doing things for other people. It didn't pay. *Just like this war,* he thought. *You fought in it because of someone else's fuckup.*

*

The same short, wizened orderly went with him each afternoon. Sometimes he laughed for no apparent reason. He had a funny walk—not the usual Oriental trot but a weird hop-hop that fascinated the prisoner.

They often sat in the sun. The orderly found that he liked this and got the prisoner a straw hat. He learned that *kam oeun* meant "thank-you," so he tried to say it. The orderly smiled. Once he indicated that he wanted to go into the jungle. The man became stern then and shook his head back and forth, watching him out of the corner of his eye as they walked back toward the hospital building. For two days after that, he watched the prisoner closely, never letting him leave his sight.

The prisoner began to yearn for a map. If he knew where he was, he might try to make another break for it.

It was crazy, he knew, but the idea was there, eating at him, and he didn't try to quiet it.

He had decided he'd better not ask the old man anything about the location of the camp. The old man was a smart old geezer and might guess what he was thinking about. Then two days later, the old man was speaking and told him, matter-of-factly, that they were 375 miles north of Pleiku. "You look surprised," he said. "Come, I know you have been wondering about this for days. You would not be a man if you didn't."

The prisoner was silent, and the old man stared across the camp. They were in the shade on the north end at the edge of the jungle.

"Do not try to escape. It would be foolhardy. We would probably not be able to find you, but you would never make it. There are 200 miles of jungle to go through before you reach the plains, and if you do not know the trails, it is impenetrable. And we hold the trails."

The prisoner laughed awkwardly.

"About this I am serious. It would be most foolhardy. There are long shots and there are long shots, but this is a one in a million thing."

The old man looked hard at him, then stared into his eyes. For a second the prisoner had a strange sensation, as if the old man were somehow beseeching instead of threatening him. They both looked away, then resumed their small talk.

*

The old man left at noon that day, but late in the afternoon an orderly came to fetch the prisoner. They crossed the camp and entered the only permanent building in the compound—a three-room house made of stone with a copper roof turned green by corrosion. Once inside he felt a coolness that he had not experienced in months. The floor was red tile, whisked clean, and the walls were white plaster with paintings hung on them. Some were Oriental—Chinese, he guessed—with dripping waterfalls and misty mountains. Then he saw one with two men rowing on a river. The men were Americans, and he studied the painting closely.

"It is a reproduction of a work by Eakins. The river is

94

the Schuylkill." The old man was standing behind him.

"A realist. This is my favorite, but some prefer his pictures of the operating room. Do you know them?"

The prisoner shook his head.

"A painter who was also a scientist. Not one of those artists who depends upon inspiration. Like da Vinci or Michelangelo he has studied anatomy, and so when he makes a man, it is a real man. Note the way he indicates the muscles in the arms—that is the way they really are. If you look at Rubens or Van Dyck, even Rembrandt, you will never see that. Only in da Vinci, Michelangelo, and Eakins."

The old man paused, then indicated some chairs around a table on one side of the room. They went over and sat. There was a clay pitcher from which he poured something into two glasses.

"We serve ourselves here. The cooks will prepare things, but there are no servants in the Peoples' Army."

They drank the liquid—it tasted of orange and something bitter that he didn't recognize. The prisoner thought that although the old man was at home without servants, he did not seem complete without them. He had seen such men before; they had a certain air about them.

"Are you interested in art?" asked the old man. "As you see, it is one of my hobbies. My degree is in engineering, but that was for my people. If I had had my way, I would have become a painter."

"Then you would have gone to Paris, not Philadelphia."

The old man shook his head. "No, I think not. I have no great admiration for the French artists. The Impressionists—Monet, Renoir—they did not paint as I wanted to. Mist and color, harmonies of sweet color—it is all tasteful I am sure, but it is hollow stuff. Good to decorate a room, but not art for a man. No, I would have stayed where I was. The Philadelphia Academy had some men I admired. Not famous men but men with solid talent. From them I would have learned what I could, then gone to Rome to study firsthand the painters I truly admire. It would have taken a dozen years, but in the end I would have been able to begin painting as one should." The old man sighed—it was barely audible, but the prisoner detected it. "But I did not. I guess that is fate. One does what one must. That is true, is it not? One does what one must. Even your President, the man who is causing all of this . . . this . . ." he gestured with his hand, unable to find the word, "even your President does only what he must. Behind him is your Senate, and behind your Senate are your industrialists and those of your people who are so afraid of that which is best for them."

The prisoner laughed.

"Oh, you think I am joking. I have been in your country. Remember that. I know of its peculiarities. And even to one like myself, who is a bit of an aristocrat, it is quite clear that the largest number of people fare better under a communist government. Come, even you must admit this."

The old man took his glass and filled it again.

"But do you know the strangest thing about this war —this I must tell you before we change topics, for to go on with this does not suit me—the strangest thing is the men whom your government sends over to fight their battle. So many are Negroes—the poorest of your people and the ones who would benefit most from a communist system. It never ceases to amaze me that these men will fight and die for that which oppresses them. But then life is truly a paradox, and he who does not accept this has not seen the world."

The old man paused, observing the prisoner's blank face. "I have invited you so that we may eat, but instead I preach. Accept my apologies."

The prisoner nodded.

*

The food was in bowls on a wooden table, which stood on the porch at the back of the house. There was an awning over the porch and screens to keep the flies out.

"It reminds me of summer back home," the prisoner said. "We would sit on the back porch and eat corn on the cob and hamburgers and drink ice tea."

"I'm afraid we have no ice tea," said the old man. "They would think it an Americanization, a poison of imperialism. But we do have this." He filled the prisoner's

96

glass again with some of the fruit drink and put some food on his plate.

The food was good—not fancy but it satisfied. Midway through the meal, the old man stopped. He had been silent while they ate but now he set his chopsticks down and looked at the prisoner.

"Tell me do you have a desire to contact your family, to let them know that you are still alive?"

The prisoner had thought about this before but only in a general sort of way. He supposed that by now they had received the usual letter that said he was missing in action and presumed dead. They would have mourned and then gone on living, and he saw no reason why he should upset them until he was safe. He was a little surprised that the commander had not thought of this.

"No," he said. "I have no wish to do that. It is better that they think me dead."

"I see," the commander said and resumed eating. The prisoner had a sudden uneasy feeling that something that he did not fully understand had transpired, but he let it pass.

After dinner they walked outside. It was a windy night, and clouds were racing past the moon.

"A night for those who want to bomb," said the commander.

"Also for those who ambush," the prisoner said, "for they won't be able to see their targets."

"Touché," said the old man.

XXIII

Another week passed. Twice he ate with the commander. Once they discussed chemistry—the old man surprised him with his knowledge—and once American politics. The old man said that he admired the structure of the government, but that the economic system had eroded the principles upon which the country was founded.

"Jefferson, Hamilton, Adams—they were your great men, men with vision. They constructed a system of government that worked admirably in their time, but they could not foresee the future. Capitalism was not yet the disease that it has become, and men still behaved as men, not as maggots. It was an aristocratic society, and the leaders had principles; not like today when the majority of your leaders are men motivated only by the lust for wealth."

The prisoner said he thought that was a bit extreme.

"I wonder," said the old man. "Can you really admit what your country has become? Look at your leaders. What are their accomplishments? What have they written? Are not their speeches crass? They are politicians, the lowest form of vermin. I must admit, though, that your country is not alone in this. We, too, have such men."

He lit a cigarette and blew a cloud of smoke.

"When I was young, it was still an aristocratic society here. Full of abuses as always, and then there were the French to cope with. Truly petty people." He lifted his hand and showed his thumb and forefinger about an inch apart, his estimation of the size of the French soul. "But in its way, it was better. There was literature and art. Buildings were designed for something besides mere utility. But this has changed, and now all that we do is for the good of all. We have gained, but we have also lost."

And you, the prisoner thought, *where do you fit into all this?*

"Ah," said the old man, reading his thoughts, "I see that you are surprised at my reactionary doubting. We all have such doubts, my friend. Ho Chi Minh had them, Cho En-lai, and for all I know, even the great Mao. He is a poet, you know, and no poet can be blind to beauty. Our world has lost much of its beauty."

There was a knock at the door, and the commander told the knocker to enter. Two men stepped in. One was No-Neck. The prisoner felt himself flinch.

No-Neck said something to the commander. The old man listened, then rose and went to the other room. He unrolled a map, spread it on a table, and studied it for a few minutes. Then he spoke to the men, tracing something on the map as he did so. The men listened intently. Then No-neck nodded toward the prisoner. The commander shook his head and continued speaking. After a few minutes, the men left. As he passed, No-Neck quickly looked at the prisoner out of the corner of his eye.

The commander rolled up the map carefully and returned to his chair. "We were speaking of beauty, were we not?" He sipped his drink, then put it down with a frown. It had grown warm. "And I was making reactionary statements. It is, of course, as in most things," the commander looked toward the prisoner accusingly, "the young who are largely at fault in this. Men such as those," he nodded toward the door. "They are good men." He hesitated. "Perhaps overzealous but basically good. But they are also narrow. They think only about their country, and what they deem best for their country. They have no souls. I . . . I cannot understand them. I cannot understand how one can live without sometimes satisfying his soul."

The commander offered him a cigarette. He took it, and the old man lifted the lighter which was standing on the low table before them, lighting the cigarette for him. The prisoner had hardly noticed the lighter before, but now it caught his eye. It was a silver elephant with a gold chair on its back. There was an elephant boy sitting on the neck; he was also gold, and his turban had a ruby in the center.

"A memento of times past," said the old man. "It belonged to my father. He managed a rubber plantation in the mountains. Penn, Class of 1919."

The prisoner picked up the lighter and examined it. The workmanship was exquisite, even the features of the elephant boy were sharp and lifelike.

"The work of a superb craftsman," said the old man.

After dinner they talked some more, sitting on the porch and listening to the sounds of the night. Occasionally there was a distant rumble and a flash far in the south.

"Some of your comrades," said the old man wryly, "blowing up villages."

"How can you be so certain they are ours?" he asked.

"Not certain—just confident. We do not bomb villages and forest. That is your specialty."

The prisoner was silent. They both looked down.

"That was unfair. I am sorry. I am blaming you for things beyond your control."

Then they sat, unable to think of anything to add. He respected the old man, so he had not rebuked him. Now they both felt awkward. Finally the old man spoke.

"It is not easy. In war nothing is easy, and who am I to judge."

The prisoner looked at him but remained silent. Until now he had been content to listen. He had no ax to grind and was happy to be away from the hospital. Besides, he did not believe in arguments. *They're stupid*, he thought, *and only waste time. It is useless to try to convince somebody of something that he doesn't want to believe.* And so he had always watched people arguing passionately with something akin to disdain. Action, physical action, had a reality. Everything else was so much baloney. But now he wanted to argue. Something about the old man drew him out and made him want to speak.

"Earlier you spoke of souls," the prisoner said finally.

"Yes, souls," said the commander. "Things of a peculiarly western origin. We do not really believe in souls."

100

The prisoner said nothing, feeling his passivity returning. The old man filled his glass again and motioned that he should drink.

"Do not let me cut you off," he said. "It is a bad habit of mine—one I have never been able to break. Finish what you began to say."

The tone was soft, almost cajoling, but the prisoner could not help but feel that the words were a command. The old man was genial, but there was an iron will behind his charm.

"How do you know that it is not satisfying to some men's souls when they devote themselves to their country? Captain Duc Thong, for example."

"You mean Duc Thang," said the old man.

"Yes, him."

The old man smiled. It was a smile of cunning.

"That is an old argument. It is one that I must admit occurred to me long ago, long before all of this. I was in China then, an engineer designing a waterworks in the mountains west of P'uchai—a small place near the border. I was a young idealist fresh from school in America and full of the writings of Marx and Engels. There was a man—the son of a coolie from Shanghai—who was sent by the party to organize the villagers. The man worked tirelessly. They loved him, and I was taken in along with them. He was passionate, logical, and obviously devoted to his cause: a saint who thought only of others. I remember thinking that if I had one-half his selflessness then I should be happy. At that time I thought him the most wonderful of persons."

The old man paused here, picking up the silver elephant again and looking at it closely.

"The man had no culture. This I saw from the first. But then I was young, in the early stages of my conversion to the ideas of Mao, and I thought that the doctrine of sharing and self-sacrifice superseded all others. I was blind, for I should have known. But then I learned.

"There was a man in the village—a landowner who sided with the Kuomintang. From the beginning he knew why we had come and what our aims were, but he did nothing. And at that stage—in the beginning—a word from him would have been sufficient to have us all executed. It would have been as simple as that. But the man did nothing. He watched us, and he listened, and on occasion he even helped us. Why he did it I do not know, except that he was probably bored, found us interesting, and thus let us play. Who is to say?

"But then the day came when the people followed us. The Kuomintang's forces fled, and the landowner remained behind. He had a beautiful home and many friends in the district. He had even built a small hospital for the people on his land, so he must have felt safe."

He flicked the elephant lighter, and a small bluish flame shot from its trunk.

"Most of the people were for leaving this landowner in peace. But as always there were a few who disagreed—men who had grudges against him. One man he had punished for theft, another for rape. They played upon the people's hatred of all landowners, said that this particular man was no different from the rest, that he was even worse because of his arrogance in daring to remain on his land. The people were as all people—good in the main but not wise. They listened, and after a while they began to believe. People in a group are not discerning. Who was the man . . . ah, your satirist Swift, who said that he loved individuals but hated people. Well, the ending was to be predicted. I was always a student of human nature and should have known. I did in fact know, but I wouldn't let myself believe because I was blinded by my youthful zeal. The people marched on the landowner's house, burned it to the ground, killed the man, and raped his daughters. They even destroyed the hospital he had built to cure their diseases. All this happened while I was in Yenan, conferring about the next attack that our forces should make. I was aghast when I returned and asked the man—the leader I idolized—how he could have allowed such a tragedy to befall a man who had befriended him. He said that the revolution must be first and all else second, that friendship was unimportant, and that the will of the people was always sovereign. 'Who was I,' he said, 'to set my wishes against those of several hundred others?' It was then that I saw the man for what he truly was. He had devoted himself to his blessed people, and he had lost his judgment as a man. He was nothing but an expression of their will. The desires of a mob inflamed by the rabble had been consecrated by this man. And yet he was not a bad man. Some even said—and these were intelligent men—that he was a saint."

He shook his head and set the silver elephant down.

"A man who gives his will over to the people has lost his soul—and one who has no soul is not really a man. But then I am lecturing again. Come, we will walk outside and look at the stars."

It was a bright night, and the sky was filled with light. The old man took it in, then made a sweeping circle with his hand.

"Glorious! I envy you, my friend. I will see five, maybe ten more nights as beautiful as this one, and then I will pass from the earth. You, if you do not do some foolish thing, may see a hundred nights such as this. But then you are probably thinking not of the stars but of your freedom —or perhaps of sharing such a night with a woman."

The old man laughed a peculiar, throaty laugh.

"I was like you as a young man. The stars speak of infinity, but I was interested in more mundane matters, wasting many such an evening in pursuit of women. Foolishness! But that passes."

They returned to the middle of the camp, and a guard met them. Then the old man left. The prisoner watched him walk away, still gazing upward at the stars.

XXIV

The guard left him at the door of the hospital. It would have been easy to escape, to slide off into the darkness of the jungle and wait until daybreak, then move south with the early light. But he didn't. He felt languid and weak. The feeling confused him. He had been growing stronger day by day, but now, inexplicably, he wanted only to rest. *It must be the climate,* he said to himself, remembering the stories he'd read of men rotting in the Far East. In the back of his mind, the voice started again, telling him that he should be struggling, that if he yielded he was done for.

When he woke the next morning, he discovered a woman working in the hospital, the first he had seen in months. She was old and wrinkled and moved quickly around the room, clopping softly on wooden sandals. She was making the beds. A little later when he looked again, he saw her outside under the small awning in front of the entrance, washing the linen and beating it against the side of a wooden tub. She was so thin that when she moved her arms the sinews stood out like ropes.

He found himself longing for something to occupy his time with, but there was nothing so he just lay in bed. He had reread the newspapers so many times that he knew them by heart, so there was little else to do. He did not want to think, because he knew that then the voice would begin again, and he would become angry, first at himself, then at his captors. He was not ready for this.

And so when the voice started again and his mind started churning, he fought to control it. *Think of something else*, he told himself. *Anything else.* The situation struck him as ludicrous. He remembered when he was a teenager, and he had struggled to stop thinking of the breasts of the girl who lived across the street. Each night toward ten, he would be in his room with the light switched off, staring across at her bedroom window. She never drew the drapes when she changed into her nightgown, and he would watch with excitement as she unhooked her brassiere.

When he had confessed to the priest, alone, whispering into the darkness, he had been told that he must change and overcome this impure habit—so he had begun to pray. Each night at 9:30, he would begin to say *Hail Marys* mixed with an occasional *Our Father* or an *Act of Perfect Contrition*. As ten o'clock drew nearer and the temptation became stronger, he would pray more fervently. "Blessed Mary, Holy Mother of God, protect me from temptation." He would think of the Blessed Virgin's goodness. If he yielded to temptation, then he was hurting her, trespassing against the ideal of purity that surrounded her. His sins hurt her. All women were like the Mother of God—all were holy—and he was staining that holiness with his impure thoughts and deeds.

He almost laughed when he thought of it now. The purity of women and the filth of sin—he had believed all that, wallowed in it and burned in the fires of his conscience. But two years later he was helping them take off their brassieres, and if there was an aura of holiness around those girls, he never felt it. No, he remembered feeling other things.

He was watching the old woman again. She had finished beating the wash and was hanging it on a line that ran between the hospital and an unused shed. The sun was higher now—it was about ten—and he knew how hot it was out there. But she worked on, as if it were a cool fall day. She worked smoothly, unhurriedly, and then when the sheets were all hung, she came back into the building and worked over the small stove in the corner. Evidently she was making the midday meal.

He dozed again. This time the women who roamed

through his dreams were older and surer, and he was very young—a child. In one dream, he was watching his mother as she worked in the kitchen. She was making cookies, and if he was good she would let him lick the bowl. He sat on the floor and watched, waiting quietly. After the batter was poured, she started to bend down to hand him the bowl. He reached up for it. Someone came into the room. He couldn't see who it was, but the person was tall because his voice was coming from high above. He waited for the bowl, but it didn't come. Finally he wanted it so badly that he overcame his fear and started to cry, looking up at the tall figure. He could not see the face, but the figure wore a black uniform with red stripes.

XXV

He woke when the bell signaling the midday meal rang. The men in the hospital ate in a special place about twenty-five yards to the right of the building where a long piece of green canvas was stretched over four bamboo poles. The eating place was in an open area near the center of the camp, and if there was any breeze blowing, one could feel it here.

The men sat around a long wooden table, and the old woman passed among them, pouring stew into their bowls and giving them rice and tea. He ate slowly; the breeze was pleasant, and the food, plain though it was, tasted good. He watched the other men. They were all soldiers, two of them officers. They had been wounded on missions or in air raids, and they were recuperating, gaining strength until they would be ready to fight again. None of them appeared to have been badly hurt, and it occurred to him that those who were seriously injured were sent elsewhere.

He looked across the camp toward the jungle, then up at the sky. It was clear blue and cloudless. Then his mind went out of focus. He was thinking, but he wasn't aware of it. Something was percolating in the back of his mind; something growing. He sensed this and knew that it was foolish to resist or even to try to discover what it was. He would know soon enough.

He daydreamed in the afternoon, serenaded by the flies as they buzzed about the room. The others in the hospital slept—he had never seen men so incommunicative. They hardly ever spoke, either to each other or to the orderlies who helped them. And when the two doctors with their canvas bag made their rounds, they had to bully the men to discover how they felt. Most of the men in the hospital were peasants, and they did not trust science. They understood rest. They were happy to be out of the war in a place where all one had to do was eat and sleep. But medicine—pills and stethoscopes and men peering into their wounds and probing their bodies—frightened them. They didn't protest outwardly, but they drew into themselves whenever the doctors came, like turtles going into their shells.

On the third evening after the old woman came, he first felt the pain—sharp and burning in his stomach as if needles were being driven into him. At first he said nothing, but then the pain became too intense and he called out for help. The others in the room all turned to look at him. No one had ever raised his voice in that room before. The orderlies came over to him, but none of them understood English, and when he pointed to his stomach they gave him an emetic to drink. The pain increased, and he began to vomit blood. He lay at the edge of his bed, his knees curled to his chest, retching in agony. They watched him for fifteen minutes; then one of the orderlies went for the doctors, who came with their ever-present canvas sack. One bent over and listened to his stomach. Then they covered him with a blanket and sat beside the bed.

The vomiting continued for an hour, gradually subsiding. When it stopped, the nausea was replaced by a hot, burning sensation. In time this passed. His stomach hurt, but otherwise he felt normal. The burning had moved lower into his intestines.

For thirty-six hours the pain continued, moving ever lower in his body. Finally he had a bowel movement, and the pain left him. His abdomen ached and he felt ill, but the pain had gone. A deep fatigue came over him, and he fell into a dreamless sleep.

*

When he woke, it was midday. He did not know how many days had passed, but he felt very weak. Sunlight was streaming in the doorway, and the other patients were sleeping or staring dully into the air before them. He noticed that a man was standing under the awning outside the doorway, beating the linen against the side of the tub. He looked about for the old woman but couldn't locate her.

Late in the afternoon the doctors came. They smiled at him, listened to his stomach and intestines with a stethoscope, then left. About a half hour later the old man came. A look of concern was on his face.

"It makes me happy to see you awake at last," he said. "You were very sick. So sick that I feared I would lose your companionship permanently."

The prisoner asked the commander if he knew what he had been suffering from. A pained expression crossed the old man's face, and he looked down for a second; then he spoke with a look of embarrassment on his face—as if he were disappointed with the world.

"It was the old woman," he said. "She put green bamboo shoots in your food, and they became hard when they reached your stomach and poked into you."

The prisoner remembered the old woman, calm and diligent, washing the linen, cooking the patients' meals. Her expressionless face came before him—her sunken cheeks and downcast gaze. She was at least seventy he guessed, and her action puzzled him. Had she been younger and a patriot or the wife of a soldier he would have understood, but this made no sense.

"She was from the village of Ben Tre," the old man

said, then fell silent. The prisoner sensed that he was waiting for a response. One of the men on the other side of the room coughed.

"Ben Tre was destroyed in an air raid—all of the people except for a dozen died, most were burned. It is an excruciating way to die."

The prisoner said nothing. He was staring across the room, watching the particles of dust dance in the late afternoon light.

The old man spoke again. "It is one of those things. It happened over a year ago, but people do not forget."

"No," the prisoner said, "I guess they don't."

His words had bitterness in them, but his voice was tired and soft. The two men exchanged glances for a second, then the commander offered him a cigarette. They smoked in silence.

XXVI

After three days he was still weak, and when he walked it felt as if his knees would buckle under him. And still, each time he passed a stool there was blood. This scared him, and he asked the old man to speak to the two doctors about it. The prisoner didn't think they knew much, but he was worried so he asked.

The old man grinned. "You do not believe in these men; I can read it in your face." He cracked the top of his boots with the quirt he had in his hand—it was the first time the prisoner had noticed it—and then laughed. "Do not worry. They do little good, but then they also do little harm. And that is all that any doctor does. They are Chinese, trained at the National University at Peking. That is why the soldiers fear them. To them they are foreigners, devils from the north. But their training is good if a bit short on theory."

That afternoon when the two doctors made their rounds, the prisoner gave them the note the old man had written for him. They studied it for a minute, discussed it, then wrote something on the bottom of the page and gave it back to him. He understood that they wanted him to show it to the old man.

That afternoon he read some newspapers that the old man had brought him the day before. This was a new batch, filled with pictures of great crowds of people carrying placards attacking the President and the Congress and demanding the end of the war.

It made him feel strange. He was alone in an enemy camp, lost so far from his lines that there was no real hope of getting back. He knew that he would be able to return home only if the war ended. Yet he did not like the pictures in the newspapers. Somehow they meant that all that had been—the burning and the pain and the dying—was somehow meaningless, a game. *If that is how they are going to end it,* he thought, *by talk at a table because politicians are afraid to lose votes, then why didn't they do the talking before all this happened?* To him it seemed impossible that anything could be more important than the war. The notion that wars were made in rooms, not on battlefields, was new, and it sickened him. He fought the feeling, but it gnawed at him. *If this is all just a game,* he said to himself, *then who is responsible for all the death and destruction? If it was a war fought for good reasons, then the suffering and dying were inevitable and meant something. But if it was a game. . . .* The idea boggled his mind, and he squashed it before it could grow.

*

The old man returned that evening. He glanced at what the doctors had written on the paper, and his expression seemed to soften.

"The doctors say that you will feel weakness for a week or so more. The bamboo shoots have lacerated your intestines, and the bleeding will continue for a few more days, gradually lessening. They have had much experience with this sort of thing. There will be, they say, no aftereffects, but you will never again want to eat *chao-hsüeh-tou*."

"What is that?" asked the prisoner.

"A dish with bamboo shoots," said the old man with a sly smile.

"Very funny," said the prisoner.

The old man's expression changed, becoming more serious. He started to speak, then stopped. The prisoner could see him thinking. When he began again, he had changed the topic.

"I am to take a trip to Hanoi in a week's time to confer about new strategies. We are now in an advanced stage of the war—we have pushed the opponents back and must think of ways to consolidate our gains without unduly disrupting the country and its people."

The prisoner looked at the old man suspiciously. The old man noticed this and stopped.

"You are acting as if I am trying to brainwash you. That is nonsense. Had that been our motive, you would have known long ago. Duc Thang handles such matters, and you have seen how he works."

He paused here, flicking the toe of his boot with his quirt. The gesture almost seemed to be a habit and the prisoner was surprised, for he had never noticed it before—he hardly remembered the old man carrying a quirt.

"I do not concern myself with such matters," said the old man, looking directly at him. "I tell you this so that you will not worry. To worry about such a stupidity would be a waste of energy, and I deplore waste."

His voice was as hard and cold as steel, and the prisoner hesitated. He felt confused and embarrassed. *This man has been good to me,* he thought, *and I have insulted him.*

"Accept my apologies," he said.

"That is not necessary," said the old man. "Under the circumstances your suspicion is understandable. I am sure that if our positions were reversed, I would feel much as you do. And in a war . . . well, it is all luck, and I could as easily be the prisoner as you. Knowing

111

this, all one can do is be fair and forgive as much as one can."

He got up and left then. Despite the old man's words, the prisoner felt that he had hurt him by his suspicions.

He stared at the walls of the room—the oil lamps that were used at night sent flickering patterns over them, shadows leaping like animals in a strange, frenzied dance. The shadows hypnotized him, and he felt himself sink into a half slumber, almost a trance. His head ached a little, a symptom left over from his weakness and the heat of the day. He felt himself drifting and imagined he was swimming in the sea far from land, the lone survivor of a shipwreck. At first he had swum south, guiding himself by the North Star, but now he was swimming no longer. His arms and legs were tired, and his spirit was weak. It was all he could do to float. He lay in the water, relaxed, and kept himself up by moving his arms and legs slowly every now and then. Waves were lapping over him, but he had stopped fighting them. He relaxed even more and began to ride them, up the crest of one, down another. He could feel the swell, and it felt strong under his body, but all the time there was the gnawing thought that he was doomed. *If you do not swim south,* said the voice, *you will never come to land.* The worry would not die, but it was weak, while the tiredness and the waves were strong. He lay back and let the waves move him as they would.

XXVII

Two days elapsed before the old man returned. He seemed cheerful, as if the unpleasantness of the last visit had passed.

"Preparations are underway," he said. "I am to go north to Bai Thuong, then by helicopter over the mountains to Hanoi."

The prisoner looked at him without expression.

"You do not understand," said the old man. "It has been eight months since I have been away from this God-forsaken camp. It has a certain charm," he gestured about him, "but unfortunately it leaves much to be desired. Hanoi, however provincial it may be, is a town."

He beamed, and the prisoner noticed how white and even his teeth were. *Amazing,* he thought, *for such an old man. His teeth look like they belong to a movie star.*

"A town, my friend," repeated the old man, "with restaurants and a theater—there are two of them—and cafés. Even women for those young enough," he nodded toward the prisoner, "and inclined to waste their time."

"How long will you be away?" asked the prisoner, not wishing to show that he was feeling tired and unable to share the old man's enthusiasm.

"Two months, two glorious months. During the days I will be busy—the staff is not quick, for everything is decided by vote, and you know how inefficient that can be —but the nights will be mine. A commander must have relaxation so that his mind is clear when he plans for the death of others."

They sat in silence for a few more minutes. Then the old man rose and bid him good night.

*

The next day was burning hot. Flies circled in the hospital room, and he sweated like a pig. In the afternoon he climbed out of his bed and walked across the camp to the small awning where there were chairs and tables. There were flies here, too, but the air was not as stagnant.

Sitting here, he could see around him. No one was moving. Here and there soldiers sat in the shade of buildings, fanning themselves. Then two men came out of the commander's cabin and crossed the camp. One of them was No-Neck. He stood out because he was almost a head taller than his companion and strode with a vigor and an assurance that seemed impervious to the heat.

The bastard is not human, thought the prisoner. *But if he were cut in the right place, he would bleed. And even if it weren't real blood, if enough of it were let out he would not walk so tall. No, he would not.*

The two men went into the jungle at the south end of the camp and were swallowed up by the green. The prisoner went back to staring into nothingness. Once a lone plane, flying so high that he could not tell which side it belonged to, flew over. He guessed that it was on a recon mission—a single-engine prop with an observer peering down through a telephoto lens, snapping pictures and praying that no one fired a bullet through the paper-thin floor of his plane. A friend who flew such missions had told him that they usually stayed so high that they saw nothing. He could not blame them. *If the plane was lower, it would be like shooting ducks,* he thought, then he remembered the mallards that passed over his house in Cleveland each November, heading south. They flew high in great *V*s and he had always found it hard to imagine birds up so high, flying such great distances.

"Don't they feel cold?" he had once asked his father after reading in school that it was cold high in the air and that was why airplanes had heaters.

"No" was the answer, "I don't think they do." Then his father went back to reading his newspaper. That was how the prisoner remembered him—hands and feet and a newspaper in front of his face.

*

Toward evening he went back to the hospital. The heat had not lessened any; if anything, it had increased. The air was more humid, and there was no breeze. The men were lying in their beds, waiting for the bell to ring announcing the evening meal. As soon as he went inside the room, he began to sweat again. He cursed and got out the last set of newspapers the old man had given him and tried to read to take his mind off the heat.

When mealtime came, he ate only a little. It was too hot to eat, and the food tasted like mud and left a bitter aftertaste. After dinner he tried to sleep but found it impossible. Finally he got up, went to the door, and pointed to the awning across the camp. The guard nodded, and he walked over. He was surprised that the man let him go out, for it was night and it would have been easy to slip into the jungle, but he guessed that they weren't worried about that now. *They know that I know that it is impossible,* he thought, *and if I were to be such a fool, then they will not bother to stop me.*

Sitting under the awning, he could feel the mosquitoes humming around him, but he had smeared himself with the salve that the soldiers used. It smelled like cloves, almost sweet, but it stopped the mosquitoes from biting.

Finally he felt a breeze rising. He had been sitting so long that he had lost sense of time, but the breeze felt good, and he became drowsy. He rose and walked back to the hospital building. The lights were out, and all the men were sleeping. He lay down and slept, not knowing that it was long past midnight and that the breeze was strange because it had come from the northeast, and all breezes in that season were supposed to come from the southwest, off the Indian Ocean. The breeze woke the old man, who noted it, shook his head, then went back to sleep.

XXVIII

When the prisoner awoke the next morning, the chill of the air surprised him. Several of the patients—those already racked by malaria—were shaking violently. The two doctors were already there, taking medicine from their miraculous canvas bag and forcing it upon the reluctant men. He looked out into the center of the camp. The sunlight was as bright as always, but the wind—still from the north and stronger than ever—was blowing dust into small clouds, forcing the soldiers to cover their eyes. A few men even had handkerchiefs tied over their noses. He watched them struggle against the wind, then turned back to the doctors and the other patients. The men were huddled under blankets, and he noticed that the two doctors had pieces of orange cloth wound around their necks, much like scarves. He laughed. To them this weather was frigid, but to him it was like a gusty April day. He hadn't felt anything so invigorating in months.

Toward mid-morning the old man came by. He smiled when he saw the prisoner.

"So, at last we have Cleveland weather, eh! God, it feels good, does it not?" The old man thumped his chest and breathed deeply. "This is football weather. It was on a day such as this that we defeated Princeton in '39. That was before your time, but you must have read of the great Princeton team, two All-Americans in the backfield and a mammoth offensive line. But that day we surprised them."

116

He stopped, and the faraway look that the prisoner had noticed before returned.

"My roommate was a tackle on the team. A great fellow—Rolfe Hugley III. A great fellow."

Again he paused, and again there was the faraway look.

"He died in '42 . . . in the war at Midway. He was a commander and the Japanese sank his ship. The youngest destroyer commander in the Navy. A tremendous fellow."

The prisoner thought he saw tears forming in the corners of the old man's eyes, but he couldn't be sure.

"But enough of the past—that was all before your time. That was the war of your father's generation. You have your own war, and I'm certain you do not wish to hear of another."

The prisoner chuckled.

"I have made a joke?" asked the old man.

"You said that it is our war as if we wanted it. Most of my friends say that it is your war. You, plus our fathers, are the ones who have brought this upon us. At least that is what the newspapers you have brought me say."

The old man laughed. "Always it is the young accusing the old. In my time I remember my father speaking of the French and the wicked men who followed them. These were the villains, and when they were expelled we would have peace. It was the old men—the ones who had entered into bargains with the French—who were responsible for our suffering. They were weak and senile and, like the old everywhere, eager to protect themselves against the young who they feared would take some of their hard-earned wealth. And so we drove the French out and killed many of these men. I remember how happy my father was at their execution and how he went to the square every day to see them shot. But then came others who strengthened the army and built planes and tanks, and all the while the people were starving and as hungry as they had been with the French—perhaps even hungrier."

"But you have joined with these men," said the prisoner. "If you see their folly, why do you fight in their war?"

The old man looked at him, but not with the cynical

117

smile that he had expected. His face was calm, expressionless, without anger or bitterness.

"I have done what I must—what any man who is not a fool would have done. You are too young to understand this fully, but in time you will. Already you have had your first lesson. It has been painful, but sometimes the painful lessons are the most important ones."

They were silent for a long time after that. The prisoner again felt that he had offended the old man, but he was too tired to apologize. The old man seemed to be thinking. Finally he spoke.

"But I have not come to lecture. I have come to discuss a matter with you. It is a delicate matter—one which you may not understand," he paused, "may not see as I see it."

The prisoner waited.

"I am to be accompanied by three men when I go to Hanoi. Two of them have already been selected. One is Captain Duc Thang. The other is still unknown."

The prisoner sensed what the question would be and knew how he must answer.

"I see your concern already," said the old man. "You are afraid that I will ask you to come and you will be compromised. I have thought of this, and you are right. If it were discovered by those on your side, they would brand you a traitor, and should this conflict ever end— and it will someday, God knows when, though—then you would be a man without a country."

The prisoner watched closely. He liked the man, but there was a quality about him at this moment that filled him with anxiety. *Somewhere,* he thought, *there is a place in his mind that I do not know. That I do not have the slightest notion of.*

"So I will not ask you, my friend," said the old man. "Truly I would have welcomed your company. The cafés, the theaters—they would be more enjoyable if you were there as my guest. But it would be unwise, and men must always do the wise thing."

The old man shrugged and got to his feet, then reached over and shook the prisoner's hand. It was the first time he had done so. Suddenly the prisoner realized this, and he became embarrassed.

118

"In two months' time I will be back, and then I will have much to tell you. Until then, good health."

The old man turned and left the room. The prisoner watched him for a moment. Something about the old man's departure troubled him. It was a foreboding, something he couldn't put his finger on but which he knew, almost with a certainty, was in the offing.

XXIX

The next morning the cold continued. The prisoner rose early, walked to the awning in the center of camp, and sat. The dust peppered his skin and stung his eyes, but it felt good. He remembered his youth and the summers on his uncle's farm. One day in particular haunted him. He had been walking in a field where the wheat was freshly mowed and there were still wispy, uncollected stalks littering the ground. The wind whipped up suddenly, and the air seemed alive with golden brown arrows that stabbed him in the arms and face. He had tried to struggle across the field to the farmhouse but had given up and sat down, putting his head on his knees, waiting for the wind to stop. He had a crazy, childish fear that he would be buried by the wheat and that no one would ever find him. But in a few minutes the wind died, and he straightened up, shook the wheat from his hair, and walked to the house. For some reason he had told his uncle of his fantasy. It was a peculiar thing for him to do, for he was a secretive boy and usually spoke to no one about his fears.

"If you're goin' to be buried alive," his uncle had told him, "it won't happen in the middle of a wheat field. Maybe in a strip mine like they got up near Ashtabula, but not in a wheat field."

At least his uncle hadn't laughed. He was only a kid, but he had appreciated that.

*

The bell that signaled breakfast woke him from his daydreams. The morning meal was being dished out indoors today because of the wind and dust. The men were lining up to get their food. He got on the end of the line and waited. When the line was about half finished, some men came in the door and watched the prisoner. He had never seen them before. There were three, and they looked alike—short and muscular, wearing black uniforms with red stripes and peaked caps pulled so low that he couldn't see their eyes. They talked to the attendants for a minute, then turned and came toward him, stopping about five feet away.

"The prisoner will come with us!" ordered the one in the middle. He followed them across the compound and into the cabin where No-Neck was sitting at the desk. The prisoner was surprised because the old man had said that No-Neck was accompanying him to Hanoi.

"The prisoner will stand at attention!" said No-Neck. The sound of his voice was the same—hard and metallic, the pronunciation precise. The prisoner could feel the sting of the whip again and the heat of the sun.

"The prisoner is to be sent to the prison camp at Phuly. He is to leave today at noon. Before he leaves, he will tell us the supply lines he has discovered and the place where he is to rendezvous with his superiors."

He couldn't believe it. It was as if the last month had never existed, and he were back standing before No-Neck on that first hot day.

He looked at No-Neck, then shook his head. No-Neck nodded to one of the guards, and they took him out and led him across the compound to the small shack where he had spent the first weeks. The door was shut behind him, and he heard the lock click. Then he smelled the stink from the latrines. The prisoner went

120

to the small window in the door, grabbed the bars, and shook them as he had that first day.

*

For a while he was dazed. He knew where he was, but he thought it was all a dream. *I'll wake up,* he kept telling himself, but when he opened his eyes, he saw only the dark, stained walls of the shed and the light coming through the barred window. Then he knew where he was, and he put his head on his knees and began to sob softly.

They gave him nothing to eat that day. Toward nightfall he remembered No-Neck's statement about the transfer to Phuly, so he waited, half hoping, thinking that it might be true, that it might be more than a lie told to weaken and confuse him. But no one came, and he knew that they wouldn't come, at least not to take him to Phuly.

On the second day they fed him rice and a cup of weak tea. It was shoved through the slot in the door by a guard he had seen many times in the camp. He said *"Chás anh"* to the man, using the greeting that the commander had taught him. The man looked at him strangely, nodded awkwardly, and left. Somehow that made him feel better. He was alone in the cell and the heat was unbearable—already he felt his strength going and his nerves weakening—but it wasn't like before because now the shack was not an island. It was connected to the rest of the camp. The links to the outside were the men he knew who carried his food and checked three times a day to make certain that he had not escaped. Because of this, the loneliness was not as great.

*

Time turned liquid and flowed over him, around and past him. He was like a stone, and it wore him smooth. He slept much, sometimes almost all day. He was accustomed to the heat now, and the flies didn't bother him. *I've gone native,* he said to himself. *Hell, after it's all over, I might even come back for a vacation just to renew old acquaintances.* At night when he was awake, he lay on his back in a place that let him see the sky

121

and studied the stars. He had never been interested in astronomy, so he didn't know the names of most of them, but that made it better because he could give his imagination free reign. He knew the North Star, the Big Dipper, and the Little Dipper, but he decided to call them by new names. The North Star would be King. The Big Dipper his wives. The Little Dipper their children.

"Child Number Two," he would say, "you are twinkling funny tonight. Do you have a sore throat?" or "Wife Number Three, you look beautiful tonight. Your eyes are sparkling."

He had never realized that there were so many stars and that each blinked in a certain way with a certain color and a special intensity. A few of them moved, and he guessed that these were either planets or satellites, but for him they held none of the magic of the stars. He remembered how excited everyone had been when the first few satellites were launched, but it had never touched him much. He had agreed with his uncle about that.

"Doesn't make any difference to me," his uncle said, rocking in his chair and puffing on an old corncob pipe. "Doesn't make my corn grow any better and doesn't make the spring any longer or the winter any shorter." He knocked the ashes out of his pipe into an old tin he kept beside him when he smoked. "People get all head up 'bout someone shootin' a piece of metal up into the sky. Like it was a miracle or something. The real miracle's right here, all about us"—he swept his hand around him, pointing to his fields filled with ripening corn—"only the damned fools'er too blind to see it. Shortsighted as a hog. Yes sir, most people are shortsighted as hogs."

About dawn, after the first rays of the sun came over the trees at the edge of the jungle, he usually fell asleep. Then he would wake at noon when the guard pushed the food through the slot in the door, eat, walk back and forth for a half hour or so, relieve himself, then sleep some more. He had decided that he would walk some each day. It would be healthier for him and would keep his muscles toned.

The thing he hated the most was the shit. *There's no way to avoid that,* he thought, *unless you scoop it up and throw it out the window.* But he had nothing to do that with except the plate that he ate from, and he couldn't bring himself to do that even though he knew they washed them. He would never have guessed how repulsive his own fecal matter could be, but he found himself avoiding the corner he had picked to defecate and urinate in—and not just the corner but the whole area, places where there were no droppings. He remembered how dogs sniffed at shit. There was a word for that. Once he'd taken a parasitology course, and he remembered that that was the way dogs picked up worms and that was why it wasn't good to let them lick you on the mouth. Then he remembered reading that a nobleman—or was it a Roman senator?—kept his shit in a box and smelled it from time to time. The man claimed that it gave him inspiration. At the time he'd told a friend that story, and the friend had laughed and said it was impossible, but he had argued with his friend that with people all things were possible.

But with the passing of days, the smell bothered him less and less until he almost didn't notice it. That was the smell of his own shit. He still noticed the smell of the latrines—*It's different, somehow sweeter,* he thought, half laughing to himself, *almost fragrant.* But still it nauseated him. *Well, at least that's something,* he mused, *at least I still have that—the feeling of disgust.* It was a human feeling disgust. He had little else in the way of feelings anymore and so he welcomed it.

That was the worst thing that was happening to him— the draining away of feelings. It was insidious. He hardly noticed it, but it was happening. Day by day he felt less and less, became more and more a thing, zombielike, sleeping endlessly, shitting in his corner, walking for his half hour of exercise, then sleeping again. Day followed night, light followed darkness, but his link with the light had snapped. No longer did he sleep at night and wake in the morning. Like an animal, he slept when the feeling seized him, then woke suddenly in darkness and went to the window to grab the bars and peer at the moon.

He remembered the dog that he had found once, the only pet he'd ever had. The dog had been wild for a long time when he found it, and although he cared for it and the dog came to love him, it never lost its wild ways. Some nights he would wake and see the dog standing by the window, peering out and sniffing the breeze. At other times when he took it for walks, it would stop and look into the distance. Voices were calling that dog, he knew, and although it stayed with him and valued the comforts of food and a warm house it had given up something and it wasn't happy.

Standing by the barred window of his cell, he remembered the dog, then his home and his mother and father. For that he was grateful. At least there was something real out there beyond the bars, the latrines and the jungle. The feelings—the anger and the impatience he always felt with them—were real. They were a long way off, far away on the west side of Cleveland and light years into the past, but even No-Neck couldn't take them away.

Scenes from his childhood drifted through his mind. He remembered the first time he'd kissed a girl. He was thirteen, and she was his cousin Linda's friend. They'd gone to a movie together—*South Pacific*—and during the entire show, he was working up the nerve to do it. And then he did it, and she looked surprised and kissed back, and they held hands on the way home. Later they'd necked for hours. His groin had ached, but he never tried anything. *Too holy,* he said to himself, half in admiration, half in derision. He never talked about it with anybody, though. He liked to keep things to himself, inside where he could feel them. *Once you talked about something,* then it wasn't yours anymore. It also belonged to whoever you talked to. And he didn't like that. He knew he suffered because of that feeling, but it was him, the way he was.

He remembered the baseball games and the basketball games, and the track meets better than anything else. Better than people and books. He didn't really have much feeling for those things; once that had bothered him, but now it didn't. *If that's the way I am,* he thought, *that's the way I am.* He had always been stubborn, sometimes stupidly stubborn. That was good and that was bad, but it was him too.

He recalled the time he'd hit two home runs. He was sixteen then, and it was an important game. The pitches had been up high where he liked them, and he'd hit the ball a mile to left center. He could still recall the feeling in his hands when the ball jumped off the bat. First it seemed to sink in, and the bat had that soft feeling like it was rubber and it was catching the ball. When it felt like that he knew he'd hit it just right.

They had won that game, and afterwards he'd gone out with the guys, and they'd gotten drunk on beer. It was the first time he'd ever been drunk, and he'd come home still in a half stupor, vomited, then fell into bed. His mother just shook her head the next morning, and his father smiled. Funny, that was one of the few good memories he had of them—his father, dressed for work in his tie and suit, looking down at him and shaking his head ruefully, and his mother giving him a glass of Alka-Seltzer and coming to his room every half hour to see how he was.

In a yellow haze he woke, dragged himself to the window, and peered out. He could see the soldiers coming and going, crossing and recrossing the camp. Once or twice he saw No-Neck emerge from the commander's cabin, stand for a minute issuing orders, then go back inside. He wondered when the old man would return. That was the one hope that he still held. The old man would not let No-Neck do this to him, and if he ever knew, then No-Neck would have to answer for it.

He laughed. He was a fool. Probably they were together in this thing. First one, then the other. It was all part of their plan.

Then he stared out the window again, again watching the men and the commander's cabin. He was confused and he knew it, but he also sensed that it was useless to try to reconcile the two halves of his mind. One side trusted because it had nothing else to trust, the other doubted and hated because it had reason to doubt and hate.

He was becoming feebler, and although he didn't realize it he was changing. He was thinner, there were dark hollows under his eyes, and his teeth were loosening. Now he sometimes spent whole days lying in the corner of the shack, too depressed to move or even to want to move. His soul was softening, but that was something which he had no experience with so he didn't detect the signs. The guards did though, and each day they reported back to No-Neck.

XXX

How much time had passed he no longer knew. It could have been a month, maybe two. When he ran his hand over his chin and felt his beard, it was full and felt strange to him. *Like Santa Claus,* he thought, *like Goddamned Kriss Kringle.* Then he laughed to himself in the peculiar way that had become second nature to him. It was all funny, a great joke—the soldiers, No-Neck, the camp, and the whole God-damned war. It was some great joke like the time Kurowski painted all the seats in the latrine with glue and sugar. No one had laughed much about that. He thought it was funny, though, and when he came to mess and everyone's trousers were sticking to their asses, he couldn't help laughing. It was all so God-damned funny: the men all looking at K and muttering, and K sitting there like Little Lord Fauntleroy, quietly munching his food then asking someone to "kindly" pass the sugar. That was a good one all right. "Kindly pass me the sugar!"

*

It was September now, and although the prisoner did not know it the men in the villages were beginning the first harvest of the rice paddies. The wind had changed: It was from the northeast as it had been on that strange night when the old man woke, and the dust flew in clouds, and the prisoner sat up half the night under the awning, in the middle of the compound. It was a dry breeze that powdered the leaves around the edge of the camp with light yellow dust. The hum of the insects was softened, and at night the stars twinkled dimly as though through a veil.

The prisoner saw this from the window, but he did not understand. All he knew was that the stars were dimmer than they had once been, and in his delirium he assumed that something was happening to his vision. His gums had been bleeding for weeks now, and each day he felt his scalp, for he was certain that his hair was falling out. *When I get out of here, my movie career will be over,* he said to himself. *Yes sir, old Marlon won't have anything to worry about anymore.* Then he slept again, curling up in the place by the west wall where he had lain so long that the ground was smoothed and rounded to his body.

All the time that he lay in the shack, his fellow soldiers were retreating farther and farther south—farther and farther from him—but he knew nothing of this. Nor did he hear of the mounting casualties or the protests or the Senate debates or the marches or the demonstrations. All that was somewhere else, somewhere where men walked in the daylight and slept at night and knew women and laughed and cried and lived. Where he was, it was dark—always dark—and there was no perfume but the smell of the latrines and no women but those he could imagine.

He did not know it, but slowly, more slowly than even the seasons change, he was moving toward nothingness and imbecility. For now when the guard looked in the cell, he saw only a strange thing that sat in the corner and gaped like a dumb animal. And when the prisoner ate, he was like an animal. The guard looked away, for it disgusted him to see a human like that, and he thanked his gods that he was not the man in the cell.

Toward December the Viet Cong consolidated their gains. Now they could relax, for the war was in their hands, and although the enemy was still strong they were certain that in the end he would yield. Still No-Neck kept the prisoner in his cell. He had ceased to think of questioning him but was convinced that he was an infiltrator, and as a man of honor No-Neck hated spies and did not believe in showing them mercy. It cost him the service

127

of one man to watch the shack, and he could have used that man for other things—to help build the new airfield beside the camp or to travel into the hills and help the villagers clear debris and bury their dead. But he did not seriously consider this. There was a prisoner in the shack, and he was the commander, and commanders made certain that prisoners did not escape. If a prisoner escaped, it was because of negligence or stupidity, and he despised those things.

Winter came and with it came cold nights. The prisoner huddled in the corner of the shack and shook as chills racked him. His teeth rattled, and although he lay down, he could not sleep because of the cold. Sleep was all that was left to him; it had saved his mind, healing and obliterating the boredom and the frustrated rage. But now that sleep was gone, he was consumed with a fury that would give him no rest.

Over and over he saw himself tearing at No-Neck's throat, stabbing him, trampling him. His delirium was filled with blood, and he thought one thing day and night: *When I am free, when I am outside, I will kill him—no matter what happens, I will kill him.*

XXXI

One day early in January, Commander Xuong returned. The air was still—the wind had stopped for an unseasonable day of calm—and the old man looked at the pale blue mid-winter sky as he stepped from the copter, nodded with approval, and walked across the camp toward the cabin. No-Neck stood and saluted when he entered. They spoke briefly, then the old man retired to his room. He would rest a while, then come back to his desk and read over the reports that No-Neck had prepared. That evening he ate alone, following the meal with a cigar that he had brought back from Hanoi. "Courtesy of our Cuban comrades," he said, smiling at the stone-faced No-Neck. *No sense of humor,* he remarked to himself, then bid No-Neck good night and walked out into the compound. He looked at the stars, then strolled up to some guards and made a joke. Just before turning in, he remembered the prisoner and inquired about him. When the men pointed toward the shack, he swore, then gave sharp commands, and they followed him to the building.

He looked at the thing on the floor, told one guard to go and get the doctor, then told the others to carry the man to the hospital. He was being reckless, he knew, but in his anger he did not think. Then he strode across the compound and went to his room.

The next morning at eight he called No-Neck before him and demanded the reason for the incarceration of the prisoner. No-Neck spoke matter-of-factly. He had followed the regulations which said that prisoners were to be incarcerated. The old man swore again.

Later that day he went to the hospital to see the prisoner. He lay on a bed, staring at the ceiling, his eyes empty and strangely large and bright. The old man spoke, but he knew that the man didn't understand. He put his hand on the prisoner's shoulder and then left, walking slowly, his limp more noticeable than ever.

All this the prisoner noted. Alone, isolated in his world of emptiness, he had seen the guards come and had heard the old man's voice and felt the hands as they carried him across the camp to the hospital. The bed felt soft and good, and the sheets were cool and smooth. Then there was the soup—the first warm food he had eaten in months. He could feel it in his stomach and imagined it seeping into his veins, warming his fingers and toes. The fury had lessened. He was not afraid of the darkness now —the phantoms with the teeth and the claws that danced through his mind, always tearing at the figure with the great shoulders and the bullet head—they were fainter

. . . shadows in the background. He felt sleep coming on, and he waited for it as child awaits its mother.

*

The second day in the hospital he felt better. Still he did not speak—it was as if there were a great wall between him and the rest of the world, a wall which he did not want to breach—but he noticed more. The men about him had faces—noses and eyes and ears—and when they talked, he watched their mouths and saw their teeth and tongues and lips. He had no feelings for them—they were things that moved, and he watched the movement. It fascinated him—the patter of their feet, the quickness and dexterity of their hands. He had been away from men for so long that he had ceased to believe in their reality.

On the third day he sat up in bed and at the noon meal took a fork and ate without help. The attendants moved away and left him alone, only coming back later to take away the plates and utensils. They had seen such men before, and to them these men were merely another kind of wounded. Some had no arms or legs, others no fingers; these had no minds. They were a fact of the war and that was all.

On the afternoon of the third day, the old man came to see him again. He spoke but the prisoner did not hear —the sound rained about him and he felt it but it made no sense to him. He watched the old man's lips, his teeth, and his eyes. He could see sadness mixed with pain in those eyes. He wanted to speak but still words would not come, and he had no wish to struggle. Then the old man was gone, and he lay and stared at the ceiling again.

Toward nightfall the light diminished, and the room darkened. The ceiling turned from white to gray. He noticed this, blinked twice, and looked toward the window. He could see men moving back and forth, dark shapes in the twilight. Just before nightfall the crickets began to chirp, loud and in chorus. He blinked rapidly for a few seconds, then a faint smile turned the corners of his mouth up and he shut his eyes and slept.

130

XXXII

He was beginning to feel things now. When people were near him, he could sense them breathing and perspiring. Now he could pick out words and sounds—the pad of feet on the floor, the clink of glasses, and the sighs of men in pain. Things were coming into focus. And with this he gradually began to sense what lay behind him, where he had been, and what he had suffered. He remembered the last day before the old man had left for Hanoi—the dust and the strange wind and the night under the awning in the middle of camp. Again he could see the three men who came to the mess for him; again he crossed the camp with them and stood before No-Neck and was questioned and remained silent. Then he remembered the shock and the silence and heat and the solitude.

He knew what No-Neck had done to him, knew that he had waited, in his fanatic way, for the moment to be ripe to rend him like a weak animal. All this he understood, and he hated the man and knew that if he could he would kill him. But the feeling was different than it had been when he was in the shed. It did not torment him and spin strange shapes in his mind. Other things were there now, things that were more real than No-Neck. He knew that there was a limit to his power—not consciously, but somewhere inside he sensed this—and so the fury dulled.

It was as it had been when he was a teenager, thinking for days on end of what he would do the first time he

131

ran a race for the high school track team. He had waited and waited, and the idea had grown until it filled his mind day and night. And then something happened—his brother became sick, almost died, and his feelings shifted. Still there was the race, and it was still important, but his imagination was somewhere else, his hopes and fears joined to something else.

On the fifth day he answered when the commander spoke to him. The old man was speechless for a minute, then he reached out his hand, took the prisoner's, and grasped it firmly.

"I am happy—so happy—to see you back, my young friend," he said.

The prisoner nodded, his neck still weak, and smiled.

"What you must think—what you must feel about all of this!" The old man shook his head.

They were both silent then. The old man seemed to be thinking. He shook his head again and spoke to one of the orderlies, who then left the room.

"We will celebrate," said the old man. "We will celebrate your return, my friend."

The old man was so filled with emotion that he was shaking. The prisoner moved his hand to touch him and the old man smiled sadly.

"Do not. Save your strength. It is all so stupid, this, this. . . ." He gestured about him. "Fanaticism. Stupid, senseless fanaticism. Always it is the same. The stupid ones—they take an idea, and then they use it to arm their malice, and they hurt, and they kill. Men. . . ." He shook his head.

The orderly returned with a gray clay bottle that was beaded with moisture. The old man filled two glasses with the greenish liquid, and they drank.

It was cold, but it warmed the prisoner's stomach and filled him with a strange joy while it relaxed him. And because he felt so good, he started to laugh. Softly, almost chuckling, he shook with gentle laughter. The old man looked at him and started to laugh too, softly and with sadness still filling his eyes.

When the prisoner finally stopped, he raised his hand to his face for it felt strange, and then he realized that tears were rolling down his cheeks.

132

XXXIII

The first days of February brought the ducks—great brown ones, flying north in *Vs* through the blue-gray midwinter sky. The prisoner was walking now, unsteadily, but walking. Each day at two the old man came for him, and they crossed the camp, walking slowly, talking or just ruminating, enjoying each other's company. The soldiers watched them pass but took little notice. Three weeks earlier the prisoner had been a thing, a forgotten animal living in a shed. Now he was a person again, the companion of their superior. Thus were the fortunes of war. They shrugged and went about their duties.

February was dry. The edges of the leaves in the forest turned yellow, and the wind blew steadily from the east. Far off, a hundred miles east on the coast, the rains were falling. Great torrents of rain from dark thunderheads born over the China Sea. These clouds blew west until they reached the central highland, pouring rain down on the waiting jungle along the way. When they reached the lower slopes of the plateau, they were pale and wispy and they dispersed—thousand of threads of white fluff racing quickly west. From the lower slopes of the plateau into Laos and then Thailand, the sky was a clear blue-gray filled with the pastel yellow of a winter sun. It was a peaceful sky, a sky that made men feel old and crave quiet. The old man and the prisoner spent much time looking at it.

"It reminds me of the sky in the poems of our greatest poets," said the old man.

"Mao and Ho Chi Minh," said the prisoner.

The old man laughed. "You must think me thoroughly indoctrinated, an aesthetic barbarian."

The prisoner mumbled an apology.

"Do not, do not," said the old man. It was the first time the prisoner had seen him embarrassed, and he smiled to himself.

"For me," said the old man, "the greatest poets lie in the past, far back. I am, as my comrades would say, unreclaimed—aesthetically speaking that is."

"Yes, aesthetically speaking," said the prisoner.

"Tu Fu—a Chinese poet of the T'ang Dynasty—he is the greatest. Others approach him—his friend Li Po, for example; his rhymes are richer. And then there is my namesake, our great satirist Tu Xuong. But for sheer poetry—tenderness and bitterness and depth of feeling—Tu Fu is unsurpassed."

He recited a poem, and the prisoner listened to the foreign sounds. Then the old man translated it.

I met you often when you were visiting princes
And when you were playing in noblemen's halls.
. . . Spring passes. . . . Far down the river now,
I find you alone under falling petals.

"Tu Fu courted the emperor, but the emperor did not reward him, and so the master was forced to roam. His life was not easy. His poetry was the fruit of sad experience, the story of what he had seen and suffered."

The prisoner suppressed a yawn.

"Poetry does not interest you?"

"Sometimes," said the prisoner.

The old man was silent again. They wandered on until they reached the edge of the jungle, then turned and walked back toward the hospital.

"Is there any news of a truce yet?" the prisoner asked.

"None yet," said the old man. "Those in your country —the young, the students and intellectuals—they are struggling to bring about peace, but the men who rule are stubborn."

The prisoner frowned.

"Do not be so hard on them. It is not easy to rule, my friend. Many in your country have forgotten that."

134

The prisoner started to speak then stopped.

"You have decided against speaking your mind," said the old man with a half smile. "Becoming politic?"

The prisoner looked at him out of the corner of his eye. "Words about such things disgust me."

"I am sorry," said the old man and looked away.

"No, no—I do not mean what you have said. It is my countrymen and what I know to be happening in my country—or at least what the newspapers you give me say."

The old man nodded, and the prisoner went on.

"To debate this thing at all times and in all places, to have men and women who have not been here decide—professors and politicians and shopkeepers. What do they know of it? Everyone gives his opinion, and it is listened to as if . . . as if. . . ."

The old man coughed, and the prisoner stopped.

"Go on, go on. It is the dust, the accursed mid-winter dust."

"In the last paper you gave me, there were two pages of interviews with people who gave their views on the war. Most of them were women—school teachers, secretaries, saleswomen, and a nurse."

"Yes," said the old man, "women have become important in the politics of your country—that is a sign of the imminent overthrow of the bourgeoisie." There was a slight smile on his face as he said this, but the prisoner did not notice.

"Each was so sure: the war is an evil thing; the President a war monger; the Secretary of Defense a killer protecting the vested interests of the arms' manufacturers. They say it is an evil plot of those who would kill and use the young. But if it were as simple as that, there would be no wars." He paused, then kicked at the dust.

"People," said the old man, "have always wanted to see things in such a way that the troublesome questions are solved. Ambiguity discomforts them."

The prisoner looked at him, only half comprehending.

"My friend, war like everything else has two sides. There are reasons, and there are reasons. I would not be so blasé as to say that no one is at fault and that a war does not involve questions of right or wrong. To feel thus—well, that is mere silliness, the foppishness of dil-

135

ettantes. I have my point of view and you yours. They
differ. We go to war and I respect you as an opponent
and you respect me. I am right, you wrong."

"It is as simple as that," said the prisoner.

"Yes, unfortunately, as simple as that," said the old
man.

"But the death and the suffering and the destruction.
It must mean something. It has to."

"Do not think too long or too hard about that my
friend," said the old man. "It will do you little good."

XXXIV

The camp was growing. The prisoner could see this. Each
day new soldiers arrived in large helicopters, usually at
midday. A crew of men were clearing the jungle on the
east and south sides of the camp. Most of the new ar-
rivals lived in tents on the east side. The tents were olive
canvas, and there were almost fifty of them the last time
he counted. He made a quick calculation. At six men to
a tent, this meant at least 300 new men. He could not
understand. The war was far to the south—there would
be reason to send men there, but here? He wondered and
thought of asking the old man but decided not to. Then
one day as they were enjoying their afternoon stroll, he
blurted the question out. The old man looked at him suspiciously for a second, then his expression lightened.

"That, my young friend, is a question which you can
understand why I cannot answer."

"Does it matter?" said the prisoner. "There is no
chance of my escaping. Who will I tell—the moon?"

The old man shook his head, but he would say no more concerning the new men.

That evening the prisoner watched the new soldiers closely from the hospital window where he sat reading old newspapers. They did not look like the soldiers who had manned the camp since his arrival. They were younger, stronger-looking, and most seemed taller—much taller than any Vietnamese he had seen. Several were almost as tall as No-Neck. Their uniforms were the same olive-green color as the veteran soldiers', but the cut was different. A few times he had seen men wearing uniforms with dark blue shirts that were new to him. He tried to remember the sound of their voices—he could not understand Vietnamese, but he could recognize it when he heard it. He suspected that the new soldiers spoke a different language, but he had never been close to them for long enough to really listen to them. He noticed that they did not mingle with the older soldiers, and that although all the men ate together, the new soldiers cooked something over an open fire afterwards. It looked like flat, yellow cakes of grain, which they ate late at night. Since his arrival in Vietnam, he had heard stories of Chinese soldiers joining the ranks, and he assumed these new men were Chinese sent as far to the south as the high command dared.

But what does it matter? he said to himself. *If these are Chinese soldiers, fine. If they aren't, they aren't. I don't really give a damn. The old man doesn't care either, although he pretends to. The only ones who could care would be some damn fanatic congressmen, and they can all fuck themselves.*

He shut his eyes and tried to think of other things—of some place else besides the camp and the hospital. The moon was a funny orange and hanging low on the horizon. He rolled on his side and looked at it through the window.

"You don't look very cheerful, old fellow," he said half aloud. "Your color's not good, a little peaked. You need some Geritol or maybe an Ex-Lax."

He shut his eyes and tried to sleep. The moon stayed before him—orange and big like a pumpkin. The moons he remembered were mostly silver crescents or big, pale, smiling fellows. His thoughts ran on, and he remembered the nights he'd spent parking with Sally Porter at Rocky River Park. She had light brown hair and slim hips, and he liked her. He remembered when he'd dreamed of marrying her and raising a family. That was when he was sixteen and stupid. She was a cheerleader—that made her hot stuff—and all the guys on the football team were after her. One day she threw him over for the captain of the team—an all-state middle linebacker and the school hero that year. He was an ape with an IQ of seventy-five.

For two months he had refused to speak to another girl. His mother said he was crazy, that he should find someone else. His father complained that he wasn't keeping the grass trimmed. But he didn't want another girl. He felt romantic and wronged and empty, and he enjoyed it.

That lasted until he met Jane Phillips. She had blond hair, wore glasses, read a lot, and thought he looked intellectual. And she was better at making out than Sally Porter. You wouldn't think it to look at her, but she was. He chuckled to himself softly in the darkness. There were girls and there were girls, but that Jane Phillips had been something else. She finally married some guy who worked for the Salvation Army or something like that— some kind of evangelist, his mother said.

He shut his eyes, but he kept seeing hips and breasts and thighs. Then he opened his eyes and stared at the ceiling. *Funny,* he thought, *this is the first time I've really missed women.* That didn't surprise him, though. He knew how he felt about them, and it wasn't all love and kisses. He remembered the girls he'd met at college—the silly snobs and the intellectual ones. They talked all the time and wanted you to call them each day and listen to their stupid shit. And something was always bothering them, or if it wasn't that he was using them, offending their precious sense of self-importance. He knew there wasn't one he had really liked. Sometimes he'd fake it for a while, but in the end he always let his feelings show. Then they acted hurt and cried. He didn't like scenes much, so he let them go and found another.

A sound interrupted his reverie—a soft buzzing that went on for a few seconds, then stopped, then began again. There was a mosquito flying around his head. He waited and listened. The buzz started again. He swung his hand, missed, and swore to himself. Then the buzz moved off. He was going around the bend—when you started to worry about mosquitoes in Nam, you were on your way to the loony bin. It was like worrying about snow in Norway. He must be turning weird.

He shut his eyes again, and women came back into his mind. He didn't know which was worse, that or the mosquitoes. He remembered his sophomore year at college. He'd been lonely then—so lonely that he couldn't work or think—so he'd found a girl. For a long time they were together, and she got an apartment and he moved in. She never talked about getting married, and it never entered his mind. Then one day she said she was a month late with her period and probably was pregnant. That had shook him up a bit, and when the tests were positive he'd panicked and talked with his parents. His mother said, "Why don't you get married?" His father said, "How much will it cost?" The girl said nothing, just sat, smiling like a Jersey cow, each day swelling up a little more and eating ice cream all the time. She seemed quite content.

Another month passed, and still he'd done nothing. Then she said that she'd talked it all over with her parents and they thought he should marry her. She said that she thought so too, and that next week they should go get the license. He didn't say anything when she said that, just sat and thought. Then he took a long walk in the cold—it was mid-December—and when he came back, she was crying and said that she thought he had gone forever. She snuggled up in his arms like a little kid then, and they did it and went to sleep.

She slept fine but he didn't, and a few hours later he was awake, staring at the ceiling. He knew he couldn't marry her. He felt like a creep and didn't know what to do or how he would tell her, but he knew he didn't want to get married.

So he talked to a friend who'd been the same route, but it did no good. The friend suggested he see the senior advisor. He went to see him—a grad student in philosophy who smoked a pipe and always wore a checked vest. The guy listened and puffed on his pipe, then asked how long the girl had been pregnant. When he said two and a half months, the advisor said that they'd better not wait any longer if they wanted an abortion because it would

139

be hard to find a place that would do it later and it would be dangerous.

But he never seriously considered that. It went in one ear and out the other. He couldn't do that—it was like murder. He'd never thought about it much, but somewhere in the back of his head he'd made up his mind that it was wrong, no matter what anybody else said or how logical it was, and so he just ignored what the advisor said.

At the end of the third month, she began to cry a lot and wouldn't talk to him. She lay in bed all day and cut classes. He'd sit in the room and try to read, and she'd start to cry; then he would go out and walk and walk and think about leaving town or joining the army or something like that. Then he'd think of her in the apartment alone, crying in the darkness, and he'd go back.

Finally she went to the priest at the neighborhood church, and he seemed to help her some. She said that she'd made an appointment for them both and that they should go together and try to work things out because it was something they'd gotten into together. He didn't want to, but he didn't know what else to do, so they went. It was a Saturday night, and when the priest came into the reception room of the rectory, he looked tired because he'd been hearing confessions all afternoon. He was a big man with close-cropped gray hair and a serious face. When the priest started to talk about arrangements for a wedding, he looked at the girl, but she just looked down. Then, just like that, he said he didn't want to get married and the priest stopped and looked at them both.

The priest said that he understood that they wanted to get married quickly, that was why he'd dispensed with formalities. He looked at the priest and shook his head. The priest sighed and looked embarrassed. The girl started to whimper. Then he said that he couldn't go through with it, that he knew he didn't want to get married, that it was his fault but that they had better make some sort of plan.

The priest looked at him for a long time, then left the room. He came back with a book that listed adoption agencies, copied down two addresses on a piece of paper, and gave it to them. He said that they should think long and hard about what they wanted to do, but if they still

140

did not want to get married, there were places where the girl could go to have the child if she didn't want to go home to her family. Then the priest shook their hands and they left.

That had happened almost five years ago, but he could still remember the room where the priest had talked to them. It was bare with drab, purplish-brown walls, and there was a picture of Cardinal Cooke on one wall and a crucifix—the cross black, the figure gold—on another wall. The place was depressing as hell, and the women who worked in the rectory spoke with Irish brogues and coughed and looked like they had just come over from the old country.

A week later he came back from classes one day, and she was gone. There was a note saying that she had gone to her parents in Buffalo, that she knew he would never marry her, and that she couldn't understand how he could be so selfish. She wanted him to sell the furniture, store her clothes, and pay the rent for the rest of the month. She would call him about the doctor's bill.

He felt free—like a dog, but free—and he knew he was glad that she was gone. His feeling for her had become ugly, and it was better for them both that she was gone. At the beginning he had needed her, but now he knew that needing wasn't enough. If somebody wanted to make him pay the price for that, he wouldn't. It wasn't a question of being fair or not—that didn't enter into it. He had seen marriages made because people did what was "right," and he didn't want that. He wasn't going to sign his life away because it was the "right" thing to do.

One day about a month later, a letter came from her saying that the doctor's bill was $450, that she had had to go to New York to have the abortion, and that it had been dangerous and painful. So he called up his old man to ask for a loan. His old man said "be a little smarter next time," then he sent her a check. A year later she sent him a letter saying that she was going to be married and just wanted him to know that she had found someone who was more of a man than he'd been.

Other girls came after her, and he went out with them and took them to dinner and went to bed with them, but it never seemed to work out. He didn't want to spend time talking to them or waiting for them or flattering them—if he needed them, he needed them, but that was it. He started to think there was something wrong with him.

Then there had been the army and training camp and WACS who all did it. You could do it any time you wanted if you didn't mind the community water dipper, but he didn't like that. And there was Vietnam and the whores —slim yellow-brown girls with narrow, cold eyes. Funny, but they were better than the WACS, and definitely better than the college girls, and a few of them were even as good as Jane Phillips. And that was about where he was at with women. He wished he'd stop thinking about them because he was damn tired and wanted to go to sleep.

XXXV

Time started to become strange to him. He would forget what day it was. It would be noon, then evening would seem to come the next hour. He woke, washed, shaved, ate, and slept, and the days spun on and on. He walked and talked with the old man, but it was all sliding together. He had the feeling that life was swimming past him, rolling on, and he was standing on a rock above it all, not getting wet but not moving either. Voices droned, and people moved. Life was sliding and pushing, but he was a still, passive thing. He did not have the strength to move or to act, and there was nowhere he could go and nothing he could do anyway. He felt worthless and sank into nothingness.

The old man noted all this. He asked the prisoner what was troubling him but got no answer and did not ask further. An Oriental would have reacted differently —he would have accepted his situation and not eaten his soul away. But Westerners were different. *No sense of realism,* the old man thought. *He feels that his imprisonment is somehow his fault and that he must try to escape even if escape is foolhardy. He wants to bend the world to his will—an American Nietzsche.* Intellectually he damned the prisoner's stupidity, but he could not be too hard on him. There was something attractive about his attitude, foolish though it was. He admired it and remembered his days at Penn with Rolfe Hugley III.

The product of overindulgent parents and a lack of realism—but it allows them to do so much, he mused. *We make do, but they refuse to. They will be driven by their damned hubris.*

And so he looked on the prisoner with compassion, wishing there was some way he could help him but knowing that there wasn't.

A week passed, then another. The camp had grown almost threefold. Now there were over 1,000 new soldiers, all tall and silent and all eating yellow wheat cakes before they slept. Daily the old man and No-Neck met with the commander of the new men. He was a stocky, businesslike man who listened to them and moved his men where they wished. The old man had seen such men before. They were trained to be respectful and would not force their will on another in his country, but if word were sent from the North they would kill all in a minute. *He has feelings,* thought the old man, *but they are as sophisticated as those of a dull child. For him there is only one right way, and he knows that way. Mao is his god and for him he will do anything.*

The old man laughed softly to himself. *Caesar and Alexander and Attila and Hitler and Christ and Stalin and Mao—always such men draw simpletons to their cause.* Then he chided himself for his anger, for things were as they were—this he knew—and he knew that the man was happy as he was, that without his stupid ideology he would be confused and weak, a peasant worrying about his rice paddies.

The veteran soldiers kept away from the new men. They were worn and tired of the war, and although they had not been in battle for almost six months they had no desire to see action. Many had been fighting since their teens and they were becoming old. Their families were elsewhere, their children growing, and still they lived the lonely life of soldiers, feeding and fighting like beasts. The life of a farmer was not easy, but it was infinitely better than that of a soldier, even the most warlike of them knew this. War had not been so terrible when they were younger—then the fighting and burning and raping fired their blood. But later they had tired of these things. Their souls had sickened and the sight of corpses now nauseated them. They longed for a bed at night and a woman. They wanted to watch the seasons pass over their fields. They did not have the courage to desert—deserters were killed when caught—and yet they hated the new soldiers because they knew that they only meant more fighting and more deaths and more months of suffering.

So the camp came to be divided—in spirit if not in fact—and time passed and tension grew. All this the prisoner sensed. He watched the new men and saw the faces of the old soldiers when they were near them and listened carefully when the old man talked of the commander of the new men. He sensed trouble coming and he waited.

XXXVI

With the beginning of the warm days of spring, the prisoner detected the first signs of discord. The old man still walked with him each day, but now he was silent and tense. For several days the prisoner did not see No-Neck and assumed that he was away. *Probably in Hanoi boning up on new ways to get information,* he said to himself. But then No-Neck returned. When the prisoner saw him, he was with the Chinese commander, and for the first time he realized how similar the two were. No-Neck was taller and younger, but they both had the same bullet head and square shoulders, and both wore the same straight-lipped, serious expression. They were not so much like men as robots—strong, efficient, metal-souled creatures who were programmed to act mechanically and flawlessly. If they had feelings or human weaknesses, they were hidden, submerged in their devotion to their ideology.

The old man didn't visit for a week, then came to see him one day much earlier than usual. They walked across the camp together, and the prisoner could see the old man looking toward the new tents, his eyes playing over them. He did not look frightened or excited, but the prisoner could sense that he had come to a conclusion about something.

"You must decide," said the old man suddenly. "You must decide soon—today—for I do not think there is much more time."

The prisoner looked at him. He understood but not fully, and the request to know more was in his eyes.

"Orders have come—I am recalled to Hanoi and God alone knows where after that. Duc Thang and the new commander will assume control. You will not be safe."

The two were silent.

"Keep walking," said the old man. "I trust no one. Act as you always act. Even now I think we are being watched."

They strolled along the edge of the camp, then turned and started back slowly. The old man was speaking smoothly and softly, and the prisoner was listening.

"I have two more days. I do not think they will do anything until I have left. After that Duc Thang will try to question you again, of that I am certain. The new commander is not a bad man, but he will not stop him."

The prisoner said nothing; he was waiting for the old man's plan, a cold fear growing in the back of his mind.

"I can arrange for you to be shipped to another camp, to be held and questioned there. They may honor the request or they may not, but it would mean that for a pe-

145

riod you would remain here with Duc Thang. Such requests are never answered in less than a month."

"What is the alternative?" asked the prisoner, for the idea of being alone and at the mercy of Duc Thang bit into him like a sharp sting. He felt his face begin to twitch.

The old man looked at him, then to the side. "I can help you try to escape."

The prisoner's eyes followed his glance. Two soldiers were leaning against a building, watching the pair intently. He noticed that they wore the uniforms with the peculiar cut.

They were at the hospital now, and the old man looked at him again. The prisoner looked into his eyes—they were narrow and hard as he squinted in the late morning light; there were lines at the corners and a scar on his right cheek. He looked very old today—not defeated or tired, just very old.

"It is the fourth quarter, my young friend," the old man said and turned and walked back toward the commander's cabin.

XXXVII

He was in the jungle. The dew was rising in steam where the hot, early morning sun shot through the trees overhead, sending shafts of whiteness into the dark green undergrowth. He crouched behind a fallen tree a hundred yards from the road. Not more than a half mile ahead were the crossroads, the clearing, and the small station. Already men—*Montagnards*, the peasants from the uplands—would be collecting their to be picked up by the old man's convoy and carried to the new camp. No one knew where.

He looked down at his clothes—fiber sandals and dirty, brown trousers—then at his arms. They were colored red-brown with the ointment the old man had given him, as was his face which he had seen in a pool of water he had passed in the forest. His hair was blackened with tar and ashes, and he wore a flat planter's hat like the hill men. If anyone looked closely, they could detect the imposture. But the *Montagnards* were taller than the lowlanders, with strange, almost western features, and the old man said that no one would notice him, at least not until they reached a big camp. That would give him time to plan his next move.

He crept toward the clearing, moving slowly from tree to tree. Then he realized that he was being stupid. Anyone who saw him moving like that would know he was hiding, so he straightened up and walked briskly toward the roadway. He reached it about thirty yards from the clearing but around a bend so that no one waiting there could see that he had come from the forest. Then he walked on.

There was a shelter—four poles with a roof of dried leaves—and under it sat half a dozen men. They were squatting in the Oriental fashion, dozing in the midday heat. Flies buzzed about them. As he walked toward them, the men looked up for a second, then closed their eyes and slept on.

He started to look for a place among them, then realized that it would not work. They were all squatting, some rocking slowly from side to side as they slept. None were stretched out, and there was no room for a man to do so. But he could not squat—five minutes in that position and his legs would give out.

He couldn't walk on—that would look strange, and he might miss the convoy. Then he would be stranded 350 miles behind enemy lines in the middle of a jungle with no provisions. He remembered too well what it felt like to go without water and food until you were too weak to move. *Besides,* he said to himself, *I don't feel especially hungry for snake meat just now. A bit too tangy for my palate.*

And so he moved into a space between two men in the far corner of the shelter. They looked at him out of the corners of their eyes as he assumed the squatting position. Then he shut his eyes and tried to endure. After five minutes his legs felt as if they were being twisted by a wrestler. He gritted his teeth and told himself he would endure it—he had no choice. Mercifully, his legs turned numb. First there was the feeling of pins and needles for a few minutes, then nothing but a dull ache that he could bear. *When I have to straighten up,* he thought, *it will look strange. I may not be able to make it.* But the worry was minor, and he shrugged it off.

Time passed—possibly an hour, he could not tell. It had grown hotter, and even the flies seemed to be feeling the heat, for they had stopped buzzing and were walking slowly in circles between the men. Now and then one landed on his face, but he did not move his hand to brush them off, for mountain men did not do this. Sweat was running down his face. He opened his eyes and looked around him. The others were moving. Two men were fanning themselves with small branches of ferns. It didn't seem to be doing much good, for their faces were bathed in sweat and their shirts were wet. He looked up at the sky. From the position of the sun, he judged that it was after noon. The convoy should be along any minute now. He remembered what the old man had told him—they would pick up men along the road to Anh Son, then head for the coastal road at Xuan Loi. From there they would turn north.

"If you look like a mountain man, you will be taken along. Later we can arrange something else. It will be dangerous, but it can be done."

He was depending upon the old man's judgment—it was really all that he could do. Strangely, though, he wasn't worried. Perhaps because he had already been through so much, or maybe because he trusted the old man, but once he had left the encampment and No-Neck, he had become calmer. No-Neck and the shed and the whip—he could not have stood that again. Physically perhaps he could, but he knew it would be too much for him mentally. That was why he had been so certain from the very beginning about what he would do.

It had been easy to escape. Late at night he had strolled toward the edge of the camp. No one had bothered to follow him. Then once in the shadows, he had run into the jungle, heading due north just as the old man

148

had told him. Even in the darkness it was easy to find the place—a giant tree split at the base. In the middle of the trunk under two rocks was the package with the clothes and the ointments for his skin and hair. There was a map too, and matches to read it by. Then he had moved due south until he reached the roadway. There was no traffic on it at night—the old man had assured him of this. He had traveled fast at a half jog until dawn broke. Then he took to the jungle.

He covered almost fifteen miles that night. He was missed, but in the confusion caused by the movement of troops from the camp, there was no chance that a search party would be sent after him. It would have done little good anyway, for most of the older soldiers were going with their commander and the new men didn't know the area.

*

He continued to wait for the convoy. Sweat and heat and flies and more sweat. He knew that all Westerners had a peculiar smell to Orientals, and he hoped the noses of the mountain men were clogged by the dust of the road, otherwise they could not fail to smell him. He chuckled to himself, remembering all the commercials for deodorant he had seen on TV. *This would be a good one,* he thought. *Saved by Ban—guarded by Right Guard, the Deodorant of Democracy.*

There was a noise on the road—the purr of an engine —and all the men turned. A truck rolled into view, followed by a second and a third. The men jumped to their feet and ran onto the road. He tried to straighten up and almost collapsed. Then he grabbed the nearest support pole and pulled himself up. In the confusion no one had noticed. If the trucks would just stop for a minute until the blood started to move in his legs again, he would be OK.

But they didn't stop. Instead they only slowed down for a few seconds. The mountain men ran after them, reached up, and were pulled aboard by those already on. The prisoner took a step, but his legs gave way. He scrambled to his feet and tried to run again. His legs worked this time, not well, but at least they worked.

149

He ran stiff-legged, like a lame animal. The trucks rolled on. They were beginning to pick up speed again, pulling away from him. All the men from the shelter were on board except him. He could see the men looking back at him, curious at his slowness.

Now his legs felt stronger, and he ran faster. But the trucks had moved back into high gear, pulling farther away from him with each second. He ran as he had never run before. His lungs burned. He could see the faces of the men in the trucks, but he would never catch them. His heart started to sink.

Suddenly and inexplicably, the convoy slowed. With a bound he came up to the last truck and was pulled in. Then it began to pick up speed again. He felt eyes upon him, but he stared ahead. Far to the front of the convoy, the old man removed his gaze from the rearview mirror and looked ahead, too. The confused driver was looking at him, but the old man ignored him. Then suddenly, he ordered him to drive faster. *Confuse them!* he said to himself. *They can only hold one idea in their heads at a time. Confuse them!*

XXXVIII

The trucks droned over the dusty road. The prisoner looked back at the trees vanishing behind them—green sliding into green until it was all an emerald gleam with the road's yellow-brown tongue in the center. The motor sputtered and ground, and several times he thought it would stop altogether, but they kept moving, rolling on.

He tried to sleep but couldn't; the road was too bumpy, and the driver kept shifting back and forth from second to third, jerking the truck each time. The prisoner gave up, opened his eyes, and looked at the other men. There were a dozen mountain men in the truck—gaunt, wild-looking peasants with flat straw hats like his. The rest were soldiers from the camp. He scanned their faces quickly but didn't recognize any of them. That was good —if he knew them, then they would be likely to know him, too.

Toward nightfall the truck pulled into another camp. It lay about 500 yards off the road and was almost a carbon copy of the place he had left. There was a shack in the center and several sheds at the north end. Opposite these was a large Quonset hut; he figured this was the barracks. Two men came out of the shack and questioned the driver of the first truck. Then the convoy drove toward the north end of the camp and stopped, and the men got out. Tents were set up, and fires started. The soldiers sat down for their evening meal. He lingered near the truck, mimicking the other mountain men who were timid and unsure around the soldiers. Hunger was gnawing at him, but he was afraid to approach the soldiers. It was wiser to let someone else do that.

Time passed, and none of the hill men moved. Then he realized that they did not intend to. Most of them seemed to have some food with them in their small leather pouches, which they tied to the cord that cinched their trousers. He watched them eat for a few minutes, then lay down and tried to sleep.

He would have given a hundred dollars for some of the mountain men's food or a taste of the soldiers' rice. But it was best not to make a move, no matter how hungry he was. If he was the only one to ask, he would draw attention, for the soldiers would think it strange that he had been foolish enough to undertake such a journey without food. Then one of them might look closely and recognize him, and the game would be over. They would probably shoot him, and there would be little the old man could do. It was better to try to sleep and wait for the morning.

*

Soon after the first light of day, the soldiers were up and preparing to move. He saw the old man sitting in a chair, drinking his tea. All around him was bustle, but the old man sat and sipped. Men came up to him, and he issued orders, but he did not move until he had finished his tea.

Like a medieval warlord, thought the prisoner. *He is not of this time. He is cunning and he survives, but he is no Maoist and the others know it. They will get him in the end.*

By the time the old man had finished his tea, the tents had been taken down, and the equipment loaded on the trucks. He stood, and a man took his chair, folded it, and carried it to the truck. Then he spoke to his subordinates and climbed into the cab of the first truck. Orders were given, and the soldiers sprang into the backs of the other trucks, then they began to move.

By noon the prisoner was ravenous and had decided that come what may he would ask for food at the evening meal. The fact that he had to sit still made him feel the hunger all the more. When he had been on the run, he had sometimes killed hunger by movement so that he could almost ignore it until weakness forced him to stop. But sitting in the back of the truck, watching the others eat, and feeling his stomach knot was a different experience.

The sun was almost level with the tops of the trees when they stopped. This time there was no camp, only a clearing with one rickety lean-to, half its roof fallen away. As before the men pitched tents and built fires for cooking. Again the mountain men kept to themselves, lingering by the trucks and eating from the pouches tied to their waists. He sat for a minute, gathering his courage, then walked toward the circle of soldiers nearest him. He could feel his heart speeding up.

When he reached them, he stood mute, not knowing what to do next but hoping that if he just stood there someone would sense his hunger and give him something. If they spoke to him, he would remain silent. This would not seem so strange, for he had often observed villagers behaving that way around men with uniforms. Soldiers took it as a sign of respect and somehow enjoyed it. So he waited.

The men finished eating and drank their tea, but no one seemed to notice him. He had begun to despair

when one of the men finally handed him a mug of lukewarm tea. He sipped it, controlling his thirst to savor
each drop. When he finished, he handed the mug back
to the man, bowed his head, and returned to his place by
the truck to sleep. He began to think that he'd seen the
man who had given him the tea before, perhaps at the
hospital. He was certain the man had recognized him,
but it was too late to worry about that now. He fell into
a restless sleep, which gradually deepened as his body
strove to compensate for his hunger and thirst.

XXXIX

The sounds of men moving woke him. He stretched, then
sat up. He felt lightheaded and instinctively looked toward the soldiers' tents to see if they were still eating
breakfast. The tents had already been taken down, and
the men were loading them onto the trucks. His stomach
ached, but he pushed the thought of it from his mind
with the remembrance of the tea from the night before
and the face of the man who had given it to him. Now he
remembered who he was—the night guard at the prison
shed. He remembered the peculiar way he held his head
and the shape of his eyes—round and large, unusual for
an Oriental. The man had seen him so often that he must
have recognized him. He waited with trepidation.

But no one came for him. The soldiers finished putting
the equipment on the trucks and hopped aboard. Then
the mountain men scrambled in, and the trucks rolled
back onto the road.

Late that afternoon they came into the village of

Muong Sen. It lay along the roadway, hovels with tin roofs lining both sides of the road. Just outside the town, the road crossed a fast-flowing stream. Here there was a metal bridge. The trucks rolled over the bridge, then pulled to the side of the road, and the men got out.

Orders were shouted, and they began to put up the tents. The wind increased, and several of the tents blew away. The others flapped lamentably, like the sails of a ship. Finally the men gave up and stood, huddling close to the trucks. He could see the officers talking to the old man. He was consulting a map. Then he said something to them, and they left him, going back to the men to bark out new commands. The soldiers filed across the bridge into Muong Sen. He noticed that they took their guns.

The prisoner stood with the mountain men and watched. Finally they followed, walking slowly about thirty yards behind the last soldier.

The villagers were standing in front of their houses, looking at the soldiers suspiciously. Children and young girls were huddling close to the old women. The eyes of all the villagers were filled with the peculiar mixture of fear and disgust that he had seen so many times when he entered a village with his platoon.

An old man came out of the last house—the one farthest from the bridge—and walked toward the soldiers at the head of the column. They stopped, and he spoke to them. The prisoner could see that he was frightened, but not so frightened as to be cowed. He looked angry as he argued with the soldiers. They listened to him, not with patience, but because it was what they had been trained to do. The man kept pointing back toward the bridge, talking excitedly. It did not take much imagination to see that he wanted the men to return to their trucks.

Finally the soldiers lost their patience with the man and pushed past him, continuing through the village. As they advanced, the villagers seemed to shrink into themselves, and the prisoner thought he saw some of them begin to shake. It was pathetic, but it did not surprise him. To see people afraid, knowing that death was near, made one understand them. It made one wary. It also led one to see how weak people really were. *If I lived in this village,* he said to himself, *I would be just as afraid.*

154

I would have seen my sister raped, and my brother shot, and my chickens stolen, and I would be afraid. The prisoner did not think that the commander would permit such things to happen, but he knew that the villagers did not know this. They had seen many commanders do otherwise.

When the men came to the last hut, they stopped. The man leading the column made a signal, and the men broke up into small groups to enter the houses. The prisoner was with the very last group of soldiers. His group split into two groups of four and entered two huts which lay about forty yards up the road from the river. It was dark inside—there were no windows—and it was a few minutes before his eyes became accustomed to the dim light. But even before he could see, he knew what it was like. He could smell the closeness and the sweet, sickly smell of several people living together with little ventilation. Then he saw some pallets on the floor—they appeared to be made of reeds—and a small table with a cardboard top scored in several places. On the wall was a picture of Ho Chi Minh, framed in gold. There was something that looked like an altar at one end of the room, and atop it was a statue of the Buddha. In front of the statue were some small glass vases filled with flowers. They smelled pungent in the closed space.

The soldier who was giving the orders gestured toward the pallets, then looked at his comrades and smiled. It wasn't a pretty smile, and the prisoner remembered that there were two young girls in the family that owned the hut—one about fourteen or fifteen, the other he guessed to be a year or two younger. The soldiers took the pallets they wanted while he stood and watched. There were three left, but he didn't really want to sleep in the room, for it would be filled with vermin, and even with the wind kicking up outside it was so close it was stifling. But again he decided that it was better not to do anything unusual, so he selected the pallet closest to the door and sat.

After a while he was aware that someone was standing in the doorway. It was a thin, middle-aged woman, wearing dirty orange slacks and a maroon shirt. She was looking at the men, afraid to make a move but wanting something in the room. Finally she mustered her courage and came in, went to the table, and took two bowls from it. Just then one of the soldiers made a noise halfway between a grunt and a laugh—evidently someone had made a joke—and the woman dropped the bowls with a clatter. They all looked at her. She stood, afraid to move. Then she grabbed the bowls and ran out the door, and the men resumed their conversation.

The wind was still blowing—he could see the dust swirling just outside the door. It was a warm wind, the kind that usually blew before a big storm. That worried him. If it rained, they would be slowed down and might have to stop for a while. The soldiers would have more time to watch him, and he might do something to give himself away.

He listened to the wind. It was whistling through the trees, causing the dry leaves to rattle. He tried to sleep but the smell of the room bothered him. He did not want to think, because he knew that all he would do would be worry. So he tried to imagine himself somewhere else: not back home in Cleveland—it would be raining there, and the streets would be empty—but at Cedar Point, the resort where he'd worked during the summer of his freshman year in college. It was a sandy spit of land that stuck into the lake between Cleveland and Toledo. There was an amusement park, an old, weather-beaten, wooden hotel, and miles of beach. In the evenings after work, he and his friends would drive into Sandusky to buy a case of beer, then return to drink and talk in the shadows of the poplars that lined the beach. When they were drunk enough, they'd take off their clothes and run into the water. It was usually calm and tepid, almost like a bath. There were hardly any waves, and the bottom was sand, smooth and even. You could walk out five or six hundred yards before the water reached your chin. He'd done a lot of thinking during those nights in the moonlight, floating on his back and looking at the stars. Even that first summer just out of high school, he had a feeling that although he was starting school in the fall, he would never finish. They weren't drafting college students yet, but something told him that would change. He told that to his buddies at the Point, and they said he was crazy. But he wasn't stupid—he could read the fear in their eyes.

He remembered how he'd felt that summer—worrying

156

about little things like what school would be like or maybe a girl, and living each day for the fun of it. After work toward sundown, he'd go swimming. Evenings when he wasn't drinking, he'd find a girl and neck, or just roam about the amusement park. He rode the roller coaster until he knew every dip and turn in it. A buddy was the operator, and he let him go on for free. Sometimes he'd ride all night.

There was a noise and he looked up, toward the door. One of the girls—the older one, he thought—was standing there, looking in. He could see the soldiers looking at her. Many of them hadn't been with a woman for at least half a year. Desire showed in their eyes, and the girl was frightened. He thought it had been stupid of the family to send her into the hut. She saw what she wanted, walked across the room, took a towel off the wall, and got a big metal basin that looked like the family bath tub. As she crossed back toward the door, he noticed her feet— she was wearing high heels. *In Muong Sen!* he thought. Then he realized how she'd probably gotten them. The soldiers looked at each other, spoke for a minute, then the one who had been giving the orders went out the door after the girl. One of the other two men took out an old deck of what looked like playing cards, and they began a game.

After about twenty minutes the soldier who had gone out returned. The men looked at him. He said something, and they laughed. Then they matched cards, and the winner got up and went out. The man who had just returned sat down and leaned against the wall. In a few minutes he was stretched out on his pallet, snoring.

When the second soldier came back, the third one went out. Like the first man, the second was soon asleep. Then the third man returned. He started to stretch out, saw the prisoner, gave him a half smile, and nodded toward the doorway. The message was clear, but the prisoner ignored it. The soldier looked at him for a second, then, apparently assuming that he had not been understood, pointed toward the door. The prisoner decided he'd better go out.

It was dark now, but the wind was still blowing strongly, and the dust that filled the air was so thick that he almost choked. He could see nothing and thought that he would

157

merely wait a while, then return to the hut, and no one would know the difference. He stood for a minute, then looked for somewhere to go to be out of the wind. He saw what looked like a shed about thirty yards down the road and started toward it. He had gone about ten yards when he felt a tug on his shoulder. It was the woman with the orange slacks. She held his sleeve and pointed to his right where he could just make out the back of a lean-to. She thought he was lost and was giving him directions. He tried to ignore her and continued walking toward the shed, but she pulled harder and began speaking to him. Then he stopped, afraid that someone might hear and come, and walked toward the lean-to. She released his arm but continued to walk beside him.

When they reached the lean-to, it was as he had expected. The girl was lying on the ground without her slacks. She was looking up, staring into space, her eyes wide open and expressionless. When she saw him, she forced a smile and held up her arms. His heart raced, and his loins tightened, but at the same time he felt disgust and pity. The woman was still beside him, and although he did not look at her face, he felt certain she was watching him. He knew that at least he had to fake it—otherwise it would seem strange, and she might talk to the soldiers.

He turned to the woman and pointed away from the shelter. She didn't move. *Protecting her property*, he thought. He took a step toward her and raised his hand, and she moved away quickly. Then he lay beside the girl. She continued to stare sightlessly ahead. After a few minutes had passed and he had still done nothing, she turned her head slightly and looked at him out of the corner of her eye. She was puzzled, and he could sense that his strangeness frightened her. Then he heard a noise above him and looked. It was the woman again and beside her was one of the soldiers. His stomach turned over, and he pushed his trousers down and began.

XL

The rain had come in the middle of the night—great wind-driven blasts of it—and by morning the road had turned into a yellow-red mire, slowing the convoy to a crawl. Where it was rocky, the road was passable, and they picked up speed, but it was flooded in the low stretches and almost like a swamp. Here the water rushed out of the forest in streams, turning the roadway into a small river. The prisoner propped his back against the side of the truck and tried to sleep. The other men were squatting, but he had given that up. He had slept deeply last night. *Like a soldier,* he said to himself, *like someone who spent six months' pay on a whore.* It was not that he remembered the girl—her eyes, yes, but the rest was a blur. But he could not forget the faces of the woman and the soldier after he was done. The woman looked strangely satisfied, and the soldier was smiling. The had enjoyed themselves the way people enjoy watching dogs. The woman had followed him back to the hut, wanting money, but he had nothing to give and finally, after berating him, she left. Later when the others had wakened, the soldier had pointed to the prisoner and said a few words, and they all laughed.

He stared into the darkness, saying to himself, *With whores, yes. But not with kids! My God, not with kids!* But then he had slept soundly and although his conscience bothered him, he knew that he had somehow needed it.

About noon they passed Khe Kien, which meant it was about eighty miles to Xuan Loi and the coast road. They should make it by nightfall. Then they would head north. That was the time to break from the convoy and move south alone. He knew this, and it made him afraid. He had thought about it for so long—freedom, his people, home—that it had become an obsession. His nerves were vibrating, so he shut his eyes to calm himself, sometimes dozing, other times staring into the shadows behind the men opposite him.

The rain kept up, beating steadily on the roof of the truck. About noon the convoy stopped, and everyone was given lukewarm tea and rice. He gobbled his. Except for some food he'd taken in the village, it was the first thing he'd had to eat in three days, and it was like pheasant under glass to him. Then he dozed again.

When he woke, the rain had stopped, and they were climbing. They had left the forest behind, and here there were rice paddies in terraces, the water reflecting the gray sky. He could see farmers wading in the paddies, and sometimes a man plowing behind a water buffalo. He knew that the land was more populated toward the coast, so he assumed they were getting close to Xuan Loi. Just before nightfall, they stopped. They had left the fields behind and were on a rocky plateau where little seemed to be growing except a few stunted, olive-colored shrubs. The convoy pulled off the road, and the soldiers began to set up their tents. The prisoner walked off, found a big rock, and climbed up on it.

He could see the edges of the plateau. It wasn't more than a mile or two wide, and on both sides the land sloped sharply. To the west lay the forest; to the east more paddies, stretching endlessly until they dissolved into a fuzzy, indistinct, glimmering brown-gray. That meant more water. He remembered once seeing a map of the coast. There was a flat marshland that extended for almost twenty miles behind Xuan Loi.

He walked back to his truck, sat down, and leaned against a wheel. He guessed there was probably about an hour's light left, but no one was setting up tents yet, and he wondered why. He could see the leaders of the column grouped around the old man's truck. A man who had joined the convoy the day before was speaking and pointing to a map. Then the men went back to their trucks, and the convoy rolled on into the gathering darkness.

The road that descended from the plateau was smoother and wider. It did not wind back and forth but angled, easily, down the gently declining grade. Soon it was completely dark. The drivers switched on their lights which were weak but at least revealed the shoulders of the road. Sometimes he could see moths fluttering in the light— small white ones and occasionally giant, red-orange, butterflylike creatures. The road was still wet but not swampy, and it looked as if it had been worked on recently, for there were fewer ruts and someone had attempted to build a rudimentary gutter on the lower edge for drainage.

They drove on through the night, the truck groaning as it descended in second gear. Sometime around midnight he woke. They were still rolling, but now the road was flat, and he could hear the sound of water splashing over rocks. That meant the roadway lay close to a river. Then he slept again and woke at dawn as the convoy rattled through the outskirts of a large town.

The other men had wakened too, the smoothness of the macadam roadway and the sight of the houses and shanties surprising them. People were awake and walking the roads now—men and women in dark slacks and shirts with broad-brimmed straw hats. Many of them rode bicycles, and he saw a few emaciated oxen pulling carts. With the dawn the rain had come again, falling in a thin mist. The road was slick and filled with puddles that reflected the gray clouds that hung on the horizon. Finally the convoy climbed a slight grade, then rolled down a road that led to broad black mud flats and stopped.

The men climbed stiffly from the trucks. The prisoner looked around him. They had passed through the outskirts of a big town and were about a mile outside of it. He could see the buildings in the distance. Around them stretched miles of semi-swamp filled with green reeds. Far off in a direction that he guessed to be east, he saw the dark blue of the sea and a faint line at the horizon where the water met the sky. Some men were gazing at this; others were scattered about outside the circle of trucks, relieving themselves. He could see a half dozen men setting up a shelter and knew that this was for the old man. Apparently they would stay a while.

161

XLI

At noon the sky was still dark. The men were hovering close to the tents, talking or playing cards. The prisoner had found a dry spot beside one of the trucks and was sitting there, his head resting on his knees, surveying the scene. He did not know where they were, but he felt that something had changed their plans. He could tell this from the soldiers' confusion. They were on the coast—that was obvious—but he did not think they were as far north as he had expected. It occurred to him that they might be going south, heading for the battle zone. The men had been in the jungle camp a long time. On paper at least they would appear rested, and so it would be logical to send them back to battle. *That's the way they think,* he said to himself, *on paper. They do not know these men or how tired they are of fighting. The commanders never bother with that, or if they do, it is only on paper, and then they put the sheet with the number of the regiment in another pile, and it comes up a day later.*

He sat back against the truck's tire and shut his eyes. The anxiety he'd felt for the last few days was leaving him—he could feel it oozing out of his body. He knew the time when he'd have to make another move was coming soon—then he'd be on his own and probably in enemy territory. If they caught him, he would be shot. But he wasn't worried—his mouth wasn't dry, nor was his stomach quivering. He was just waiting, that was all, relaxing and waiting.

In the evening they ate. It was rice cakes and tea again, and the men ate in silence. He wondered if they ever got angry, then remembered how the guys in

his outfit had raised hell when the chow was lousy. Someone wrote his congressman, and then it got better—for a
little while. These guys didn't write their congressman,
maybe that was why they were winning. People said it
was the South Vietnamese, that they didn't really want to
fight. There was something to that, he knew, but they only
copied what they saw.

He chuckled to himself. *Man, you're turning into a
hawk. They'll dig you at the Legion.*

*

He bedded down early in the back of the truck. The
soldiers slept in tents, but the mountain men had none, so
they stayed in the trucks. The benches were hard, and
the floor between them even worse, but at least it was
dry. He had been sleeping for about an hour when a
light hit him in the face, and he sat up. He heard words
and realized that someone wanted him to get out. His
heart speeded, but something told him it wasn't anything
big. *Not here,* he thought. *Not while the old man's still
around.*

There were two soldiers motioning for him to follow
them. They took him to the old man's tent where they
stood beside him, waiting. The flap swung back, and rays
of light from inside shot out. Then the old man appeared,
dressed as always with his collar buttoned up to the top
and his boots polished. He gave a command and the soldiers left. Then he nodded to the prisoner to follow him
and went into the tent.

The prisoner was surprised at this. It was a reckless
move, and the old man didn't do foolhardy things. There
was a map spread on the table and they walked to it.
The old man studied it, then pointed to an *X*. He looked.
It was Dong Hoi, a town on the coast road about 175
miles south of Xuan Loi.

"Here is where we are, my friend," said the old man.

The prisoner looked at him; he did not understand.

"There were orders yesterday afternoon, and so we
have turned south."

The prisoner asked what it meant, and the old man
shrugged, then looked thoughtful.

"I do not know—one never knows—but I think it is the

163

beginning of the big push to the south. Sooner or later it had to come, and now it is time. The enemy," he looked at the prisoner for a second, "the enemy has weakened. Most of your countrymen have gone, and the time is ripe. It is spring—soon the rains will make the roads impassable, but now they are still adequate, and so we are moving."

The prisoner was bewildered, but in a vague way he sensed that this was good for him. Whatever else it meant, he would be farther to the south and closer to his countrymen. Every mile in that direction helped him.

"You can see that this is better for you," said the old man. "For your side and for those with you it is not good, but for you and for the people"—he smiled, he always smiled when he said "the people"—"it means that an end is in sight."

He looked at the commander, not realizing the expression on his face.

"Your patriotism, my young friend. It is showing. What would your honored leader say?"

The prisoner smiled broadly, then left and returned to the truck.

XLII

The next day they rolled down the coastal road. It wove and twisted, sometimes hugging the coast, other times drifting two or three miles inland. The sea was a muddy brown, and the land beside the road was swampy and filled with reeds and eelgrass, appearing almost black in the sunless air. Toward noon they stopped for about twenty minutes, and he could see the officers surrounding the old man's truck, looking at maps. Then they got in the trucks and moved on.

They had gone about twenty minutes when he heard a high-pitched whistle and a muffled thud; then the swamp about fifteen yards to the left of the road exploded, and mud and water flew skyward. Then there was another thud and another, all wide to the left. The trucks moved faster, and the explosions got closer and closer. Then he heard the sharp rat-tat-tat of machine-gun bullets and watched, almost hypnotized, as a path moved toward the roadway, the water riddled with small splashes as if hail were falling. The other men in the truck scrambled under the benches, and he followed, pushing his way in just as the bullets bit into the roof of the truck.

In a second the planes had passed over. He could see the holes where bullets had dug into the wooden floorboards. He looked at the part of the bench that had been in the bullets' path. It was splintered, and the man underneath was lying face down, his arm twitching wildly. The trucks roared on, careening around curves and over bumps as the thuds continued, eventually growing fainter, then stopping altogether. One man went over to look at the man who had been shot. His arm had stopped twitching, and there was a pool of blood beside him. The prisoner had watched it form and grow larger as the truck moved. The soldier stood up, looked at his comrades, then shook his head and returned to his place.

With the coming of darkness the truck finally stopped, and the men climbed out. He could not see much, but it looked as if they were in the midst of trees, and he heard a sound like the lapping of waves. The men buried their comrade, then ate a meal of cold rice cakes and tea. They were silent, and although they had spent the day sitting, they seemed tired and soon slept. He lay down among them and did the same.

*

The next day they continued south, moving quickly, and were attacked twice. The aim of the bombers was bad, and this time the bombs exploded almost fifty yards from the roadway, and there was no machine-gun fire. He guessed the pilots were flying high. *More worried about their hides than their targets,* he thought. Again they spent the night in the midst of trees near the water. Far off, dead south, the sky was lighted with a golden glow that brightened and dimmed, pulsing like a heart. He thought of the map and guessed it was Da Nang, a big port on the sixteenth parallel. That would put them at least 150 miles farther south than the VC had been when he had fought in his last battle. Now he knew for certain that the old man was right.

*

The tranquillity of the morning filled him with awe. The sky was first tinted pink, then crimson so bright it hurt him to look at it. Above that was turquoise, almost green near the horizon. A few birds were flying far out over the ocean, black specks winging north. He watched them until they disappeared. They were the first birds he had seen in months.

Soon the others woke. Breakfast was made and eaten hurriedly, then they rolled on. About noon they came to the outskirts of Da Nang.

*

The streets were empty, and there were no houses—only blackened beams and rubble. Block after block nothing was standing. Sometimes they had to stop while the roadway was cleared. The men in the first truck usually did this, but once they all had to get out and move the charred skeleton of a bus. He thought there would be bodies, but there were none, and he realized that the bus had been sitting there for a long time.

Finally there were signs of life. First a lone woman riding a bicycle, then a few other army trucks moving in the same direction as the convoy. Still, there were no buildings standing. It gave him a strange feeling. He had seen whole villages destroyed before, but they were small —never more than a few dozen houses in the midst of rice paddies. The villagers had usually been nearby, hovering on the edge of the jungle, waiting until the soldiers had gone to reclaim their land and the few belongings

166

that remained. But the sight of an entire town reduced to black ashes and emptied of people for as far as he could see gave him a feeling of numbness. He thought of the west side of Cleveland, Detroit Avenue and Lakewood, and saw them turned to rubble, a desolate black desert of crumbled brick.

Now he could see other trucks, rolling in the same direction on other avenues. They seemed to be coming from all directions, all converging toward the same spot. With them were more bicycles and more people. Most of the bicycle riders were women. The only men he saw were soldiers, either on other trucks or riding in jeeps.

The truck slowed then stopped, and the men got out. There was a great open space, miles across, and in the center of it great numbers of small booths. Soldiers were strolling up and down in groups, laughing and buying things from the women. He had rarely seen so many people in such a small space before, even at football games. They seemed countless, all talking and buying, the men drinking and smoking, the women cooking for them.

The mountain men stood in a group, overwhelmed, and he stood in their midst. He did not want to be alone; he was afraid that even in the crowd his strangeness would attract attention.

Finally the mountain men walked away from the trucks and down the rows of booths. He went with them. The women called to them, holding up bowls of rice and skewers of meat. The mountain men looked at them suspiciously. They had little money, and these were city people. Finally one of the men stopped, and they all bunched around him. They were in front of a booth where two women were selling wine. It was brown, almost the color of mud, and he could not imagine what it was made of. A mountain man took a roll of paper money from the pouch around his waist, stripped off two bills, gave them to one of the women, then took a cup. He drank it in one gulp, then looked at his fellows and nodded. They began taking out bills, and the women ladled more drinks out of large clay jugs. The prisoner stood at the back of the group. He had no money and knew that here, unlike in the villages, he could not take what he wanted. The men had finished and started to walk on, when one of them realized that the prisoner had

167

had no wine. He called to him and made a gesture with his hand as if he were drinking, then rubbed his stomach to show that it was good. The prisoner looked at him, then shook his head, affecting an expression of sadness and pointing to the man's purse.

The man took his roll of bills out, gave two to the women, and pointed to the prisoner. They gave him a cup and he drank.

The liquid made him gasp—it started a fire in his throat and seemed to burn into his stomach. He struggled to keep from choking, and his eyes teared. The mountain men laughed and one of them slapped him on the back. Then they sauntered on.

The sun was higher now, and he could feel its warmth. He had taken only one drink, but he felt drunk. The liquor had been strong and his stomach empty. Besides, he was not a good drinker. For a second he was afraid that he would give himself away. He looked around him quickly, but none of the men seemed to be looking at him —they were all busily eyeing the booths and the women selling things. Their eyes were filled with the naïve hunger and awe that simple country people have at fairs. He had seen it in Ohio when he was a teenager and had gone to the county fair and watched the farmers strolling about in their overalls and work boots. The mountain men would notice nothing, for they were too overwhelmed. And even if they did sense something strange about him, they would attribute it to their confusion. They would be too embarrassed to speak. He began to relax.

*

The men walked up and down the rows of booths until almost nightfall. They went on and on, row after row. Most of the booths sold food or drink, and after a while the prisoner began to sense a pattern in them. The booths offering drink were always at the end of a row where skewers of salted or spiced meat and bowls of rice were sold. The soldiers would buy some meat and rice, take a cup of wine, and stand, eating and drinking. There were a few booths selling articles of clothing— trousers or sandals. He saw one place that sold hats.

The mountain men just stared at these. After they had

168

bought the drink, they had tried nothing else. *They're on this trip to make money, not spend it,* he thought as he walked with them, watching their eyes.

They had trouble finding the truck again because they had lost their sense of direction. He remembered, however, that it lay directly opposite a booth with a red flag flying from it. When the men became confused, he motioned the strongest one to him, climbed on the man's shoulders, and looked over the field until he spotted the flag. Then he pointed in that direction, and they started back.

The soldiers had already finished eating when they returned. That would mean no food, and he was already nearly starved. He groaned inwardly and collapsed against the truck, watching the others eat. They took some dried meat out of the leather sacks tied to their waists and began to chew on it. Now and then they would pass around a clay bottle of cold tea that one of them had saved. He could hear his stomach growling and tried to sleep, thinking that if he did so, the hunger pangs would go away.

They didn't. He woke and stared ahead. It was dark, and the mountain men were stretched out and sleeping, their snores making a raucous serenade. The man closest to the prisoner was lying on his side with his back to him. The man's belt was twisted so that the pouch containing his money and food trailed behind him on the ground, almost like a tail. The man was breathing regularly, and the prisoner could hear him snoring, so he was certain that the man was asleep. He knew that if he were caught, it might be the end. But his hunger was too strong to endure, and almost before he had thought about it, he found himself reaching for the sack.

He opened it slowly, reached in, felt the meat, and started to remove it. It was all in one piece, though, and too big to get through the mouth of the sack without pulling. He waited a moment, then gave it a little pull and the meat came out. He pulled the mouth of the bag shut, then moved back to his place, turned his back to the man, and began to eat.

He was working on his third mouthful when he saw the shadow. It extended over him, looming large, the moonlight casting it distinctly over the ground. He rolled

169

to his right and sprang to his feet. The mountain man was looking at him with narrowed eyes, the blade of his knife glinting in the moonlight. The man lunged, and the prisoner leaped to the side, then hit the man with a punch thrown with all the strength that remained in him. The man flew backward and lay still. The prisoner let out his breath and reached to pick up the knife from the ground. But before he could do so, the others were around him, holding his arms firmly. Then they took him to the soldiers.

XLIII

The soldiers were angry when the men woke them. They listened impatiently, then one of them ordered the prisoner to sit by the side of a nearby truck and told the mountain men to go back to sleep.

When dawn came, the soldiers woke and began to make breakfast. From his place beside the truck, the prisoner could see men doing the same all down the line of tents as far as he could see. They lit fires and began to boil tea. Others were washing, a few doing the tai-chi exercises that meant they were Chinese-trained. The booths had emptied at nightfall, the women all bicycling off into the darkness, the beams of their bike lights gleaming like a thousand golden fireflies. In the early morning light the field looked strange—row after row of booths, some with banners attached, whipping in the brisk breeze. He was amazed by the emptiness of it; back home there would have been thousands of birds, chirping and searching for the scraps of rice and meat. Here there were none. Only silence. Other than a few mice and some lizards, there was nothing but deserted counters and empty mud paths.

He was becoming nervous. Soon the soldiers would come to question him. He watched them take down their tents and store them in the trucks. Then they packed the cooking utensils and stood, waiting to leave. A signal was given, and they got into the trucks. He could see the other men in the convoy doing the same. The truck nearest him began to move, and there was a shout from the cab as the driver gestured for him to move away.

His spirits rose—they were going to do nothing, nothing at all. The trucks began to move out, and he ran after one. Hands pulled him aboard, and he settled back to enjoy the ride. It looked like a good day. He laughed out loud and the others looked at him, but he did not stop. He felt inside his shirt. The meat was still there. In all the chaos he had kept it. He would not be hungry to-night.

*

Through noon the trucks rolled south. The day was bright, and the air pleasantly cool with a soft breeze blowing from the southeast. A few times the prisoner saw planes high up, but they came no closer, and there were no bombs. This was strange to him—all the time they were advancing farther and farther south, but there was no resistance. He wondered if the men on his side had given up the battle altogether. That was inconceivable to him. He remembered the bullets and the pain and the friends he had seen blown to bits before his eyes. All to win a few feet of land—land on which the enemy was now rolling south, as if they were going on a Sunday outing.

By nightfall they had reached another marshy stretch about ten miles outside a large city. Beside the highway were the large cement runways of an abandoned airfield, streets of gray amid the brown and green of the marsh. Reeds were growing over the concrete where the water had risen and claimed back the land. He could see abandoned planes and hangars. The trucks slowed down, then

171

pulled off the main road and took a curving macadam road that eventually led them onto the runways. Then they climbed out of the trucks and set up camp.

The prisoner wanted to speak to the old man again. After waiting until the tents had been set up, he wandered toward the commander's tent and waited for the chance.

The old man came out of his tent and looked at the sky. It was blue-black and filled with stars—a night much like those nights back in the jungle when he and the prisoner had talked. The prisoner whistled softly, and the old man looked in his direction, nodded, and gestured that he should remain where he was. He sat and waited. Soon two soldiers came for him, and he was led to the old man's tent again.

This time there was no map, only two chairs and a small table with some food on it. When the soldiers had gone, the old man told him to sit and offered him something to eat. He had to control himself to keep from wolfing it down. The old man watched him.

"I see you have not been flourishing on rice and tea."

The prisoner looked up at him and nodded, his mouth too full to speak.

"Eat my friend. Do not speak. I will tell you what you need to know later."

When he finished, the old man poured him some wine. It was brownish like the wine he had drunk two days earlier, but not as strong. Then they leaned back, and the old man spoke.

"We are within 300 miles of Saigon," he said, watching for the prisoner's reaction.

The prisoner frowned.

"You can see for yourself the fierce resistance we encounter," said the old man, inspecting the toe of his boot.

"The army of the South must be massing for a counterattack," said the prisoner.

The old man shook his head. "There will be no counterattack. Everything is ours. The South Vietnamese Army—the people who were willing to die for their freedom—they are difficult to find. Perhaps if we search, we may find them, but I do not think they will seek us." He poured more wine into the prisoner's cup. "From the first, my friend, it was really you—the Americans—against us. This we all knew—most of all the people whose country

172

you were, how shall I say . . . visiting. They knew who was fighting. Not why—God alone knows that—but who. Now most of your comrades have gone, and so there is no longer any war."

The prisoner took a swallow, then jiggled his cup and watched the brown liquid slosh from side to side.

"There has been an evacuation. Surely you know of this. Now there is no more money for bombs, and without bombs the airplanes you have so generously given are not of much use. And so the end has come."

"The end," said the prisoner.

"Yes, happily, the end."

They became silent.

"There will be resistance only at the capital. But we will not fight there. We will go to the outskirts and wait. Then, like so many rats deserting a sinking ship, the leaders who have so valiantly struggled to preserve the freedom of their people will flee, taking with them their women and their gold. And then we will enter the city and all will be over. It is an old story—always the same."

The prisoner held up his cup, and the old man poured him more wine.

"All the words, all the promises and the vows—*pff,*" the old man pursed his lips and blew softly, "like the wind. In the end it is force, and force is a strange thing. Today it is ours; tomorrow who knows? In 2500 we will all be overrun by Lapps."

"By Lapps?" said the prisoner.

"Yes, Lapps with herds of reindeer aided by Eskimos with herds of . . . of. . . ."

"Of seals," said the prisoner.

"No," said the old man, "walruses! Seals have no tusks —they would be useless in battle."

The prisoner nodded.

"Have you read much history?" asked the old man.

The prisoner shook his head.

"It was Spengler, who said that the West would fall. Vico said that it was all a cycle—a big circle. Your poets have written of that—Yeats and Joyce."

"Irishmen," said the prisoner.

"Ah, that is right," said the old man. "But the common language—I thought you would call them yours."

The prisoner tried to recall something he had once

173

read by Yeats, but he couldn't. He looked at the old man who seemed to be thinking.

"You must begin to plan, my friend. There is no sense in doing anything until we are farther south—probably not until we reach Saigon itself. But then you must be ready, and you must move swiftly when the time comes."

The prisoner started to stand. He was wobbly because of the wine and laughed as he reached out to grasp the center pole of the tent to steady himself. As he did so, he dislodged a sheet of paper that was fastened to the pole with a clip. He picked it up and then tried, unsuccessfully, to reattach it.

"Do you know what that says?" asked the old man.

It was a rhetorical question. The prisoner shrugged but did not answer.

"It says that all enemy soldiers encountered are to be taken prisoner and sent north."

The prisoner shot a glance at the old man, then went out into the darkness.

XLIV

The next day they encountered the first mass of refugees. They were moving north on the same road, men and women on bicycles, some pushing carts with their belongings. He wondered where the people could be heading since most of the towns that the convoy had passed were only blackened ashes. The people stood to the side as the soldiers passed. Their faces were tired, but they did not look frightened. Some of the girls waved to the soldiers who waved back.

The road was broken up here, and for long stretches they drove through thick dust which rose in great clouds as they passed. In the afternoon they crossed a bridge and came into a beautiful town, the first large town he'd seen that was not in ruins. The buildings were white in the sun, and the red and green tile roofs looked bright and cheerful. They drove along streets with wide side-walks, some covered with tables and chairs. Some of the buildings had awnings which still hung intact.

Block after block they rolled past shops and restaurants—all deserted. The sky had turned a bright blue, and there were white, fluffy clouds. The sea, which the prisoner could see glimpses of between the buildings, was a brilliant blue-green.

Finally they came to a square at the center of town and stopped. The soldiers got out, formed ranks, then began to walk quickly toward the ocean. For two more blocks there were more streets; then suddenly, the road-way ended on a terrace high above the beach. The prisoner was behind the soldiers, but he was taller than most of them and could see, over their heads, a crowd of people on the beach, lining it for what seemed like two or three miles. The prisoner could not see their faces, but he could tell that they had all turned to face the city and the soldiers. A few small boats were moving out in the bay—a small sailboat and a couple of barges powered by out-board motors—and these were packed with people.

A command was given, and the soldiers stopped. The scene was eerie. Before them lay broad, stone steps which descended to the beach, then a hundred yards of white sand, and then the rows of people who seemed to be moving closer and closer to the sea. He could see the officers discussing matters. One of them left, and every-one else waited. Finally the old man came, the soldiers separating as he walked through their ranks. When he came to the officers, he was given field glasses. He sur-veyed the beach and the horizon, then exclaimed some-thing excitedly and handed the glasses to another officer, pointing far out to where the water and sky seemed to fuse.

The prisoner squinted, but he could see nothing.

Several more small boats hove into view, coming

175

around a green spit of land dotted with white villas. The crowd surged toward them, and several people began swimming out. The soldiers started down the steps, walking slowly. A great cry went up from the people. On and on walked the soldiers, the prisoner in their midst. With each step they took, the panic of the people increased. Several broke from the line along the water and ran up the beach. Others stood their ground, paralyzed, hoping that the boats would reach them before the soldiers did.

The prisoner could see their faces now. The women were screaming, and the children clung to them, crying. The men stood dumb, sometimes looking over their shoulders into the bay, at other times staring with wide eyes at the soldiers.

A boat reached the surf. People dashed madly toward it. The men made it first; they tried to pull their wives and children aboard, but the other men fought with them. Some of them looked like soldiers. Then the boat started to move back out into the bay. People held onto the sides and were towed along, but as the boat picked up speed, these people began to let go. Some of them continued to swim feebly after the boat; others gave up, floated for a few minutes, then sank.

The soldiers made a rush toward the water, and the remaining people backed into it until it came up to their necks. Men and women were holding children over their heads. Some of the children were caught in the waves and borne back onto shore where they sat bawling in the shallow surf. Finally the command to retreat was given, and the soldiers moved back twenty yards, then stood.

They waited. Ten minutes passed, then twenty. No more boats came. The line of soldiers split, forming a path about ten yards wide through their midst. Down this path the people began to file, staring ahead, pushing and pulling their children. None of them dared to look at the soldiers until they had reached the stone stairs, where a few looked over their shoulders as they scurried up. The file was orderly and silent, flowing over the sand and up the gray steps like a conveyor belt. The prisoner watched the people, then turned and looked back out at the bay. The sun was still glinting off the turquoise water. The few clouds had blown over, and the sky was a pure, deep blue. The prisoner squinted and saw a head in the water about forty yards from shore. One of the people who had lost his grip on the last boat was trying to make it back to shore. The tide was pulling against him, and he was floundering. He struggled for a few more minutes, sank, came to the surface again, then was gone.

XLV

They stayed two days in the city. The men searched the buildings and found much liquor and cigars but little else. The people went back to their homes, but nobody went back to the big hotels and the villas. They remained as they had been on the day when the soldiers entered the town—silent reminders of the other side and its ways. No one wanted to reclaim them because to reclaim them meant that you had been a sympathizer, had entertained "Thieu's clique" and their American friends, and this meant that you were an enemy of the people, an agent of Saigon.

The prisoner chuckled when he saw the soldiers spread out on the terraces and sun decks, sipping from the bottles they had taken and smoking expensive cigars. These things were new to the men, and they had no sense of moderation. They drank until they passed out and smoked constantly. Once he spotted the old man watching them, smiling wryly. He tried to catch the old man's eye, but there were several other men with him who looked like officers, so he kept back.

The nights were clear, and a full moon shone brightly over the bay, coating the edge of each wave with silver. *A lovers' moon,* the prisoner thought, sitting alone on a terrace. Discipline had relaxed, and the men were wandering through the city. On the first night they had done little because of their fatigue, but on the second day he had seen many of them speaking with the women, and tonight red lanterns hung in windows, and there was laughter in the air. He leaned his chair back and rested his feet on the railing, vaguely aware that for the first time in a long while he was feeling lonely. Before he had always been too frightened to allow himself that luxury, and the loneliness of solitary confinement was something different—there was a reason for it, and it filled you with anger because you knew it was unjust. This loneliness was softer, more like nights back home in the States when he was without a date or alone in a strange city. It was melancholy, but it had a sweetness to it, and he savored it. He had two cigars that a soldier had given him, and now he wanted to smoke one, but he had no matches. He twisted around and looked for others, saw no one at first, then heard voices coming from the other side of the terrace around the corner of the building. He walked toward them.

There were a half dozen men sitting. He could not see their faces or their uniforms very well, but two of them were speaking. He went up to them. When they turned, he felt a shock go down his spine and his hair stand on end. One of the men was No-Neck. He looked at the prisoner for a moment, then continued talking to the man near him. The prisoner's instincts told him to run, but he controlled himself and gestured to the man closest to him that he wanted a light for his cigar. The man reached into his pocket and gave him a box of matches, holding up one finger to indicate how many he could take. He took the box, struck a match and quickly lit his cigar, then left. When he rounded the corner of the building, he began to run. He could almost hear his heart pounding, and twice he fell in the darkness, but his fear drove him. Finally with a great effort, he stopped himself. To go off in the night, still behind enemy lines, was folly. No-Neck had not recognized him—he was still safe. He would follow his plan and continue south with the old man and the convoy.

He hunted for a place to sleep. Finally he found a small porch on a building near the parked trucks. There were several chairs here so he pushed them together to make an uncomfortable bed. He lay down, but he could not sleep. His heart was still beating wildly, his lips were dry, and he felt nauseated. The scene with the men on the terrace kept coming back to him, and each time he pictured No-Neck his hair stood on end. Then he remembered striking the match. He was sure No-Neck had not been looking, but if he had been, he would have seen him in the light, and that would have been the end. *But he did not,* he said to calm himself. *If he had, he would have roused the other men, and they would have taken me prisoner.* He kept saying this over and over to himself, and when dawn came and the men began to load their gear and then board the trucks, he kept in hiding. Finally, at a moment when there was much chaos, he climbed aboard the nearest truck, slunk into the shadows, placed his head on his knees and pretended to sleep.

XLVI

By mid-morning the prisoner realized that they were no longer heading along the coast but had turned southwest and were moving inland. The land was still flat, and again there were rice paddies and small villages. As they drove through the villages, people stood beside the road and looked at them curiously. Now and then he saw a red VC flag with its yellow star, hanging from a pole sticking out of a window. They stopped a few times for water, and one time some women came and offered them rice and meat, but no one took any and the women left quickly.

He could see men working in the paddies, and sometimes the trucks passed carts pulled slowly by small buffalo. Life seemed undisturbed by the change in power, and he kept thinking of the terrified people in the seaside town. That had been a resort, and the townspeople were known to be Thieu sympathizers; these were villages and the people farmers. The VC respected farmers; the people knew this and were unafraid.

In the afternoon it became warmer. He did not know the date but guessed it to be the end of March or early April. It was too soon for hot weather, but still the air seemed stagnant and heavy compared to that of the coast. The land remained flat, and now there were more roads intersecting the one they were moving on. Frequently planes flew overhead. They looked like South Vietnamese planes, but they showed no interest in the convoy. The day grew hazy, and many of the men slept. Gradually the prisoner's fear subsided, and he slept, too. He awoke once when No-Neck came toward him with whip in hand in his dreams, but then after a few minutes he fell asleep again.

*

The trucks drove on through the afternoon and into the evening. They were moving at a good clip and covering much ground, but the prisoner, lost in his dreams, did not know this. Toward midnight they stopped, and the men hastily made a camp and slept. With the dawn, they moved on.

It was another warm, hazy day. Steam rose from the paddies as the morning sun heated the water. The land was perfectly flat, and the prisoner could see for miles behind the truck—a greenish-brown plain, dotted with paddies, gleaming dully in the sun's oblique rays.

Toward noon the sun broke through, and the heat increased. The men slept, but the prisoner stayed awake. He had slept too much and his head ached. He watched the fields and the sky. Here and there the black-brown hump of a buffalo appeared, a farmer with a straw hat trailing the animal with his unseen plow buried under

180

the water. He racked his brain for what little he had learned of Vietnamese agriculture. He knew they lived on rice, that their methods of farming were primitive but effective, and that the south had the richest farmland. He would have liked to know more, but there had been no time for that. The Army never taught their soldiers much about the people whose land they fought on. Instead, they had studied maps and learned how to calculate the range of mortar fire, how to deploy on a hill, and how to fire a rifle.

"You are fighting to keep the Communists out. To stop the Reds." That's what they told them at boot camp when someone asked for reasons. Usually no one asked. They just did what they were supposed to and learned how to shoot and bomb and protect themselves.

He remembered what K had said. "It's nice to be philosophical, only it doesn't mean much when someone's shooting at you."

That had made sense. He could understand that. He thought about some of the protests he had seen back home before he left and those he'd read about in the newspapers the old man had given him. He'd never had much feeling about all that—maybe because he was a fatalist, but mostly because he thought protests were futile gestures.

What do they know about it? he thought. *Have they been there? Have they seen this country? Do they have any idea what the other side is after and how far they'll go?*

He had always figured that the people at the top knew what they were doing, or at least that they had a clearer idea of how things went than a meatpacker in Sheboygan. It just made more sense, that was all. He still felt that way—even after all the killing and destruction he had seen.

You have to have leaders, and you've got to listen to them, he reasoned. *Otherwise you get chaos. And sometimes they're wrong. Yes, that happens sometimes.*

He stopped there. That was as far as he wanted to go. After that he'd worry about protecting his own hide. There would be some tough situations coming up, and he didn't need a philosophy or a moral solution. He needed

181

a way to get out and get back where they didn't want to chop him into mincemeat.

*

In the late afternoon the trucks stopped, and he saw the village for the first time—twenty or thirty huts and a tall building with a green roof in the middle. It looked like a pagoda, but it was taller than any he had seen. It looked as if there was glass in the windows, for light glinted from some of them like a mirror. None of the pagodas he'd seen had glass windows—someone had told him the Buddhists thought glass imprisoned the spirit.

The old man took control here. A map was spread out on the hood of the lead truck. He spoke to the officers one at a time, tracing something on the map with the handle of his quirt. The prisoner had not seen him carry it in weeks. *He's back in the field,* he thought. *Back playing the generalissimo.*

The village lay about three-quarters of a mile ahead. The main road skirted it, twisting to the southeast so that the buildings would be on the convoy's right as they passed. A hundred yards away the trucks stopped, and the men got out. Commands were given, and they took their rifles and began to walk toward the village. The houses looked deserted. The prisoner could see a few chickens pecking about but not much else. The men started to chase the chickens, but the officers yelled at them, and they stopped. In a few minutes they had come to the center of the town and the pagoda. One of the officers went up to the door—it was carved green wood decorated with brass—and pounded on it with the butt of his rifle. There was no answer. He waited for a minute and pounded again; then two men stepped up and shot the hinges off the door, and a dozen soldiers with rifles entered.

The prisoner stood behind the mass of soldiers and watched. There was no sound except for the occasional cluck of the chickens. Then a figure appeared in the doorway. He was dressed in white shirt and trousers. Several others followed him, all dressed the same. Their clothes seemed to be some kind of uniform, but the men did not look like monks.

182

The men in white were herded to the side of the pagoda, then ordered to stand still. The old man appeared and together with two or three officers began questioning them. They spoke calmly and looked unafraid. The old man and his subordinates showed no emotion. Perhaps ten minutes elapsed; then the old man turned, looked at the other officers, nodded, and left. A space was cleared in front of the men in white, and a dozen soldiers lined up, took aim, and fired. The men fell. Some were still alive, so a second round was fired. The prisoner stared at the man who had given the commands to the soldiers. It was No-Neck.

When it was all finished, the men in white lay still, their shirts and trousers dotted with spots of red. No-Neck barked another command, and the firing squad turned and started back to the trucks. The rest of the soldiers followed. The prisoner remained in the shadows until No-Neck had passed, then joined the last of the soldiers. Before he reached the outskirts of the village, he turned and looked back at the pagoda. The men in white lay, like so many slaughtered sheep, and the chickens were still there, pecking at the ground. A few chickens were among the bodies, jabbing tentatively at the faces and hands.

The soldiers climbed back into their trucks, and the convoy rolled on.

XLVII

Three days later they reached a low-lying, swampy region. There were rice paddies here, but they looked as if they hadn't been tended for some time. Airplanes buzzed overhead, most of them heading due east. At one crossroad a jeep shot out and intercepted them. The men were VC. They conferred with the commander for a few minutes, then drove away.

It started to rain—first a drizzle, then a real cloudburst. Planes continued to buzz overhead, lower now, underneath the black clouds. They weren't fighters. Most were C-141's, big cargo planes used to transport trucks and heavy equipment. Sometimes they flew so low that he could read the numbers on the wings. They were all American planes. He kept looking for one with the insignia of the South Vietnamese Air Force, but he saw none. A few of the soldiers took pot shots at the planes until the officers ordered them to stop.

At about three in the afternoon, they began to climb up a slight grade. The convoy halted when they reached the plateau at the top. He didn't know why, but something told the prisoner that this was it—the place where his stay with the convoy and the old man would end. He climbed out with the other men and looked around. Before them was a great city. The rain was still falling, but the clouds were not as dense, and the part of the city farthest from them—maybe fifteen miles away—was in sunlight. He could make out parks and wide streets. It was too far to tell if there had been any destruction in the city, but it did not appear to have been bombed.

The men began to set up their tents. A large tent was pitched on the highest point, and the old man and the officers went in. When they came out an hour later, they seemed happy, laughing and thumping each other on the back. A few of them looked drunk. A tall pole was planted, and a VC flag was run up. The rain had stopped, and the clouds had moved on so that now the plateau was in sunlight and the city lay in shadow. The men saluted the flag, and the old man made a speech. Then there was a cheer, and mugs of brown wine were passed around. They drank and cheered and sang songs.

Nightfall came and they ate. The men sat outside their tents, some under lanterns playing cards. They had never done this before because lanterns made them easy targets, but they didn't seem worried tonight. There were small circles of lights stretched out on both sides of the encampment almost as far as he could see. That meant more convoys and camps like the one he was in. Then he looked toward the city. There were lights but not many. The wind was blowing gently, whistling through the tents and the small shrubs on the plateau. A few times he thought he heard faint explosions and screams coming from the direction of the city, but he could not be certain that it wasn't his ears playing tricks on him.

He slept lightly that night. He did not know where they were, but he knew it was far to the south—the closest to the American-held territory that he had been since his capture. The time for him to make a move was drawing near. He did not yet know what he would do, but his brain worked feverishly. He thought he would take food and drink—the old man could get these for him—and simply vanish into the night. The old man could get him a map, and with that and the food he'd make it. It would be risky, but with all the refugees on the roads he would not be noticed.

He imagined himself crossing into American territory —the faces of the men when, standing before them dressed like a gook, he asked how the Cleveland Indians were doing. They would take him to some lousy colonel who would question him for an hour, then he'd shower and change into khakis. Then he'd be shipped out on

R and R. Maybe to Hong Kong, maybe Tokyo. In two weeks he'd be back in the U.S.

The thought almost made him faint with excitement. He calmed himself. *I have to rest,* he thought. *Have to save my strength.* When dawn came, he was still wide awake, and all the sleep he got was one hour before breakfast.

*

The day was filled with sunlight. The men looked over the city and talked among themselves, pointing to this or that place. He could see an airport on the outskirts of the town to the southwest of the plateau. The C-141's were landing and taking off from it, one leaving about every twenty minutes. He tried to listen to the conversations of the men to see if the name of a town was mentioned, but he could learn nothing. He could not judge its size, but it was a large town. He tried to place it on the fuzzy map which he held in his head. The place was inland, that he knew, but the only towns of any size that he could think of were Ban Me Thuot, Pleiku, and Da Lat. He knew that there was an airfield at Da Lat, but he was almost certain that Da Lat lay amid mountains in rough country. The land around this town was flat for as far as he could see. And it was flat behind the plateau, too—flat for at least a hundred miles. At first it was inconceivable to him, but gradually he realized that they had done exactly as the old man had said. They were on the outskirts of Saigon, and they were waiting.

XLVIII

Night came, and the prisoner waited for his chance to speak with the old man. He moved close to the command tent and sat, his head on his knees, alternately sleeping and watching. It was a clear night, and the big planes continued to fly. Their engines filled the air with a dull rumbling that he had mistaken at first for the sounds of bombs. They took off from the distant runway, then banked and flew parallel to the edge of the plateau almost at the height of the camp about a half mile out over the plain. He could see the lights of the cockpits, and when one flew closer, he thought he could see the pilot and copilot. The planes flew off into the night and were visible in the moonlight for a long distance, until finally they vanished into the blackness to the east.

He grew restless and walked back and forth. He wanted to talk to the old man. He knew that now was the crucial time, yet he could not go to his tent. Finally at about ten, the old man emerged to take his evening stroll. He walked erect with the strong, firm step and slight limp that the prisoner had come to recognize. When the old man passed him, he coughed. The old man looked at him, made a gesture with his hands—a slight spreading of the fingers that told the prisoner to remain in the shadows—then walked on. Several other officers were following him. One of them was No-Neck.

More time passed. The prisoner gave up for that night and found a place to lie down and sleep. He dreamed that he was flying through the night air in a great plane.

Everything was illuminated by a moon that seemed almost as bright as the sun. He could not see where the plane was going, but he felt its motion and the hum of the motors.

He woke at dawn excited and more anxious than ever. Again he stayed close to the old man's tent, so that when he emerged for breakfast, he could not help but see him. The old man was alone except for an orderly, but he looked around the area carefully before motioning for the prisoner to come to him. Then they went quickly into the tent.

"It is dangerous," said the old man, and for the first time the prisoner noticed a look of fear in him. "There are new men in camp—security officers from Hanoi. Men whom I do not know and cannot be sure of."

"And Duc Thang is here," said the prisoner.

"Yes, he is here," said the old man. "They will need him and his kind when they take over the capital."

The prisoner winced. Already he could see the firing squads and the prisons filled with "Thieu's clique" and the friends of "Thieu's clique" and the friends of the friends of the friends. It would not be pretty.

"I need a map," he said quickly, "and food. Maybe a little water. With these things I can reach my Army's lines."

The old man looked at him steadily. His calmness had returned. "Do you know, my friend, where those lines are?"

"To the south," he said. "They cannot be far."

"No," said the old man, "the place is not far. You can see it from the edge of camp."

The prisoner fought down an impulse to cheer. It had been so long, and now he was so close.

The old man shook his head. "It will not be as easy as you think. Even from here you can see the place—but that is the trouble. There are no longer lines. Thieu holds only the capital and the airfield, that and a few provinces to the south—some patches in the delta, perhaps Ca Mau. No one can tell for certain."

"Then it will be easy," said the prisoner. "No one will care, and I will walk to my freedom—like a man . . . like a man taking a stroll on a Sunday afternoon."

The old man laughed. "Like Eakins' friend Max

188

Schmidt, you will go sculling to your freedom, gliding on the river of your dreams."

The prisoner smiled and laughed. He did not know exactly what the old man was speaking of, but no matter, it would be easy. If the distance was so short, no one could stop him.

"Do you know, my young friend, the history of your art?"

The prisoner shook his head. He was restless, and the old man was becoming tiresome.

"Mid-nineteenth century. Yes, that was the time. They are called the Luminists. A minor school but some masterpieces. There is one by Bingham. Two fur trappers drifting down the Missouri River on a raft, a dog sitting at the helm. The boat and the men are clear, etched with bright light; the background and the river, a haze—soft and romantic."

The prisoner did not understand and showed his impatience by looking through the doorway into the bright light of the morning.

"Ah, my friend does not wish to hear of his art, of his wonderful Yankee heritage. Everywhere, my friend, everywhere and at all times something may be learned. Even from such a painting."

"Tell me," said the prisoner, "I'm an ignorant yokel —a hick from Ohio." His scorn was strong, but the old man chose to ignore it.

"Like Bingham, my friend, you see only the center— yourself, me, perhaps this camp. These things you understand. The rest is all a haze, and you see it romantically. You think that because Saigon is close, the way will be easy. You think that because the streets of the city look quiet and there is no fighting, all is safe there. But you do not see clearly. And if you are to find your way back, you will need to see."

The prisoner shook his head and frowned, walked to the chair in the corner of the tent, and sat. The old man looked at him sympathetically for a second, then noticing that men were passing in front of the tent, motioned that the prisoner should stand. The sight of a mountain man sitting in the commander's presence would cause speculation. He waited a moment, then resumed speaking.

"Between us and the city is fifteen miles, and squad-

189

rons of soldiers patrol that area. Some of the squadrons are my men, but some are Thieu's men—the last of his men, fanatic soldiers terrified of the end they know is coming. If men from our side encounter anyone, they will either shoot on the spot or take prisoners to be sent north. Probably they will do the latter, but there is no certainty. If Thieu's men find you, they will kill you without asking questions. There is little to choose from."

"I will get through," said the prisoner. "I will find a way."

"And should you get through," said the old man. "What then?"

"I will go to the American camp. I will rejoin those of our forces who remain in the city."

"There is no American camp," said the old man, shaking his head. "All the Americans are either in the embassy or at the airfield waiting for planes to fly them to safety. The embassy is guarded closely. The guards will let no one enter, most certainly no one dressed as a native. The airfield is in chaos. A solid ring of Thieu's soldiers surrounds it. They let men from the embassy pass through, but no others. Thousands wish to fly away—tens of thousands—but there are not enough planes. They will never allow you to pass. They will shoot you on sight as sure as . . . as. . . ."

"As sure as shootin'," said the prisoner ruefully.

"Thank you," said the old man.

The prisoner got up and walked to the other side of the tent, then returned to the chair and sat. He was too close to quit now—and too close to be patient. He had to do something or he would explode. The soldiers had more leisure time now, and already many suspicious glances had been cast in his direction. It would not take them long to find him out. He was angry with the old man. He did not want counsel that advised patience—he wanted someone to help him escape.

"We will have to think on this, my young friend. Plan. Otherwise you are merely going to your doom."

The prisoner looked at him angrily. Again the old man looked hastily toward the opening in the tent.

"We must be careful. You must not come so openly. Not in the morning. Come at night—tomorrow at about nine. I will be waiting, and we will talk some more.

190

Things may have changed somewhat by then. Perhaps the passage to the city will be safer. But you must wait."

The prisoner stepped out of the tent and walked away, blinking in the bright sunlight. His sense of caution told him to walk toward the trucks immediately behind the tent so that few would see him, make his way between them to another spot, and then emerge again into the open. But this time he was not cautious—he was angry and reckless, so he strode straight across the open space, walking between the groups of men who were talking and playing cards.

XLIX

That night the prisoner brooded. Several times he contemplated taking matters into his own hands. It would not be difficult. All he had to do would be to walk to the western end of the camp where there were many boulders and where he had seen a rough path descending into the valley. No one would notice a missing mountain man, and he would move cautiously, watching for patrols. Besides there would not be so many at night. And by morning he would be in Saigon. One night was all it would take.

But the old man's caution kept coming back to him, and he was confused. He trusted the man and was sure of his friendship, but the warning did not seem logical. He had seen the big planes taking off. Even now he could hear them rumbling in the night. Each hour there were fewer Americans in the city. A dread was growing in him that he would be left behind and would never reach safety.

The voice in the back of his mind—the voice that had been still for so many months—began again. It told him that the old man was not really trying to help him, that the old man was trying to keep him, that he was different from Duc Thang only in method. *If you wait,* said the voice, *then they will have you. It will be the whip again. They are insane—all VC are insane. They think you have information. Why do you wait? What are you afraid of? You would flee if you were not a coward.*

He could not stay still because then the voice was at him, eating into his soul like a cancer. He walked among the soldiers. They were sitting in small circles around the campfires, drinking and laughing. He looked toward the old man's tent. There were lights inside, which turned the tent into a lantern. He could see the shadows of men sitting and drinking. Now and then one would go outside to urinate and then return. It looked as if they were taking turns at giving toasts, for one after the other they stood and held their glasses high, and he heard cheers. He saw No-Neck's shadow. He must have been standing close to the light, for his form projected black and distinct against the canvas, and his shoulders appeared six feet wide. When he raised his glass to give the toast, his arm seemed to go up and up, shooting off into the darkness like a giant's. The prisoner imagined that all the men in the tent were under the control of that arm.

Duc Thang is really the commander, said the voice. *They listen to him. He is the strongest, and he is using the old man and the others. He is telling the old man to keep you here. He must have some use for you, some plan. You will be a prize exhibit in their cage—"The Imperialist Coward, the Frightened Running Dog."*

The prisoner swore and turned away from the tent, again walking through the soldiers. Finally he stopped. He had come to the fuel depot, and he sat and leaned against the drums, staring into the darkness. Time passed, perhaps fifteen minutes, maybe a half hour; he did not know how long because his feelings were running riot. He began to get the uncomfortable sensation that someone was watching him. He looked around. About ten yards away a group of six mountain men were squatting in a circle, drinking from a bottle which they passed among them. One of them had his head turned, and he could see the gleam of his eyes. He felt certain it was the man whom he had taken the meat from. He stared at the mountain man, but the man turned away and rejoined the conversation with his friends. Quickly the prisoner slipped off into the shadows and headed toward the other end of the camp.

He sat in the darkness and looked at the stars. They were bright, winking down at the plateau and the city beneath. He listened. The sound was faint, but he was certain that it was gunfire, drifting up to the plateau from somewhere down in the valley. He guessed that it was only a few miles away but couldn't be sure. He strained to hear. It came in quick bursts. In between there was silence, and he heard only the soft hum of the wind and the rumble of the planes heading east.

The voice started eating at him again, berating him. *Coward, coward . . . afraid, afraid. . . .* It grew louder until finally he jumped up. It was now or never. He could not wait. He would go to the old man's tent and get a map from him. He would not bother with food and water.

When he came to the tent, he saw that the light inside was still glowing but that the officers were gone—all except the old man. He could see his shadow as he sat in a chair, reading. His first impulse was to rush up to the tent and enter, but he realized that if a guard saw this, there would be trouble. He might be taken for an intruder. He found a stone and threw it against the tent.

He could see the startled shadow move; then the old man came out and looked around. The prisoner whistled softly, and the old man looked in his direction. The old man saw him but shook his head and started to go back into the tent. The prisoner whistled again. The old man stopped, turned, and waved to him to come. He did not look pleased.

When the prisoner entered, the old man turned the lantern down lower so that their shadows would be indistinct.

"Tonight is not safe. I asked you to come tomorrow. I have had no time to plan your escape. You must be patient."

The prisoner fixed a steady gaze on him. His confidence in the old man was dwindling. He suddenly felt the strangeness of the other man—his high cheekbones and hooded eyes, the yellow of his skin. He did not seem like a man to the prisoner but like an Alien being. The prisoner shivered.

"You are endangering us both. If you give yourself away, there will be no chance. You will ruin us both." The old man swore and turned his back.

Confusion came over the prisoner again, but only for a moment. He had made up his mind, and nothing would stop him.

"Now! It must be now. Tonight!"

The old man turned and looked at him. He shook his head. "I cannot help you tonight. It is folly, romantic impetuosity. You have waited a long time. One more night will mean little."

"Be damned!" he said. "I will do it all myself!" He turned and started to leave. But before he could reach the opening at the end of the tent a figure entered. It was No-Neck, and the prisoner knew that he was recognized. He saw No-Neck go for the gun in his holster and sprang at him. They fell to the ground and rolled over, knocking the table and maps down. He held No-Neck's wrist with one hand and his throat with the other. No-Neck was struggling violently, bashing the prisoner in the groin with his knee. The prisoner held on as a dying man holds onto life, but he could feel the strength going from him with each blow of No-Neck's knee.

There was a thud. No-Neck quivered, then lay still. The prisoner rolled onto his back, breathing heavily and biting his lips to keep from moaning. He could see the old man standing over him, pistol in hand, and he could see blood on the handle of the gun where it had struck No-Neck.

L

The old man was shaking, but he controlled himself, walked quickly to the end of the tent and shut the flap. Then he went to the lantern and turned it down so low that it gave only a glimmer. He searched through the jumble of maps on the floor, spread one out by the lantern, and beckoned the prisoner.

"This is the only safe route," he said, tracing a path beside the serpentine line of the Saigon River. "Your best chance is to get to the city and then contact the embassy. How you will do that I do not know. People are sending thousands of messages each day. It is unlikely that they are read. But it is your only hope. At the airport it will be impossible, but through the embassy there is a chance—a slight chance but a real one. If they believe that you are an American, they will take you with them."

The prisoner studied the map. The route was clear, and it would be easy to find the river even at night.

"Your best hope is to bribe someone."

The old man rose and walked over to a chest in the corner. He rummaged through it and returned with the silver elephant cigarette lighter.

"This is worth much. At least five-hundred American dollars. I doubt if that will be enough, but it will give you a starting point." He handed it to the prisoner who put it inside his shirt. "Find a jeweler," said the old man. "There are many jewelers in the capital. They will know the value."

The prisoner nodded and stood. It was time to go. The moment had come. He reached down for the limp body of No-Neck.

"No," said the old man. "I will attend to that."

"It is my responsibility," said the prisoner. "If the body is found, there will be questions."

"It will not be found," said the old man. "I have friends and they are loyal. This is a thing that I can do. Besides, my friend, Duc Thang is not yet dead."

The prisoner looked closely. He could see the man's shoulders rising and falling as he breathed.

"If you let him live, he will accuse you."

"I will not let him live," said the old man. He held out his hand, and the prisoner grasped it.

Then the prisoner was gone.

LI

The prisoner moved through the darkness swiftly and silently, heading due south. From the plateau it had been easy to see the river, glinting in the moonlight. Once he started down the hill, it was a different matter. The path wove and twisted between rocks and through small thickets of trees. He feared that he was losing his way and stopped several times, trying to get his bearings by the stars. He imagined men lurking behind every tree and rock—patrols out searching for deserters and infiltrators. A half dozen times he took cover and waited only to find that he had been mistaken, frightened by a splash of moonlight on a rock or the sound of leaves moving in the breeze. After almost two hours of walking, he still had not come to the river, and he became alarmed. Again he looked at the stars, but they were no help. There was no way of knowing how far to the east or west he had strayed, and so even if he were now heading due south, he might miss the river altogether and enter the broad plain of rice paddies that he had seen from the plateau. There would be no cover there, and he would be an easy target for a patrol. He could wait for morning, but that would place him in even greater danger.

Suddenly he saw a glow coming from behind a large boulder. He crouched down. He had almost stumbled into a small encampment. Sweat began to cover his forehead. He crept forward on all fours until he could peer around the boulder. There were two tents, and one of them was lighted from within. He squinted and saw a half dozen men sleeping on the ground in front of the tents. Then the light within the tent went out, and all was blackness again.

The old man's caution went through his mind—*Folly, romantic impetuosity*. There was no way he could move any farther because the camp lay on the path. He could leave the pathway and try his luck, but then he might wander aimlessly for hours. His mind was racing, and he knew that he had to decide quickly. He looked at the figures again and counted seven this time. The moon was low on the western horizon, a faint yellow. It seemed to be smiling at him as if to say that this was all a big joke, a game, nothing as serious as he imagined. He crawled forward and began to move slowly around the perimeter of the camp. It seemed to take forever. When one of the men rolled over, his heart jumped, but the man was only moving in his sleep.

Finally he was directly behind the tent and could see the path again, leading down the hill. He kept crawling for twenty more yards then cautiously stood and walked on.

The path leveled off, and he moved faster. Suddenly he saw the river a quarter mile to the southeast. It was flowing so smoothly that it made no sound, and he knew that if he had not been lucky enough to look in that direction, he would never have seen it. He made his way through some trees, then down a slight grade to the water's edge where he found a narrow path snaking through tall

197

grass. By the first light of dawn, he had reached the outskirts of Saigon.

*

The river was broader here but very shallow. He could see sand bars in the middle, and near the shore the water rippled over rocks and ran smoothly through stands of reeds. Twice he passed under small bridges. He kept looking for boats or men fishing but saw no signs of life. Then with a sputter, a small boat hove into view. He crouched down quickly and watched as it passed, heading upstream. There were four men on it, and it was powered by an old outboard. The men were dressed in dark blue clothes, and one of them wore a large straw hat. As the boat sailed out of sight around a bend, it suddenly occurred to him that he need not have hidden. *They are not Cong,* he thought. *I am an American, and we are on the same side.* The thought was so strange to him that it took a moment for it to register.

Several more boats came into view, their motors chugging noisily. He waved to them, and one of the men waved back. Then he followed the path until it swerved from the river and came to an end in a field of withered grass. Across the field he could see a road leading toward the center of the city. He strode on. He had been walking all night, and the constant tension had wearied him, but now he felt refreshed.

Bicycles and small carts pulled by men passed. He looked at the faces of the people. Some of them looked worried, but most were expressionless, and several were smiling. He passed a small stand where a man and a woman were selling tea and bowls of rice. In front of the stand there were tables filled with people who were reading newspapers and talking. Several children carrying books passed him. They were walking single file, and the boy bringing up the rear—the smallest—was giggling and pulling the pigtails of a girl in front of him.

Finally he entered the center of the city. Traffic was bustling in the wide streets, and there were small islands in the center of them where traffic policemen stood, blowing whistles and swinging their arms vigorously. There were office buildings—some six or seven stories tall—and

198

beside them were squat, white buildings with front yards. They looked like homes and seemed strange sitting there in the heart of the city.

He stopped and tried to orient himself. He knew from the map that the embassy was between the cathedral and the Presidential Palace. He had thought the cathedral would dwarf the other buildings and that he would have no trouble finding it, but he had not reckoned on the size of the office buildings. Finally he walked up to a man and asked. The man looked at him strangely, then gave him directions in English. The prisoner nodded and walked on. He passed a shop and looked at his reflection in the window. His face was still darkened, but he had a beard, and this together with his straw hat gave him the appearance of a fierce Mexican bandit. He would have to wash the dye off—that would make it easier for him to get into the embassy.

*

It was a large white building, amazingly modern, standing at the end of a street lined by a dozen mansions, each with a manicured lawn and a cyclone fence separating it from the street. There was a mass of people around the embassy. He was still three blocks away, but already he could hear their cries.

When he got closer, he saw swarms of policemen standing behind a barricade, and behind the policemen were Marines holding rifles. At the front of the embassy was a large glass door; he could see men passing back and forth behind it. He heard a whirring sound and looked up. A big helicopter hovered overhead, then landed on the roof of the embassy. The crowd grew frantic. There were screams, and people held up their hands.

People came out of a door on the roof of the embassy and climbed into the chopper. Some of them were women and children. He could not be certain at that distance, but many of the people seemed to be Vietnamese. The westerners among them looked like embassy officials—men wearing gray suits and carrying briefcases. The door of the chopper snapped shut, the blade began to whirr,

199

and it lifted off. The people surrounding the building watched as it flew over the rooftops, heading east.

They seemed stupefied for a minute, then started to scream. The prisoner was closer now, and he could see the women crying and wringing their hands. The men were pushing, trying to force their way to the front of the crowd. Those next to the barricade surged forward, but they were forced back by the police. Two men hurdled the barricade at the far end, then ran toward the doorway. But before they had gone twenty feet, the police fell on them, battering them with clubs. The men fell, blood running down their faces. No ambulance came, and the policemen returned to their places, leaving the bodies where they had fallen.

The prisoner made a few halfhearted attempts to push his way through the mob, then gave up and walked to the steps of the office building diagonally across from the embassy.

From here he had a better view. He could see the crowd fanned out, almost circling the building, and behind the wooden barricade the police and the Marines. The police circled the entire building but the Marines were only before the main entrance where the crowd was thickest. Most of those at the front of the crowd were men; some of them were wearing army uniforms. He imagined their fear. Once the VC entered the city it would be open season on them. Anyone who had a grudge would point them out. If order was restored quickly, they might be safe. But if it wasn't, most of them would be killed in the first few days. He had seen it before—from the other side—and he knew. Civilians were crueler than soldiers. Suddenly they would remember all the times these men humiliated them and took their women and ate in their restaurants without paying. They would scream for their blood, knowing that the louder they screamed, the more loyal they would appear to the victors.

He remembered "liberating" a small village near Ban Houe just two weeks before his capture. On the very first morning that the Americans had held the town, there was a line of men outside his captain's office. They were all denouncing their neighbors as VC. The captain was a career man—a southerner and a real redneck. To him they were all gooks, and he just swore and closed his

200

door. Later that day the villagers burned the houses of the mayor and the men who had run the town for the VC. They drove the families out into the street, then stripped them and drove them out of the village. The commander didn't believe in interfering, so his order was to "let the loyal villagers flush out the Communist sympathizers." The soldiers were to interfere only to prohibit excessive destruction of property. The next day they began to find the bodies—men, women, and children. The loyalists had killed those they didn't drive out the first day and thrown their bodies on the field they used as a garbage jump. The commander got angry then because he knew that they would have to dig graves, otherwise the stench would become unbearable. The prisoner had been assigned to the burial detail and had seen the bodies—the eyes gouged out, the torn genitals, the mashed skulls. Some of the women had been pregnant. Their bellies had been kicked in.

*

He watched the crowd and the guards for an hour. By that time he knew that it would be impossible to get through to the embassy. All the time the crowd was growing larger, and each time a chopper left the people became more frantic. Only once had he seen anyone pass through the crowd and enter through the front door. That was an impeccably dressed Oriental escorted by several policemen. He was questioned for a few minutes at the barricade, then someone went into the embassy and returned with an official who nodded when he saw the man. When the two men entered the building, someone from the crowd threw a piece of fruit that splattered on the glass door.

LII

He moved quickly down the narrow, twisting streets adjacent to the cathedral. He was hunting for a jeweler. Once he had money, he could try something—he didn't know what that should be, but he had to try.

He came to a corner and hesitated. The shops should have been in this vicinity. Of this he was certain, but he had been looking for a half hour and had found nothing. Girls wearing short skirts were standing in the doorways. They looked at him contemptuously. Mountain men had no money for prostitutes—they were violent and dirty, and the girls preferred westerners. But trade was poor, so some of them waved to him and beckoned. It occurred to him that they would probably understand English and might know where the jewelry shops were. He went over to one of them.

She was short and strong-looking and wore a white silk blouse and black slacks. The blouse was unbuttoned so that it showed most of her breasts. She smiled the smile of a prostitute and said something in Vietnamese. He shook his head and asked if she knew where the jewelers were located.

She looked surprised—she had never met a mountain man who spoke like an American. He repeated the question, and she called to another girl who was standing on the opposite side of the street. The girl laughed, then came over to them. She was chewing gum and looked about fifteen.

"Jewelry shop," he repeated, but they still didn't understand. He thought of showing them the elephant—that would make it clear—but then quickly dismissed the idea. To show one's wealth in a strange city was to ask for a slit throat. Suddenly he realized the trouble.

"Place to buy wedding ring," he said.

The two looked at him and smiled. They understood that. Then they talked to each other—it was obvious they were arguing over territorial rights. Finally the older one abruptly took his arm and led him down the street. The other called after them. He guessed that the younger girl was calling the older one names, because twice she stopped, turned, and yelled something back.

The street of the jewelers was nearby—only three blocks from where he had found the girl. It was narrow and twisting, covered with cobblestones. The buildings were three and four stories tall, shutting out the sunlight. The girl led him to a big shop with dozens of diamond rings and jade necklaces displayed in a window covered with a metal screen. They rang the bell, and a man came to the door, inspected them, then let them in.

He wore silk clothes and a skull cap and had the air of superiority that indicated that he was Chinese and not Vietnamese. The girl started to speak, but the prisoner cut her off and pulled the elephant out of his shirt, setting it on the counter. The jeweler picked it up and turned it over slowly. Then he tested the flint. Finally he shrugged, made a grimace, and shook his head. He said something to the girl. She turned toward the prisoner and said, "Fifty American dollar."

"Tell him that he is crazy—a swindler, a thief," he said. He could see the surprise in the man's face when he heard the words in English.

When the girl translated, the man turned his back and walked to the other end of the counter. The prisoner knew that he was interested, otherwise he would have led them to the door. After a few minutes he came back, looked at the elephant again, and made another offer.

"One-hundred American dollar," said the girl.

The prisoner shook his head again. The man looked at him, smirked, then said something to the girl. She laughed but said nothing.

"One-thousand dollars," said the prisoner, holding up his hands with all ten fingers extended.

The jeweler broke into laughter. He pointed to his head and made a motion to show what he thought of the other's sanity. Then he walked back to the other end of the counter again.

Several scared-looking people hurried past the window. The jeweler and the girl watched them, and the prisoner wondered what they were thinking. They could not be as calm as they seemed. When the Cong came, it would be hard for them both. The Cong would close the shop— jewelry was a capitalist vice—and they might take all of the jeweler's money. The man was fat and his hands soft—he would not fare well on a farm. The girl would also be sent to the fields. She might be better for it, but it was probably not a change she wanted. There would be no more silk dresses, and she would have to get up at dawn.

The prisoner picked up the elephant and started to leave. The move was irrational, for the merchant needed no more stock. He would never sell what he had now, and it would be much better to have cash, but the prisoner counted on his greed. *A born businessman,* he thought, *can never pass up a deal.* He stood just inside the door and put the elephant back inside his shirt, making certain that as he did so he turned it so that it glinted in the little bit of light coming through the window.

The merchant said something, and the girl said, "Six-hundred American dollar."

The prisoner nodded, took the elephant back out, and set it on the counter again. The jeweler went through a door that he locked behind him. In a few minutes, he returned and began counting out the money. The prisoner watched him closely. When the jeweler had finished, the prisoner shook his head, and the man took out two more bills, adding them to the stack. The prisoner saw the glimmer in the woman's eyes as he picked up his money and started for the door. Outside he looked through the window. The man was examining the elephant closely and smiling to himself.

LIII

The girl followed him for several blocks before she understood that he wasn't going to give her any of the money. Then she began to swear at him and tried to strike him in the face. He raised his hand, and she ran off. *She'll be back,* he thought, knowing that she would probably have someone with her. She would not give up that easily. He hurried in the opposite direction; he would circle back to the embassy.

After a half hour he found himself at the back of the building. The crowd was immense, and the people more hysterical than before. Attempts to hurdle the barricades were more frequent now, and the bodies of battered people lay like corpses in the empty area behind the gray sawhorses. The police were doing all of the work; the Marines just waited, rifles ready, in front of the doorway. He wondered if they would really shoot and what the reaction would be then. It would not take much to turn the mob wild, and the policemen could not really be that concerned about the safety of the embassy personnel. *Not unless they promised to take them out, too,* he thought.

He took a seat at a café half a block from the embassy. There were outside tables, small blue ones covered with green umbrellas. A waiter came out, and he ordered a coffee. Again he noticed the surprise on the man's face when he spoke English.

After he brought the coffee, the waiter remained. The prisoner could sense his curiosity.

"Monsieur speaks English well," the waiter finally said, looking at him intently.

He ignored the man, and the waiter started to leave when it suddenly occurred to the prisoner that the man might be able to help him. He called him back.

"Have you worked here long?" he asked.

The man nodded. "A long time—through many changes. Before the Americans there were the French— from them we have this," he waved his arm about, pointing to the café and the tables and the hotel across the street. The outside was decorated with iron grillwork, and there were balconies before each of the windows on the upper floors.

"And from the Americans?" said the prisoner.

The man smiled. "Much money. Many dead but much money."

"And the Viet Cong—from them what will you get?"

The man held up his hands, palms toward the sky. "Who can tell, my friend? I should worry, but I don't. What would be the point?"

The prisoner nodded and sipped his coffee. It was good, but it struck him that it was very strange to be sitting in a café, sipping coffee, while an army sat poised like a hawk ready to swoop down upon a flock of chickens, and people rioted in front of an embassy, ready to barter their souls for a chance to leave the city.

The waiter went away for a few minutes, then returned. He stood beside the prisoner's table and watched the action in front of the embassy. Just then a half dozen people formed a flying wedge and rammed into the left side of the barricade. The police battered them, but two got through and went all the way to the doorway. The Marines clubbed them to the ground with the butts of their rifles.

The waiter shrugged and turned to the prisoner. "Fools. They are trying the impossible."

"When men are desperate, they will do anything," said the prisoner.

"To run against a barricade is stupid," said the waiter. The prisoner noticed that he was walleyed—it gave him a strange appearance, as if he were looking two ways at once.

"Is there another way?" asked the prisoner.

The waiter looked at him, then back to the crowd.

"For those with money, yes. But they must have much money."

The prisoner took out the bills the jeweler had given him and riffled the edges like a man about to deal a hand of cards.

"Only to get me in the door," said the prisoner. "The rest I will manage."

The waiter took half of the bills and told the prisoner to return at ten the next morning. The prisoner left and wandered through the streets until he found a cheap hotel, tipped the desk clerk to make certain that he would wake him at nine, then went to his room and fell asleep immediately.

*

He woke at the sound of knocking at his door, stretched, then grunted that he knew it was time. He felt rested and strong. He walked to the sink and turned on the tap. A trickle of rusty, cold water dripped out. He let it run, but it didn't change color. He couldn't be finicky—he needed to wash the dye off his face. There was one towel and a piece of soap. He lathered and scrubbed his face, then checked the result in the mirror. His face was lighter but still hardly white. It would take a good argument to convince anyone that he was an American if he looked like that. He tried a second time, scrubbing until his face was sore, but the results were the same.

He gave up and looked through the window. The streets were emptier now. He saw a group of men standing outside the window. One was reading from a newspaper while the others were listening. Then the man stopped reading and pointed off toward the north. The prisoner realized that they were discussing the Cong. They looked concerned but not terrified. Finally one of the men made a joke, and they all laughed. Then they went their separate ways.

When he came downstairs and gave the key to the desk clerk, the man asked him if he wanted the room for another night. He thought for a minute, then said, "No." If he was lucky, he would be in the embassy by then. It seemed to him that if he said "yes" and reserved the room, he would somehow be jinxing his chances.

He walked quickly to the café, took a seat, and waited. A half hour passed, then another. By 11:30 the man still hadn't come.

Another hour passed, then two. Finally he called a waiter over and asked if he knew the man with the strange eyes who served in the afternoons. The waiter shook his head and went away.

At five he gave up and went back to the hotel. He knew the man had tricked him, but he did not want to believe it. He tried to sleep, but anger and anxiety kept him awake. He kept thinking of the helicopters leaving. He could see the people boarding them, and he could imagine himself among them. He was so close—to fail now would be horrible. He tried to think of another way but couldn't. Somehow, by some device, he had to get inside the embassy. The old man had said that it would be impossible at the airport, and the old man was probably right. He had to get through those glass doors.

*

The next day he went to the café again and waited for the walleyed man, but he never came. The prisoner asked about him, but no one knew him. He was a new man and had been there only a month—new waiters came and went all the time, they said. The prisoner was possessed with an urge to rush through the city, searching for someone or something to help him, but he did not know where he could go. All he would probably accomplish would be the loss of the remainder of his money. He sat and sipped coffee and watched the crowd.

After a few hours he discovered that the scenario had changed from yesterday. The helicopters didn't come as frequently, and there seemed to be fewer men inside the embassy. One tall, worried-looking man kept coming to the door to peer out, but otherwise he only saw a half dozen people. Every half hour or so a group of people would be escorted through the crowd by the police, and a little later they would appear on the roof and climb a ladder into the bay of a dark green chopper. Like the day before, most of the people leaving were Vietnamese. There were men with their wives and children. When they passed through the crowds, the other people looked at them savagely. Sometimes people in the crowd would call to them, but the people being escorted by the police never turned their heads. The women were silent, their faces expressionless. The children were usually crying, terrified by the clamor.

In the evening he went to a nearby restaurant and ate a big meal. He had not eaten at a table covered with a tablecloth and attended by a waiter since his capture. The food tasted unbelievably good, and when he had finished, he ordered another course. After he finished this, he felt bloated, so he walked for a half hour. Then he returned to the café near the embassy and continued to watch.

The choppers came and went in the gathering darkness, like great hummingbirds. The crowd was quieter now, and some were sleeping. He saw the same faces he had seen for two days. It dawned on him that they, like him, were waiting and watching. They knew that it was impossible, but they remained. He thought of the stupidity of it. Away from the city, walking the roads of the countryside, they would be safe. There were hundreds of thousands of refugees, perhaps millions. No one would ask questions, and if they did, it wouldn't matter. The chances of being identified as "a tool of Thieu" or "a friend of the capitalists" would be slight. But instead the people waited, hoping for an impossible salvation. If they were caught in front of the embassy when the Cong entered the city, they would probably be rounded up—maybe shot.

He left the café and began to wander. At first he walked aimlessly, but eventually discovered that he had unconsciously veered to the northwest—the direction of the airport.

LIV

There was a main terminal, then an open space before the field. The place was swarming with people, and a cordon of soldiers ringed the field. It was almost midnight, but the people were all awake, milling around. He could see a dozen big transport helicopters in the distance, glinting like giant green insects in the floodlights. The entrances to the terminal were blocked by squads of policemen, but a constantly moving stream of frantic, screaming men and women surged past the sides of the building and onto the edge of field. There they merged with more people, all straining and pushing foward. They seemed to be cursing and clawing each other. The sound vibrated; it was hysterical and angry. He made his way to the stream of people passing the left side of the terminal. It was hard work. His breath was pressed from him, and he felt people clawing at him. Then he reached the edge of the stream and leaped into it. Like a leaf, he was borne along, and a few minutes later found himself in the midst of the crowd at the edge of the field.

The people were packed together so tightly that it was impossible to raise his arms. He was twenty-five, perhaps thirty yards from the edge of the crowd where the people ended and the cordon of soldiers began. The soldiers stood side by side, rifles poised. They looked strong and unafraid. The crowd was enormous and desperate—they would have swept over a weaker force. But these men were a different matter. *If they had been like that at*

210

Hue and Da Nang, then the Cong would never have got-
ten below the sixteenth parallel, he thought.

For a minute he was frozen in the crowd. He felt powerless, an ant among a million ants. Then he felt his strength grow and began to push his way through the people. He had his eyes on a place at the very front toward the left side. Something told him that that was the place—why he did not know, but he was possessed and did not bother to question himself. He knew.

When he reached the front of the crowd, he stopped, catching his breath and regaining his strength while he surveyed the scene again. The soldiers looked as strong and sure as ever, the crowd as desperate. He looked out at the helicopters. The closest was perhaps forty yards from him, the farthest three-quarters of a mile. The field was unpaved and dusty. The rotors of one of the choppers began to spin, and a hum grew that mingled with the cries of the crowd in a weird contrapuntal chorus. The chopper slowly left the ground, and the eyes of the people lifted up with it. It rose straight up, then slowly headed east, crossing above the crowd. Heads turned and people raised their hands, half in defiance, half in the futile hope that somehow the people already on their way to safety in the helicopter would reach down and carry them along.

Just at that moment a half dozen men at the front of the crowd to the right of center broke through the soldiers and dashed madly toward the helicopters. Two choppers began to rev their engines, their blades spinning and sucking the dust into a thick, yellow cloud. Soldiers dashed after the men, some firing. The rest of the crowd pushed against the cordon, but the soldiers held them. Then everything seemed to stop as everyone watched the men and the pursuing soldiers. Two of the men had been shot and had fallen. Three others were cut off and were standing with their hands in the air. One was left, still about twenty yards ahead of the soldiers. They couldn't fire at him because he was directly in line with the helicopters that were loaded with people and ready to lift off. The rotors of the choppers were spinning faster now, and the choppers were hovering an inch or two off the ground, awaiting the signal to lift off. The man dashed toward them, blindly running for his life. One of the soldiers went down on his knee, took aim, and fired. The man was hit. He leaped skyward like a gazelle, then fell, and the soldiers were on him.

The prisoner grasped the shoulders of the man in front of him, then pushed him forward into the nearest soldier. The soldier fell, and the crowd surged through, the prisoner in their midst. They, too, dashed toward the choppers that were beginning to lift off. He ran with them for fifty yards. Bullets zinged over his head and bit into the dirt beside him. One man fell, then another. He suddenly veered to the left, cutting back like a halfback on a wide sweep, picking up speed. The shouts of the crowd grew fainter. He passed the first row of choppers and ran on; he could see the faces of the people already inside behind the narrow, rectangular windows.

More bullets zinged past him. Ahead of him lay an open space and then the last of the helicopters. He ran harder. Then he was there, standing beside the open bay door, facing a soldier dressed in khakis. The soldier was an American—young, maybe twenty, and scared.

"I'm an American!" the prisoner screamed. "For Chrissake let me on! I'm American!"

The soldier stared at him. Behind were two others with drawn pistols in their hands.

"Christ, I'm from Cleveland!" he yelled.

The men didn't move. The prisoner looked over his shoulder—a dozen Vietnamese soldiers were closing in. They were about thirty yards away, and he could see the guns in their hands. He turned to the young soldier again.

"Cleveland!" he yelled. "The Browns—the Indians—for Chrissake the fuckin' Browns—Jim Brown! Lake Erie! Euclid Park!"

The soldier reached down and pulled him on board, then the chopper lifted off.

LV

The doctor looked at him. All the other refugees in the room were Vietnamese. He had wanted to go with the Americans, but they wouldn't let him. He did not argue. It wouldn't matter now anyway.

The doctor took his pulse, looked down his throat, and thumped on his back. Then he made some entries on a chart, handed it to him, and pointed to another man sitting at a table. The prisoner went over and handed the chart to the man. The man took a blood sample. Then he was handed a jar and told, through gestures, that he should urinate. He looked around for a bathroom, and someone pointed to a screen. He went behind it and tried. Nothing came out. He walked back to the man who had given him the jar and tried to hand it back to him. The man shook his head and wouldn't take it. He stood there for a minute, feeling like an idiot. Then he swore. "Look, you son of a bitch, I haven't had a drop of water in twelve hours—there's no piss in me."

The man got up from his desk and went away, then returned with a glass of water. The prisoner drank it and handed the empty glass back to the man.

"I'll need more than that."

The man ignored him.

*

After three hours the physical examination was done. He was sent to a barracks and slept for a few hours; then

213

he went to the mess tent to get some food. There were Coca-Cola machines, and Vietnamese kids were crowding around them. Some of them had ice cream cones that were melting and running down their arms.

He ate a few sandwiches, then looked for a newspaper but couldn't find one. It was hot, and the sun was bright. He could see the white sand of a beach and the ocean beyond. He knew he was in the Philippines, but that was all he knew. It was crazy, but to the world he was a Vietnamese refugee.

He remembered the flight, the whirr of the chopper and the crowd below him. He had watched them fade into the distance, afraid to look around him, afraid to look anywhere but at the ground. It did not seem real, and he thought that if he did something wrong it would end, the helicopter would vanish, and he would be back in Saigon, running madly from place to place. The only crewman who spoke to him was the guy who pulled him aboard. He was a cracker—he could tell from the soldier's drawl. His hair was clipped short, and his fair skin reddened by the tropical sun.

"Y'all were mighty lucky there. Mighty lucky." The prisoner smiled, too tired to reply.

"Used to watch the Browns on TV. That spade's the best damn running back I ever saw. Yessir, best damn back I ever saw."

He just nodded.

The flight took all night. The sun came up, and they flew into it. They were over the ocean, heading due east. An hour or two later they put down on a carrier. A half hour later they were aboard a transport plane winging toward the Philippines.

*

Toward evening two MP's came for him. They spoke to him, and he told them his story; then they led him to another part of the camp where a man took his name and told him to wait. A half hour later he was inside an office, and a major was questioning him. This man was named McMurtry, and he said he was from Spokane. McMurtry wrote everything down, then smiled and shook his hand. Suddenly the prisoner had to fight back tears.

214

"You'll be here until tomorrow morning, then you'll probably go to Tokyo for R and R. If you want to make a stink, you can probably get sent straight to the States."

He thought about it for a minute. The idea of the States scared him. The faces of the people, the questions, his parents and friends. He did not want that yet, so he said Tokyo would be OK. He asked if they could wait a couple of days before notifying his folks, and McMurtry said he would arrange it.

LVI

He looked down at the clouds that covered the Sea of Japan. They were white and fluffy, and he imagined what it would be like to walk on them—great fields of soft cotton-snow. They were endless—a vast meadow of whiteness with no footsteps, no tracks or dirt. Once he had read an account of a mountain-climbing expedition. He couldn't recall which mountain it was or the names of the men. The final assault party had been forced to stop, but one of the men went on alone upward into the cold and snow. He had always wondered about that. What would a man going up alone into the unknown think? Would he be afraid? The man must have known he was courting death, yet he had gone on, even fought with those who would stop him. They never found his body.

*

He was still thinking about the man and his mountain when the plane descended through the clouds and began to circle high over the airport. He could see the smog of Tokyo rising in the distance when an announcement came.

"Ladies and gentlemen, this is Haneda Airport. You will be met at the airport by a bus which will take you to your hotel. Please remain seated until the seatbelt sign is switched off."

Then the plane started into its final glide toward the runway.

*

The excitement had left him, and now he felt empty. Gradually he was coming back to himself. He had looked in a mirror that morning and studied his face. There were new lines and a few gray hairs. He felt his teeth. Some of them were in bad shape, and they were all stained yellow-brown. Otherwise he was fine—that was what the doctors told him. "In amazingly good condition." No one asked about the scars on his back.

The hotel was in the middle of the business district. It was a big hotel, and he was on the thirty-fourth floor. There was a television set in his room, and the view was fine. His second day there he found a Bible written in Japanese. They gave him a map of the city, but he didn't bother to study it. He was too tired, and he didn't care anyway.

He stayed in his room and slept. Sometimes he watched television. He couldn't understand what was being said, but it didn't matter to him; he just watched. He especially liked the cowboy movies. He thought John Wayne sounded great in Japanese. It didn't suit Jimmy Stewart, though, and when Randolph Scott, wearing a rebel uniform and leading Somebody's Raiders, exhorted his men in Japanese, it was very funny. He laughed a long time.

He ordered a bottle of scotch from room service, but only drank about a quarter of it. It tasted bitter to him— he guessed that was because it had been a long time since his last scotch. He remembered the taste of *mao tai*, though, and made a note to himself to order it. He'd wait a night or two. He wanted to save that.

216

On the second day they sent a car for him, and he went to an office in a big building where a CIA man asked him questions. The man was bald, and his skin was so tight that the prisoner thought it would tear when he moved his jaw. He kept imagining that the man's face would split open and the inside of his head ooze out like ketchup.

"What did they ask you?"

He told him.

"Did you tell them anything?"

He said "no."

Then the man asked him what they had done to him. He didn't want to talk about it, but he gave him the bare facts. The man wrote it all down, and while the man wrote, the prisoner looked through the window and watched the traffic pass on the street below.

Then the CIA man asked him about the old man—he wanted to know his name and rank.

"Never found that out," he said.

"Are you sure?" said the man.

"Yup," he said.

The man stared at him then, and he looked straight back into his eyes and thought, *This is one of those SOB's who knows all the answers.*

Finally the man looked back down at his papers and continued with his questions. He wanted to know the names of the camps and their locations. The prisoner said he couldn't remember. Then the man asked where he was captured and what outfit he had been in. The prisoner told him.

The man made a phone call. After he hung up the receiver, he wrote something else down. "I suppose you know that everyone else in that company was killed in action."

The prisoner shrugged.

"Their last reported location was Canh Trap," said the man. "That's almost thirty miles west of where you said you were captured."

He said nothing.

"Strange," said the man.

He smiled and got up and started to leave.

"We may call you again."

217

The prisoner said nothing and went out the door.

That night he got drunk and went with a whore. It wasn't any good, and he had trouble sleeping afterwards. In the morning he read an American newspaper for the first time. It was full of stories of the US pullout and the reaction of Americans to it. He started to read these, then put the paper down and asked the desk clerk if there was a museum with western art nearby. The man looked in a directory, then wrote something on a slip of paper and told him to take a taxi and show the paper to the driver.

*

The cab wove through jammed streets, then circled a park and pulled up to a rambling tan building. He went inside and asked the girl at the information desk if there were any paintings by Eakins.

She told him to go to the second floor. He climbed steps and entered a room filled with mannequins dressed in clothes from different periods. There were soldiers from the Revolutionary War and a likeness of Washington, then Civil War soldiers, southern belles, and movie stars.

The room was empty except for a man and a woman and two small children. They were looking at two mannequins—one was Abraham Lincoln, the other looked like Dwight Eisenhower. He stopped for a second and looked, too. The children turned to look at him, and one of them, a little boy, whispered something to his sister. She giggled and ran back to her mother and hid behind her.

He walked on through two more rooms, then into a big gallery. This was the room he wanted. He stood in the center and looked around. There were perhaps fifty paintings in the room. He began to circle it. Halfway around the room he came to an Eakins. It was a sketch of a man running, showing his legs in several different positions. The muscles were portrayed on one leg, the placement of the bones on another. He stood in front of the picture and studied it for a long time. It was signed in the corner in neat, clear letters—Thomas Eakins. He thought it was a good picture, but he didn't know much about pictures. He looked for others by Eakins, but there weren't any more. After sitting on a bench in the center of the room for a few minutes, he left.

*

It was about noon, and he still had the afternoon to kill. The sun was bright, the sky filled with fluffy white clouds. He started to hail a cab, then changed his mind and walked across the street and into a park.

It was a weekday, and he was surprised at the number of people there. They were walking quietly or sitting on benches beside paved pathways.

The park was green and rolling, and he walked on and on. The sun felt good on his face, and there was a soft breeze. Finally he came over a slight hill and stopped. Before him lay a forest of cherry trees, their pink blossoms fluttering in the breeze.

He found a bench and sat. His mind was spinning slowly, and it was all spreading out before him. He remembered his last battle, the hours in solitary, the whip, No-Neck, and the old man. Then after a minute, their talks, the trip south, Saigon, the embassy, and the airport came in another wave. Somehow, in some way, he was trying to make sense out of it. He struggled against himself, trying to stop his mind from working, but he couldn't. It kept coming back to him that it meant something—it had to. He knew it didn't mean what most people thought—not to him anyway. He didn't care about the Communists or stopping the spread of Communism. He had never cared much about that. And if he had ever believed that he was fighting to protect the freedom of the people of South Vietnam, that idea was long gone. It had lasted about one week.

He thought about the newspapers he had read that morning. Every lousy congressman had something to say, every damn journalist and housewife. What did they know? Had they seen the burned villages or felt the bullets? Had they known K or the old man or No-Neck? They said it was a senseless war. Probably they were right, but that didn't mean anything either. All wars were senseless, and no war was. Why didn't they ask a VC soldier? He was afraid of dying and hated fighting, but he fought, and it wasn't just his leaders who made him

219

fight. If there were different leaders, he would have fought anyway. And then he would stop and rest awhile —maybe a year, maybe fifty or a hundred years. Then he would start again. It was crazy but it was so, and you could damn it and fight against it, but it wouldn't do any good.

Then he thought about the old man. He could see his face and his boots. He remembered the things the old man had said and the night they had looked at the stars. He wondered where he was and what had happened to him, and he realized that he would probably never meet another man he liked as much. *No*, he thought, *nor a woman either*. And in a strange way, he knew that he was glad for it all. *Maybe men fight wars,* he thought, *because you can never be closer to a person than when you are struggling with him—either to kill him or to help him overcome death*. The idea seemed strange to him, and he held it only for a minute. Then he looked at the cherry blossoms. A sudden gust of wind shook them, and some petals fluttered to the ground like pink snow-flakes. He reached down, picked up one, and felt it. It was soft—one side glossy, the other like velvet. He smelled it—there was a faint acrid odor.

He looked at the sky. The clouds had blown away, and it was a clear, pellucid blue. *The stars will be out tonight,* he thought. Before he had been confused and he was still confused, but now he was calmer. He stood up and headed for the edge of the park. There he got a taxi back to the hotel, ate alone, and drank a bottle of *mao tai*. When he finished, night had fallen, and he went outside to look at the sky. It was more beautiful than he had expected—the stars were endless.

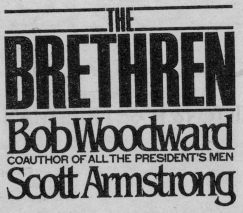

The Provocative National Bestseller

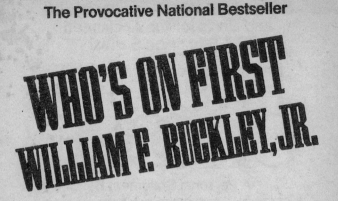

WHO'S ON FIRST
WILLIAM F. BUCKLEY, JR.

"Timeless thriller ingredients: murder, torture, sex...
Soviet defection, treachery. And there in the middle of
it all is good old Blacky: charming, insouciant,
escaping one dragnet after another without rumpling
his trenchcoat." *Boston Globe*

The cunning and sophisticated hero Blackford Oakes is
back in a new adventure involving a beautiful
Hungarian freedom fighter, Blacky's old KGB rival,
a pair of Soviet scientific geniuses, and the U.S.-
U.S.S.R. space race.

"A fast-moving plot....As in all good espionage novels
there is thrust and counterthrust....Mr. Buckley is an
observer with a keen wit and a cold eye."
Newgate Callendar, *New York Times Book Review*

"The suspense is keen and complicated....Constantly
entertaining." *Wall Street Journal*

"A crackling good plot...entertaining." *Washington Post*

AVON Paperback

52555/$2.95

On First 2-81 (1-1)